ABOUT RAE

Rae Cairns writes crime with heart; thriller and suspense novels featuring everyday people facing extraordinary circumstances. *The Good Mother* is her debut novel and draws on her background as a youth worker mentoring disadvantaged youth in Northern Ireland during the final years of 'The Troubles'. Rae has also co-managed a crisis refuge for street children, worked as Program Director for the Sydney Olympic Youth Camp and holds a degree in Performing Arts. When she's not playing around with the lives of her imaginary characters she loves to read, hike, travel, go to the beach and sing. Rae lives in Sydney with her husband, two children and her dog, Alfie, who snores at her feet when she writes.

THE GOOD MOTHER

RAE CAIRNS

BANDRUI
Publishing

For Amy and Ben, you inspired me to dream.
Love you both to infinity plus one.
And for Peter, you encouraged me to chase those dreams.
Love you now and always.

PROLOGUE

NORTHERN IRELAND, 2014.

Never, not even during the darkest moments of her life, had Sarah Calhoun believed she could become a killer. But staring down at her mother's ring, she finally understood. There was no action she wouldn't take.

No lie. No betrayal. No sin.

No matter who you were, there was always something, or someone, who could push you to the point of no return.

She reached for the band of gold and twisted it round and round. She had to do this, or even more would die.

He'd given her no choice.

One life to save many.

ONE

Sarah bounded up the sandstone stairs of her rundown Federation cottage, her breath sending puffs of white into the morning air. She checked her time. Two minutes shaved, definitely getting closer to form. Stretching out her quads, she savoured the salty scent wafting up the hill from Bronte Beach. A buoyancy moved through her, surfing the endorphins years of running had hardwired her body to crave. But it was more than that. For the first time since the divorce, she'd found a space her family loved, had finally given her kids back a home.

She deactivated the front door alarm and entered the hallway. Tinkling giggles drew her to the family room, where she found Sophie, her eight-year-old, squealing with delight as their labrador puppy licked black paste off her fingers.

"Honey, Vegemite isn't very good for Fudge. And what did we say about eating on the floor?"

Sophie jumped up for a hug, her toffee-coloured bob brushing Sarah's bare tummy.

"But Fudge hasn't had a picnic before, and I wanted to show him how."

Before Sarah's arms had a chance to fully enclose her, Sophie ran off and entered a tug of war over a blanket the puppy had dragged halfway out the dog door. Sarah couldn't help but laugh. Buying her kids a puppy was one of the best parenting ideas she'd had. She moved to the fridge and removed the lunches she'd packed before her run. The familiar grind and gurgle of the coffee machine joined the hullabaloo.

"Mum, can you sign off my homework?" Ally emerged from the study, waving a bunch of papers. Sarah did a double take. Just this week her older daughter had edged a centimetre taller, but it was her twelve-year-old's face, left exposed by the knotting back of her blond curly hair, that caused the tug in Sarah's chest. Her look no longer cute like Sophie's but maturing into the alarming beauty of a teenager. Too soon her girl would move out into the world. How would Sarah protect her then?

"Earth to Mum," Ally waved a pen in the air. "Signature? And don't forget I finish dance rehearsal late today."

"Ally, that hem is too short. Go change into the new uniform I bought you."

"This one's already longer than every single one of my friends'."

"I'm not their mother. Go change."

Ally glared.

"Now."

Her daughter smacked her homework on the bench and stomped upstairs to her room. Sarah caught the rolling pen before it fell to the floor. Ally didn't understand yet. It was better not to stand out, not to be noticed. She corrected a wrong answer on the homework, then signed. Maybe she should enrol Ally in more of the dance classes she loved. That would keep her busy, and it had worked with Riley. Even at sixteen, soccer took up every spare minute of his life. Sarah glanced towards the dining table. Where was Riley? Normally he'd be inhaling a pile of Weet-Bix by now. She checked her watch.

"Riley, get a wriggle on," she called into the hallway. They'd all better get moving if she was going to make her client meeting. While her coffee finished brewing, she gathered the papers scattered across the bench into an orderly pile. Her gaze caught on a sticky note stuck to an orange folder she'd never seen before. *Mum*. She flipped the folder open and scanned the handwritten letter attached to the front of a document. Her face began to burn. She strode to the stairwell.

"Riley." Silence. "Riley, get down here now!"

No feet came pounding. Nothing. She checked the space where his school bag should have been. What had he done? She dashed back to Sophie. "Was Riley awake when you came down?"

"I haven't seen him since last night."

Sarah grabbed the folder and ran for the stairs. With each stride up, her knuckles whitened around the file. How could he go behind her back? This wasn't part of their plan.

She rushed into her son's bedroom. "Riley Ethan Barker!"

The dark room was quiet. The jagged shadows of his soccer trophies loomed from the shelves. He'd left early for school, snuck out before she awoke. She sucked in a breath laced with the outdoorsy scent of his deodorant, then sank onto Riley's unmade bed, staring at the letter in her hand.

Dear Mum

I know you won't like this, but please, please, please try to understand. I need to go on this FIFA Youth Development camp. Only two players were selected from Australia, and there will be scouts from all over the world there. Dad has filled out all the forms and paid for everything. It's being held in Dublin, Ireland. All you need to do is sign the travel permission form. I know I should have told you earlier, but I thought you'd freak out. Please say yes.

Love Riley.

Sarah closed her eyes. The stink of burning gasoline overwhelmed her senses. Screams. A crack. A flash. A spray of blood across the floor. Surging to her feet, she parted the curtains and threw open the window. Riley could not go to Dublin. Everything she'd done to protect her family could come unstuck.

A herd of schoolboys passed on the road below, chattering and hollering. Her boy should have been among them, heading for the bus. *Goddamn Evan.* He knew she'd never let her sixteen-year-old travel alone. Especially not to Ireland. What was her ex-husband thinking? She plumped up a pillow that had been discarded on the floor and returned it to the headboard. This couldn't wait; she needed to visit Evan and put an end to this trip now. She tugged the quilt into place and headed downstairs to her phone. She'd have to ask the other researchers to cover her meeting.

The elevator doors opened onto Evan's fifteenth floor law office. Every chair in the waiting room sat perfectly spaced, each picture frame squared and matching in tones of red and grey. Everything uniform, predictable and masculine. Everything that is, except for the pastel floral arrangement adorning the reception desk, and the diminutive Mrs Farley sitting behind it. Now in her late sixties, Evan's secretary was five foot if she were lucky and used her glacial eyes to preside over all who entered Evan's domain.

Sarah smoothed down her suit jacket and moved towards the desk. "Good morning, Mrs Farley." Never Gladys, not even in her fourteen years of marriage to Evan was Sarah allowed that familiarity.

"I'm sorry, Ms Calhoun, Mr Barker is in meetings all day. Can I make you an appointment for tomorrow?"

Sarah swallowed down the urge to deliver a snappy retort. "This can't wait. I need to see him now."

"Mr Barker said you would say that." Mrs Farley reached to the shelf behind. "You'll need these." She passed over a pile of magazines. "Please take a seat."

Sarah tossed the magazines onto a side table and perched herself on the chair facing the long corridor. Every cell in her body wanted to burst into Evan's office and demand he see her straight away, but it would be a mistake. His biggest issue during their marriage had been her "irrationality". Her overzealous protectiveness. He'd only listen today if she were calm. She crossed her legs and concentrated on mapping out what she was going to say. Music interrupted, piped from speakers spread around the ceiling, the familiar melody of *Clair de Lune* grating across her skin. Evan had played it over and over while each of their children had grown in her womb. Her right foot tapped in the air. Back then he'd been everything she believed she wanted - safe and honest, a family man. But he'd always needed more than she could give. Uncrossing her legs she shifted upright in her seat. That was unimportant now. Being a good father had always been his priority. It was the reason she hadn't fought shared custody. So, what was going on now?

She fixated back on his office door. Riley was scheduled to leave in four weeks. What could be more important than their son's safety? She stretched her head side to side. When *Moonlight Sonata* started over the speakers, she pushed to her feet. "I'm going to the bathroom. If Evan comes out, please ask him to wait."

Mrs Farley gave a dismissive nod.

When Sarah reached the ladies room the snick of a lock sounded behind her. She turned. Evan Barker's eyes, the same shape and colour as those of their daughters, studied her from behind on-trend square black glasses.

"Sarah."

"Evan."

His mouth pulled into a thin line. "Please don't start until you've heard me out."

He waved her into his office and sunlight caught on his new platinum wedding ring. Why hadn't she thought to get Evan's wife on side first? Felicity oozed calm, and she understood how to keep Evan happy, better than Sarah ever had. The door clicked shut. It was too late now. Sarah sat while Evan moved to his chair on the other side of the desk. He rubbed at the manicured stubble on his chin for a moment before he spoke. "Look, I understand you might feel uncomfortable."

"Uncomfortable? Allowing Riley to go on this trip is irresponsible."

Evan looked to the desk, a faint sigh slipping out of his mouth. He removed and folded his glasses. Sarah's foot jackhammered against the floor while he took care to place the glasses in their case. His gaze returned to hers. "This trip is the chance of a lifetime. And Riley's earned it, through his dedication and hard work. I'm struggling to think of one good reason why he shouldn't go."

"It won't be safe."

"Why not?"

"For starters he'd be on his own, on the other side of the world for four whole months." Sarah forced her rising voice to lower. "He's not an adult yet."

"He's not a baby either. Riley is smart and talented, and he's worked hard for this. You can't stop him following his dream. He'll never forgive you."

At least he'll be alive! Her fingers dug into her thighs to stop her shouting the words out loud. Evan had no idea how precarious life could be. "Our job is to parent, not be his friend. The world can be a dangerous place."

"It's Ireland, for Christ's sake, not Afghanistan." Evan ran his fingers through his hair. "Look, I understand it felt unsafe when you worked in Belfast, but Northern Ireland has been at peace for years. And even if it wasn't, Dublin is in the Republic, a whole different country."

"Please, Evan, you don't understand the risks."

"I've looked into the program. Have you? Or did you merely react with your need to wrap the people you love in cotton wool? You give me one logical reason why Riley will be 'at risk' in Ireland, and I'll back you."

Sarah stared into her lap. Gerry's terrified expression flashed like a still-shot in her mind. She'd never shared with Evan about that night, about Gerry, about Michael. No way she could confess it now. Not after all these years.

"I shouldn't have to explain it. If you thought like an adult—"

He stood and threw both hands in the air. "That is not a reason." He turned to face the ceiling-high window that looked out over Sydney Harbour. Words tumbled in Sarah's head, but not one false argument she concocted made sense.

When Evan turned back, his expression had hardened. "Riley needs to follow his dreams, not fear there's a bogeyman around every corner. I will not let your fears control his life. I've promised Riley I will back him, no matter what. Even if we have to take you to Family Court."

Sarah flinched as if struck. Evan wouldn't, would he? She took in the tight set of his mouth. Her pulse sped up. "Surely you don't mean for custody?"

"No, of course not. All we need is a Court Order of Consent. Because Riley is sixteen, they will take his wishes into consideration. Unless you can give serious and well-evidenced welfare concerns, the court will rule in my favour."

Evan meant it. If she refused permission, he would take her to court. This couldn't be happening. Riley couldn't go to Ireland. What if they found him? She launched to her feet.

"You are making a terrible mistake. This isn't about my fears. It's reality."

"Only your version, Sarah."

She hitched her handbag onto her shoulder. "If anything bad happens to Riley in Dublin, anything at all, I will never forgive you." She turned away and marched from the room. There had to be another way to stop this. She had to protect her son.

TWO

Sarah reached the top of the cliff overlooking Gordons Bay and bent in two, gasping for air, a stitch gripping her side. Other late afternoon runners passed her by. She'd pushed as hard as she could up the hill but still couldn't get traction on her anger. She wasn't the controlling paranoid nightmare Evan made her out to be. Everything she did was to care for and protect their children.

And what was he playing at, threatening her? She'd recognised that look on his face, the one when he'd threatened court action. He'd worn the same stony expression when asking for the divorce.

"Please don't do this. What about the kids?"

"It's them I'm doing this for. So they don't think this is all marriage can be. Two people living separate lives, sharing nothing real but raising their children."

That had stung. Evan had been her best friend at university, then he'd stepped up when she needed him most. She had tried to match the passion he'd always held for her. To love him as a wife should. But after fourteen years he realised she couldn't, that she never would. He'd been right to end it.

Damn it though, Evan was not right about this. She threw her backside to the flat shelf of rock at the tip of the headland. An escarpment of wild grasses and ochre-striped sandstone sloped away. She guzzled down a few good gulps from her water bottle and stared at the sea. A bank of dark cloud was closing in from above. The blue-grey water churned, wild and seething in the increasing wind. A sea eagle swooped down to snatch its prey from the grass. It missed and circled round again for another try.

Perhaps she should call Evan's bluff? She hugged her legs. But if they ended up in court she would lose.

Unless she told the truth.

Waves boomed from below, smashing against the cliff face and sending up a fine mist of spray. A strike of sheet lightning lit up the almost black water, and the sea eagle flew off. No, the truth would unravel everything. The only way out of this mess was if Riley himself chose not to go. It was her responsibility to lead him to that decision.

She checked her watch. One hour until she had to collect him from training. She pushed to standing, bracing against the buffeting wind, then tucked her chin in and ran for home; her only focus on devising a way to change her son's mind.

"May Day. May Day," Ally yelled from the front passenger seat of the people mover, her hands clutching at her neck. "Need. Oxygen. Now."

Sophie giggled from the back seat and held her nose against the pungent scent of Riley's training gear while he smacked his hands against Ally's headrest. "You're such a douche."

"Riley, enough." Sarah nudged her daughter's thigh. "You too, Ally, we're almost home."

She pulled to a stop in the driveway, disarmed the house alarm and everyone tumbled out. "Girls, showers. Riley could you help me for a sec?"

She worried her cheek while waiting at the boot. Riley hadn't mentioned the letter. The only time he'd spoken at all during the car ride home was his outburst at Ally.

Riley reached past her. "Leave the bags, Mum, I can get them all."

Sarah climbed the stairs. At the top she turned and watched her boy grab the shopping it would have taken her two runs to do. Since turning sixteen, he'd broadened and shot up; he now towered over her by a good foot. Of the three, Riley resembled her the most, with his dark hair and broad smile. A smile he used a lot. Evan's positive outlook had rubbed off there. Hopefully it would hold now.

She moved to the porch swing, catching a glimpse of ocean between the houses across the road. Riley's soccer boots thudded to the side of the front door. She resisted the urge to straighten them and instead patted the seat next to her. "Sit with me a minute."

He stood one foot in, one foot out of the house, bags still held in his hands. "Sorry, I shouldn't have called Ally names."

"You know that's not what I want to talk about. Just leave the shopping at the door."

14

He sat next to her, tucking his hands under his thighs. The chair swung gently.

"Look at me, Riley." She waited until he turned. "This morning, leaving that note for me, was not okay. You should have asked me in person, discussed the offer when it first came in."

"But Dad said—"

"Stop." Her palm pressed flat at the air. "I'm not interested in what your father said. This is between you and me. To go overseas, you need both parent's permission."

"But it's a once in a lifetime opportunity. I promise I'll be sensible and careful. All I want to do is play soccer."

"This isn't just about what you want. It's my job to keep you safe, to decide if you are ready. I'm really disappointed in how you dealt with this."

Riley planted his feet, bringing the chair to a stop. He took a breath as if to speak but then slouched forward. Sarah ignored the unease bunching the muscles of her back. "Honey, I know how amazing and exciting the soccer scholarship sounds, but this year has been huge for us all. I want you to think whether it really is the right time. Things have just settled down, and the girls would miss you terribly. You're only sixteen. There will be more opportunities in the future."

"So that's a no?"

"It's an 'I'm thinking on it'. And you should too. I want you to show me you've taken everything and everyone into consideration, then we can talk about my decision, okay?"

Riley's chin sank to his chest, and he nodded. Her hand ached to take his, to tell him of course he could go. To see the light return to his face. But that wasn't what parenting was about. Her job was to protect him, to guide him towards the right dreams. She stood and kissed him on top of the head. "Time for a shower."

Her son trudged to the front door, his shoulders folding in on his body. "Riley, honey." He stopped at the doorway. "I love you."

"Love you too," he mumbled, then retrieved the shopping bags and lugged them into the house.

Sarah lowered back to the swing. Riley had looked utterly crushed. The thought of hurting them all, the guilt, would over-whelm him. No way would he go through with the trip now. She squeezed her eyes shut and pushed aside her own guilt. She had done what was necessary. Allowing Riley to go to Ireland was simply not an option.

A large cardboard box lay open on the dining table, the aromas of garlic and pepperoni sitting heavy in the air. The pizza lay mostly untouched, the cheese congealing on the board. Sarah sipped at chamomile tea, the scorching liquid doing little to settle the churning in her stomach. Dice clattered across the table, breaking through the quiet.

"Yahtzee! Take that, Riley, there's a new master in town, and her name is Sophie." Riley's expression remained blank. Sophie's smile faded. "I was just kidding."

Sarah studied her son. He hadn't eaten a bite. He'd been like this for four days, since their talk on the swing.

"It's okay, Soph, you win." Riley pushed back his chair. "I'm going to bed."

"But we haven't finished."

From the other end of the table, Ally blew on freshly painted fingernails. "Better get used to it, Sophie."

Riley glared at Ally. "What's that supposed to mean?"

"You don't care what anyone else wants."

"What?" He advanced towards her, and Ally stood, hands fisted at her side, nails forgotten.

Sarah stepped between her children. "Ally, what on earth are you talking about?"

"I know all about Ireland. I heard you on the porch the other day. Then last night, Mum, you were crying in your room. You never do that." Ally swivelled back to her brother. "First Dad leaves, now you want to go?"

"Enough." Sarah widened her eyes in warning at Ally.

"But you told him—"

"Ally, I said enough."

Her daughter's face reddened, and Riley folded his arms. "What do you care anyway?"

"I don't."

"Then butt out. Stop trying to get brownie points from Mum."

"You are such a selfish poser." Ally's voice lifted in pitch.

"And you're a whiny little brat."

"I hate you so much."

Sarah turned. "Don't you ever say that."

"But if he cared about us, he'd want to stay." Ally's eyes filled.

"Oh, honey," Sarah squeezed her daughter's shoulder, "he's not doing it to hurt us."

"You always side with him." Ally's voice cracked. She threw off Sarah's hand and pushed past Riley. "I can't wait for you to go. In fact, I hope you never come back!" She ran upstairs.

"Maybe I won't. I'm so sick of living with a bunch of drama queens!" Riley swept the Yahtzee box from the dining table and charged off up the stairs. A moment later his bedroom door slammed shut.

Silence descended, its weight settling on Sarah's chest. Drama queen - is that what he really thought? Evan's words edged into her head. *I will not let your fears control his life.* Was that what she was doing now, allowing her paranoia to infect her family, and divide her children? She'd checked the *Belfast Telegraph* every day this week. Its headlines had been filled with mundane stories about reality stars and the re-naming of a bridge. Half of the old paramilitaries were now politicians meeting with the Queen. Maybe Evan and Riley were right, and she was over-reacting. She looked to Sophie noiselessly packing away the game.

"Honey, leave that and come here." Sarah gathered Sophie into her arms and squeezed. "You okay?"

Her daughter's shoulders lifted with the depth of a drawn breath. "Mummy," her gaze searched, "why is everybody fighting?"

Dammit, she'd really messed up.

Sarah rapped her knuckles softly on Riley's door then entered the dark room. He lay sprawled across the bed on his back, turning a soccer ball over in his hands. The flush of light from the hall illuminated the gloomy expression on his face. She flicked on the overhead light. "Can we talk?"

He stopped turning the ball and held it to his middle. "It's okay, Mum. Ireland was a stupid idea. Forget about it."

Sarah fingered the document in her pocket. She'd gotten what she wanted. She could leave his room now, and he would stay home, safe, under her care. And then what? He grew up to be less of who he could be because of her ghosts? She pulled out the photo and sat on the edge of his bed.

"Did I ever tell you about your great grandfather, Aidan McBride?" Riley shook his head, but his eyes remained fixed on the ceiling. "He lived in Ireland, so we only met once, but he was the first person to encourage me to run competitively. He said if I worked hard enough at my passion it could bring me the world, like football had for him." She handed him the picture labelled Ireland Olympic soccer team, Paris, 1922. "That's Papa McBride," she pointed, "standing in the centre at the back."

Riley stared at the photo. Silent.

"I might have given up competing so I could pursue my career overseas, but I do get it, you know. Running is like a part of me, something I can't live without. Just like soccer is for you, yes?"

He gave a small shrug but wouldn't meet her eye.

Sarah brushed her knuckles gently down his cheek. "I messed up, Riley. Sometimes, I still think of you as my little boy and forget the incredible young man you've become." The space between his eyebrows wrinkled. "I'm proud of you for getting this scholarship, and I'm sorry if I made you feel otherwise."

Riley pushed the ball aside and sat up. "You're letting me go?"

"Yes. As much as I struggle with the idea of you being over

there on your own, you've earned this. Just promise me you'll stay safe."

"I promise." Riley wrapped his long arms around her, and she held on tight. She'd done the right thing. The fresh sparkle in her son's eyes proved it. So why was she barely able to breathe?

"Ladies and gentleman, this is a final call for flight QF11 to Los Angeles. Could all remaining passengers please make your way to boarding gate eight. Your aircraft is awaiting immediate departure."

Sarah held herself firm around the middle. The *laksa* she shared with Sophie an hour ago sat like a glutinous mass in her gut. At the time, she'd forced the mouthfuls down, prolonging their last meal as a family before Riley left. Now the taste kept repeating.

Riley dropped his backpack to the ground. "I guess this is it."

Ally and Sophie surged forward and wrapped themselves around him. After a long hug Ally gave him a quick peck on the cheek then picked up his backpack and stood to the side. Her face tight, her back stiff and tall. Sarah's heart gripped. Ally was trying so hard to keep it together.

No such control for Sophie. Tears poured down her cheeks. She handed Riley a drawing of the family. "So you don't forget."

He knelt to take it off her. "How could I forget you, Noodle?" With the edge of his sleeve he wiped the wet from her face. "I'll be back before you know it."

Sarah glanced at the departure board. Riley's flight status

had changed to "Go to Gate". In a minute her baby would head through the arch to customs and that would be it. She stood rigid, the only movement in her body the fidgeting of her toes against the soles of her shoes. She could still ask him not to go.

Evan's wife Felicity, her tiny frame covered in the perfect shift dress, guided Sophie from Riley then moved in for her own goodbye.

"He's going to be okay." Evan's hand touched briefly on Sarah's shoulder.

"He'd better be."

"You did the right thing."

"We'll see."

"Speaking of the right thing, Max came by last night. Said he might come today."

She stiffened and scanned the people nearby. "I hope you told him no."

"He's your father."

"Max walked away from that years ago."

Evan's hands lifted in surrender. "I told him you weren't ready. But he has been trying."

"And that's why I've allowed you to give him time with the kids, but today is for family."

She pushed all thoughts of Max away and checked the time on the departure board again.

Evan moved into an easy embrace with Riley. They shared a laugh, another hug, and parted.

Riley's gaze met Sarah's. It was her turn. Her feet stayed planted. How could she go four months without knowing who he spent time with, what he was doing, if he was safe?

He stepped in, his scent enveloping her, and an ache hit the back of her throat. He wrapped toned arms around her back and pulled her into a hug. She held him close, squeezed tighter when she knew she should pull away. He dropped his chin to her shoulder. She had to let him go. She kissed his cheek then eased back from his hold. "Have you got everything? Passport, wallet, boarding pass? It could be cold on the plane. Did you pack an extra jacket?"

"Mum, we went through all this at the check-in counter. Everything is in my backpack."

Her fingers lifted to his long fringe and brushed it to the side. "You've got the changeover at Heathrow. But when you go out into the arrivals' hall in Dublin, look for the official sign with your name. Don't get in a taxi."

"Mum."

"And make sure you call me as soon as you land, so I know you made it safely."

The weight of Riley's large hands rested on her shoulders. She wanted to grab on and drag him from the building. Why did he have to grow up? His hands lifted to her face, holding her cheeks, just like he used to do at five when he had a solemn promise to make. "Mum, I promise I'll be okay."

Evan leant in. "Sarah, he has to go. His flight is going to start boarding any minute."

She reached in for one last hug. "I love you so much."

"I love you too."

Ally stepped up and threaded Riley's backpack onto his arms. Sarah's throat burned as he walked towards customs. When he reached the arch, he turned and grinned at her. "Thank you."

Her mouth wouldn't push into a real smile. "Stay safe."

"See you all in four months." Riley gave a final wave and then he was gone.

Sarah hugged herself, her fingers digging into her waist as she stared at the empty doorway.

Evan nudged her gently. "Are you okay?"

"Can you watch the girls? I'm going to the bathroom." She ducked her head and ran. By the time she locked the cubicle door, tears and snot dripped from her chin. She sat on the toilet seat lid, her face in her hands.

Please God, if you're up there, please protect my boy. Let this trip be everything he dreamed of, then deliver him back to me unscathed. I will give anything to keep him safe. Trade everything to protect him from harm. Take whatever else you want but please leave my children be.

THREE

"I won't let you do this, Sarah!"

Yasmine hadn't drawn breath. And wouldn't, if their sixteen years of friendship were anything to go by. Sarah pulled the phone away from her ear and pushed the office door closed with her foot. The two of them had met when Horizons Research hired them as the company's first ever community engagement workers. Neither had pictured themselves working in the business sector, what with a social work and psychology degree between them, but life events and newborns had pushed both to seek a safer, more predictable form of work. They'd bonded immediately. Now on a surprise fourth round of maternity leave, Yasmine was devoting her investigative and influencing skills to fixing Sarah's love life.

"You are not cancelling again."

"Yas, please, I've had a huge day. All I want to do is go home to a hot bath and a glass of wine."

It was Friday night. Evan had the girls for the weekend,

Riley had been settled in Dublin just over a month, and the two projects that had been hanging over her head were finally completed and sent off to the clients. The last thing Sarah needed was a blind date.

"Babe, it's been two years since you and Evan split. It's time to get back out there, to live a little. Travis is gorgeous and funny and kind. He's perfect for you."

"I don't want a man in my life. The girls have had so much upheaval lately, they have to be my priority."

"Don't give me that. The girls are at Evan's tonight."

"Yes, but tomorrow Ally—"

"It's okay to prioritise yourself sometimes. Besides, it's too late to cancel. Your date is already on his way."

"What?"

"What's the worst that can happen?"

"He turns out to be a sociopathic serial killer?"

"Very funny. Put on a little lippy and let that gorgeous hair of yours down. You never know, you might even enjoy yourself."

She ran her hand over her head. Her hair was scraped back into a bun at the nape of her neck, flyways poking every which way. She looked like a harried office worker, not a date-ready single woman. "Sorry Yas, I'll find a polite way out, say something has come up with the girls. Believe me, I'll be doing him a favour."

A knock interrupted, and Rebecca entered the office. Sarah took in the receptionist's ironed-out hair, full make up and little black dress. Now that was date-ready. The girl's face was alight, like she was about to combust. "There's a man here to see you."

Sarah sighed at the innuendo colouring her tone. "Yasmine,

I have to go. The doctor is here. I promise I'll be kind. Bye." She hung up before Yasmine could get in another word.

When her office door swung open again, Sarah fixed a smile in place and looked up. A suited man in his mid-forties filled her doorway. Her expression faltered. Yasmine wanted her to live a little, but surely this was taking it to the extreme. The raven-haired man was well over six foot and looked like he'd gone a round with a broken bottle and lost. The left side of his face had two red jagged scars, one circling the corner of his mouth, pulling his lip down a touch. The other, even more brutal, ran the full length of his face from chin to the outer tip of his brow. Then there was the challenge in his green-eyed stare, the intensity impossible to hold. She dropped her chin and shifted papers about, tidying her already immaculate desk.

"You must be Travis, Yasmine's friend. I'm so sorry, but I can't make our date tonight." In reflex she looked at him again. Despite the scars she could see why Yasmine found him attractive, although Sarah was getting none of the funny and kind. He hadn't shifted a muscle. His continued scrutiny dried her mouth. She removed her jacket from the back of the chair and slipped it on. Her hands struggled with the buttons.

"I did try to let Yasmine know, but it was too late." She didn't dare make eye contact again. Instead she reached for her bag, bumped past her desk, and made for the door. The stranger planted his feet wider, blocking her exit.

Sarah's tone cooled. "Excuse me."

"I am neither Travis nor Yasmine's friend, which it seems, is lucky for me."

His deep Irish lilt rumbled through her chest. Her senses

heightened. That accent wasn't just Irish. The man was from the North. A chill climbed the back of her neck.

She took in his conservative suit and tie.

For goodness sake, Sarah, he's probably just a new client. Removing her bag from her shoulder, she retreated to the other side of the desk.

"Sorry, let's start again," she waved him to the chair. "How may I help you?"

The man didn't budge. She tucked her hair behind her ears. It was like being under the disapproving glare of a school principal, one who always assumed you were up to no good.

Finally, he stepped away from the doorway and flipped open a wallet showing an identification card and badge. "Detective Inspector Alec Stone, from the Northern Ireland Organised Crime Task Force."

Sarah's focus darted between the police crest hologram, the words "Police Service Of Northern Ireland" and his photo. The warrant card appeared legitimate except for one thing. "The RUC, the Royal Ulster Constabulary, are the police force of Northern Ireland."

"They were. We changed names in 2001."

Her gaze dipped to the carpeted floor. What was a policeman from Northern Ireland doing in her office? Her head shot up. "Riley?"

"Nothing has happened to your son, Mam. I'm sure he is fine in Dublin."

She exhaled, lowered herself to her seat and stilled. All she'd said was a name. But the Detective knew exactly who Riley was to her. And his location. Why would her son be of interest to the Northern Irish police? She crossed her arms. "I think it's time you tell me exactly why you are here, Detective."

"I'm investigating the murder of Gerry McCann." She stared back at him. Her insides thrashed, searching for escape. "You were flagged as a person of interest when you unexpectedly departed Northern Ireland on the night of the young man's death. You were Gerry's youth worker at the Harmony Reconciliation Project, were you not?"

She looked to her desk, shifted the papers about. "I was, yes."

He sat and opened up a notepad. "And at the time you were engaged to one Michael McNaulty?"

"Yes, but I don't see—"

"At this juncture, I should inform you that Michael McNaulty and his brother, Daniel, are the prime suspects in Gerry McCann's murder." He poised his pen. "Ms Calhoun, where were you on the night of Friday July 18, 1997?"

This couldn't be happening. She stole a glance at the detective but couldn't read him at all. Her fingers drew to her middle finger, twisting the ring she'd inherited from her mother. If he really knew what happened to Gerry that night, she would have been subpoenaed, not visited ad hoc like this. He was fishing. "Since when do the police send a detective halfway round the world to conduct enquiries?"

"I was notified by Dublin Customs when a Sarah Calhoun of an Australian address was listed as next of kin on Riley Barker's arrivals form. I checked the title deed for the given address and found that the birthdate matched our records for the Sarah Calhoun we wished to interview in relation to this crime."

"You didn't answer my question."

Detective Stone paused, his forehead wrinkling with a frown. "I'm following this lead on my own time," he leant forward, "but it would be in your best interest to cooperate."

Sarah stood. "I'm sorry, but you've taken a wasted trip. I came home to Australia because I had ended my engagement with Michael and was eager to get on with my life. The breakup was traumatic, and I wish to discuss it no further."

"You left the country in an unplanned hurry. Your work colleagues at the Youth Centre reported it was extremely out of character for you to leave them in the lurch. If you tell us what you know, we can protect you."

A rapping on the door cut in. "Sorry to interrupt, Sarah, but there's a Travis here to see you. He says he's your date?"

A rush of air escaped Sarah's lips. God bless Yasmine. She picked up her handbag and made her way to the door before the detective could fill it again.

"My date is here, I'm sure you can see yourself out." She walked out of the office, another false smile plastered to her face, this time relieved Yasmine had railroaded her into going on her first date since the divorce.

The unhindered views of Middle Harbour, the crisp white table linen and soaring Puccini aria should have made for the perfect night out, but Sarah was oblivious. Every detail of the conversation with Detective Alec Stone filed through her head like a music track caught on repeat. *If you tell us what you know, we can protect you.*

"So, Sarah, Yasmine tells me you have three children?"

She gnawed at a loose piece of skin at the side of her thumbnail. What exactly did Detective Stone know about that night? Was she a suspect? She swallowed and smoothed down her skirt. The investigation wasn't official, and she'd given the Detective nothing. Hopefully he was on his way to the airport, and that would be the end of it.

"Sarah, are you okay?"

She tucked her hair behind her ear. "Sorry, what did you say?"

"I asked about your children."

"Oh, sorry. I have three. Riley is sixteen. He's on a soccer scholarship in Ireland. Ally's twelve going on twenty and a bit of a bookworm, and Sophie's my baby. She's eight. What about you? Do you have children?"

Travis seemed nice. He reminded her a lot of Evan. Right down to the absence of any spark. Poor man, he'd probably rather have root canal than sit here a moment longer with her.

"...and then there's the twins, Joe and Pat."

"Twin boys," Sarah smiled, "bet they're a handful."

He nodded. An awkward silence opened up. Okay, the man had endured her enough. The least she could do was give him an out. "I'm sorry, Travis, I'm not much company. The drink was lovely, and you've been very understanding, but would you mind if we call it a night?"

He blinked with a flicker of relief and stood to help her with her coat. "I'll have to work on my material."

Her face flushed. His kind grin only drove the guilt deeper. "It's not you. It's just been one of those days."

"Let me give you a lift home."

"No, it's okay. I'll get a cab." She dug out a twenty-dollar note and placed it on the table. "For my drink. I hope you have a good weekend, and sorry again about tonight."

After a final half smile, she wound through the tables and exited the restaurant, certain she would never hear from Travis again.

Sarah groaned and flipped over. The bed sheet bunched in untucked lumps against her back. It made no sense that Gerry's case was being re-investigated now, just because they'd found her after all this time. There had to be a way to find out what was going on.

She slipped from the bed and parted the curtains above her desk. The bluish light from outside softened the dense black of her room. The walnut desk, a scratched and dented antique that had been her mother's, looked out to the Pacific Ocean. Watching the soft white-capped waves roll in under moonlight usually helped calm her mind, but tonight she barely gave them a glance. She sat, opened her laptop, clicked on the search engine and paused. If she did this, she wouldn't be able to unlearn what she found. Then she remembered the Detective's dogged stare.

She typed in Gerry's name. A few newspaper articles came up, all from 1997. Gerry's body had washed up in the waters of Carrickfergus three days after his death. They'd dumped him like a piece of rubbish.

She closed her eyes, took a slow breath, then returned to scanning the screen. The newspapers contained nothing recent, no clues to explain why the case had been reopened. She changed the search parameters and this time found Belfast's online coroner reports. Gerry's file was marked as closed. She'd need to lodge a personal request to have it opened. Not going to happen.

Next she typed in Detective Inspector Alec Stone. A list of newspaper articles appeared on screen. Mostly the *Belfast Telegraph* and the *Irish Times*. Detective Stone was making a name for himself going after Ireland's organised crime gangs, north and south of the border.

Sixth down the search list was a different sort of article, from a blog titled *The Justice League of Belfast*, a commentary on the Police Service of Northern Ireland.

Justice or Vengeance, does it matter?

Detective Inspector Alec Stone, a name synonymous with Belfast's fight against terrorism and organised crime, is a hunter for justice. By all accounts he is a dedicated and respected veteran of the Police Service of Northern Ireland (PSNI). Recently he made headlines for his steadfast pursuit of Daniel McNaulty, whom many suspect is the current Commander of the Real IRA's (RIRA) Belfast Brigade. McNaulty has been arrested, but unsuccessfully prosecuted, twenty-three times in the past five years, many of the charges instigated by Stone.

Is McNaulty guilty, or is the detective on a misguided vendetta as McNaulty is loudly proclaiming?

After a little digging it would seem Detective Stone does indeed have a personal agenda. The RIRA Omagh bombing in 1998 killed twenty-nine people. One of the victims was Detective Stone's aunt, a woman who had helped raise him after his mother's death. Law enforcement suspected McNaulty of sourcing the bomb components. Suspected but never proved. Now Detective Stone hounds McNaulty relentlessly.

It would therefore be reasonable to question the detective's motives - is Stone seeking justice or vengeance? This matter should be promptly investigated by his superiors.

That explained Detective Stone. It also explained the vibes of distrust emanating from him. She'd almost married into a family he believed responsible for the biggest single atrocity in the history of the Troubles. Queasiness seeped into her belly. Had Daniel really moved that high up in the IRA?

She typed in Daniel McNaulty. Her finger hovered over the enter key.

It's just information. It can't hurt you.

She pressed down. What appeared on the screen sucked all air from her lungs. Page after page of arrests for despicable alleged crimes.

Not only had Daniel taken over the helm of RIRA activities in Belfast but he also directed a far-reaching criminal empire involved in racketeering, prostitution, drugs and people smuggling. Some reports linked him with the Russian bratva.

Her palm covered her mouth. Where was Michael in all this? The only mention of him was as Daniel's defence counsel. What about all his beliefs in peace and the law?

Pausing before typing his name, her hands trembled. Did she really need to know anymore?

She closed the computer, climbed back into bed, and settled deep under the covers.

Sending that detective away had been the right thing to do. Daniel was even more dangerous than before. She had no place walking back into his crosshairs. Especially not with Riley in Dublin.

Surveying the Monday morning chaos in the kitchen, Sarah's eyelids grew heavier, craving the sleep that had eluded her since Friday. She scrubbed her hands across her face. When she looked up her daughter was sneaking cornflakes to Fudge. "Sophie," Sarah shook her head. "Do you want toast?"

"Yes, please."

After setting a slice of bread in the toaster she poured herself a mug of coffee. "Where's Al?"

Sophie pointed to the ceiling. Ally had withdrawn lately, avoiding family contact ever since Riley's departure. Tonight, Sarah would make time to get to the bottom of it, when her head wasn't pounding.

She gulped down a mouthful of coffee and toyed with the idea of ringing in sick to the office, knowing all along she never would. The smell of burning snagged her attention. She plucked out the toast and spread it with Vegemite, hoping Soph wouldn't complain.

A cold drop of water slid down the back of her neck. She still needed to dry her hair and get dressed. The doorbell chimed, cutting through the raised voices of her girls now fighting over whose turn it was to walk Fudge. The bell rang again. Navigating her way around the scattered school bags, she moved to the front of the house, tightening the belt of her dressing gown before opening the door.

She balked. Standing before her was Detective Stone.

"Look, Detective, this is going too far. First you come to my place of work and now my home. I told you I know nothing about Gerry's death. If you turn up again, I'm reporting you for harassment." As she closed the door, his foot slid in the gap. "Get your foot out now, or I will call the police."

"Then I will interview your ex-husband. Find out what he can tell me about your ex-fiancée."

Her pulse skidded. Evan knew nothing about Michael. And he couldn't. Ever. She gripped her dressing gown together at the base of her throat. "Fine. But you'll have to wait out here while I get dressed and get my girls off to school."

She glared until he removed his foot and slammed the door closed.

Sarah tore her focus from the vile photos the Detective had fanned across her dining table. Tears burnt the back of her throat. Her gaze travelled across the dirty breakfast dishes heaped high on the white bench and came to rest on a bouquet of yellow and white flowers. Her ragged breath steadied, remembering her girls' excited squeals when they presented her with the jar full of daisies. She closed her eyes. The last photo flashed on her lids. *Oh God.* The girl looked just like Ally, all gangly and thin. That broken child was someone else's precious girl.

Heat surged through her, the walls advanced. She lurched for the bench and heaved the liquid contents of her stomach into the stainless-steel sink. Her gut convulsed in spasms as that last girl's vacant stare seared itself into her brain.

"Are you ready now?"

Detective Stone's measured voice cut through her shock. If Daniel could inflict the evil captured by those photos, trade in the pain and suffering of those innocent girls, how would he punish her for betrayal? A cold fist took hold in her chest. He would annihilate everyone she loved.

She tore off a square of paper towel, wiped her mouth then turned. "I'm sorry Detective, but I can't help you."

"You can. You know something. Imagine if they were your girls—"

"Enough!" Sarah gathered up the photos and pushed them back across the table. "I let you have your say, now it's time for you to leave. I don't want you to contact me again."

"If you think you can hide forever, you're wrong." His card landed on the kitchen table. "I'll leave this for when you come to your senses."

The air swelled with his disdain and anger. She waited for the attack she deserved, but instead the man turned away. A moment later the front door shut.

Sarah stared at the pile of pictures he'd left behind. How could she live with herself now she knew what Daniel had become? What Michael was party to? Her shaking hand pressed at her chest, and her eyes shifted to the jar of flowers. She swallowed hard. Holding the McNaultys to account was not her job. Lunging forward, she tore up the images into tiny unrecognisable pieces and threw them in the garbage. Then she gathered up the half-full rubbish bag and buried it in the outside bin.

FOUR

Five days had passed since the detective's visit, and Sarah
was struggling.

She'd fought her legs for every step she took from the shops
to her car to the kitchen. Every time she closed her eyes that
young girl's face looked back. Or Gerry's.

She added the meat to the sautéing vegetables in the
saucepan. She just had to make it through dinner and get the
girls to bed, then she could sit with the one glass of wine she
allowed herself each night.

Sophie's arms circled Sarah's waist from behind. "What's
for dinner?"

"Dolls' eyes and toothpicks." Sarah turned into the hug,
holding tight a little longer than normal.

"Why do you always say that?" Ally asked, looking up from
the homework she had spread out across the dining table.

"It's what my mum used to say to me." Sarah shook her head

at Sophie who had ducked away and opened the fridge. "No more food before dinner."

The fridge door closed with a thud. Sarah returned to the sizzling pan and stirred. The aroma of frying onions, garlic and mince swirled through the kitchen. She stared out the window.

Memories elbowed in of her mum teaching her to cook. The hours spent together measuring and mixing, and her mum's gentle guidance through the puzzle of teenage friendships and boys.

God, she missed her.

Then the final moments with her mum encroached - her mum clutching at her chest, crumpling to the grass; the tailgate of the ambulance racing away. Sarah's fifteen-year-old self so sure everything would be okay.

"Can I help cook?" Ally's chin rested on Sarah's shoulder, her touch a tether back to the now.

Sarah poured a can of tomatoes into the pan.

"You can make the *Béchamel* sauce. Soph, can you please feed Fudge?"

Sophie skipped outside.

With Ally working in the kitchen beside her, Sarah's mood lifted a touch. Perhaps her daughter had finally moved on from Riley's departure. "How was school today?"

"Good."

"Best part? Worst part?"

"Worst part's easy. Maths. Mr Smythe goes on and on in his monotone voice. Best? English, I guess. We had a discussion on Anne Frank. You know, the Jewish girl from World War Two?"

"Her diary was one of my favourite books." Sarah stirred the simmering meat mixture, leant against the bench and watched her girl confidently add butter, flour and milk to a pan.

"The thing I don't get is how people ignored what was happening to the Jews. Our teacher explained how citizens were scared of the Nazis and that's why they did nothing, but that's so wrong! I mean, if that were happening here, we'd hide them, help them escape, right? How could the people who did nothing live with themselves?"

Gerry's piercing scream of pain filled Sarah's ears. For a moment she couldn't move. Ally stared back at her.

Pull yourself together Sarah, it was in your head. She turned and poured herself a shiraz.

"It is hard to understand, sweetheart, but I'm not sure we should make sweeping judgements of people's actions."

"Why not?" Ally's tone rose an octave. "They either helped people who were their neighbours and friends, or they let them die."

Sarah blocked the voice wailing from her past.

She looked Ally straight in the eye, willing her to understand. "It's not always black and white. What if, by speaking up, they caused their own families to be imprisoned or killed?"

Ally's nose wrinkled in disgust. "You're always telling us to stand up to bullies, but when I say it, I'm wrong?" She shoved her books into a pile. "Whatever. I'm going upstairs to work."

Sarah turned off the stove and lowered her body to the kitchen stool. Her mind filled with visions of Gerry's face. Tears stung the rim of her eyes. From the very beginning she had tried to help him, thinking she knew better, sure she knew just how to guide his life down the right path.

But instead, with decisions and actions she'd do anything to take back, she had placed him directly in harm's way...

Careening through the doors of the Harmony Reconciliation Project office in Belfast, she shivered with relief at escaping the bitter winter wind and drizzle. She shrugged from her puffer jacket, unwound the magenta scarf Michael had given her and flung them both haphazardly on the metal hat rack by the door. She scanned the unusually quiet youth work division - its thread-bare carpet, mismatched desks and the musky smell of rising damp bringing a smile to her face. Turning to her corner of the room, her mouth stretched wider. A huge bunch of red and white roses overwhelmed her desk, their sweet perfume scenting the air. She rummaged for the attached card. "Mo chroi, you've made me the happiest man alive. Xxx."

Mo chroi, Irish for my heart. She twirled the foreign metal on the ring finger of her left hand, still getting used to it. The cool hard silver band was simple and beautiful, two hands embracing a heart. The perfect engagement ring. She moved to the kitchen, filling a jug with water for the flowers.

On her return to the main office a scrawny boy-almost-man with sandy-brown hair styled into spikes paced the room, hands jammed deep into his pockets.

"Hiya, Gerry." Sarah took in his appearance. His usual cocky stance had deflated into a slouch. His deep-set silvery eyes were barren of hope. Clearly the meeting between the parish priest and Gerry's parents had not gone well.

Gerry flopped to the tattered couch, his head dropped back.

"It's of no use, Sarah. If Father Collins couldn't get through, no one will."

She dragged over a chair and sat in front of him. "Hey, we knew this wouldn't be a piece of cake. Your parents love you. They're scared to rock the boat. The IRA can't make you sign up. We need to try a new tack." Her gaze fell on her ring. "And I have just the idea. Michael McNaulty," her mouth softened, "my fiancée. He'd understand this better than anyone. He's in his last semester of law at Queen's but he's from Crossmaglen, and he's smart like you. What do you think? Perhaps if you meet and talk, he will have ideas on how to change your parents' minds."

"Daniel McNaulty's brother? Daniel's dead on around the estate. Do you think he'd talk to my Da?"

Sarah cleared her throat and stood. "How about we meet here tomorrow after school? I'll bring Michael, and we'll see what he can do. Hang in there, Gerry. Keep studying. I promise you'll look back on this and realise it was all worth it."

"Okay," his face broke into a toothy grin, "but only seeing as a lawyer snagged the likes of you."

"Off with you now," she said, laughing. "I'll see you tomorrow."

Sarah gazed blankly at the kitchen floor. If only she had known back then where Michael's true loyalties lay, she would have kept Gerry far away from him.

Sophie ran back into the room, cheeks flushed with cold. Sarah turned her face away and quickly wiped her sleeve across her eyes.

"Fudge sat, Mum, he sat by the bowl until I said he could eat!" She rifled through the cupboard next to the sink and held up a bag of dog treats. Sarah gave a nod, and her daughter raced back outside.

Tightness banded her throat as she stared at the open door. Remorse was all very well, but it couldn't protect her children. She blew her nose and rose to her feet. She couldn't do anything to change the past, but this time, no matter what it took, she would keep her two worlds apart. Returning to the stove, she reignited the gas and concentrated on salvaging dinner.

The bubble bath's muskiness blended with the earthy scent of the candles lighting the bathroom. Every exhausted muscle loosened as Sarah eased into the hot foamy water. She leaned her head back on the tub and closed her eyes. For the first time in ten days nothing but candlelight flickered through her lids. Guilt still sat in a knot, buried in the pit of her stomach, but she was learning to live with it.

Her phone pinged, and her eyelids fluttered open.

Ignore it. Relax. But her brain wouldn't switch off. *It's just an email, probably work.* She slid deeper into the water, and her hair floated around her face. The follow up reminder pinged.

Oh fine. She shuffled to her knees and reached for the mobile. When she tapped the screen a Facebook request email appeared. She rolled her eyes. *Ground-breaking, stuff Sarah, highly important.*

She was about to discard the phone when the name on the request snared her attention. She blinked, re-read it and leapt to her feet, sloshing water everywhere. After a cursory dry, she threw on a dressing gown and made for her desk. She opened her laptop and brought up Facebook.

"Daniel McNaulty wants to be friends on Facebook".

No photo. She lunged for the keyboard, clicked on her own homepage and released the air she hadn't known she was holding. She had followed the golden rules - no intimate info or kid photos. The only personal information listed was that she lived in Sydney. She was a needle in a haystack of 4.5 million other people.

But hairs remained raised at the back of her neck. Why now? Had Daniel found out about Detective Stone's visit? Was it even him? She pushed the computer lid closed and moved away. Whatever it was, she'd stay away from Facebook. Whoever sent it would never know she received the request and the whole thing would go away.

Please, just let it go away.

Sarah stepped from the lift and trudged through the open plan section of the research division. Around her, people chatted and buzzed between cubicles, phones chimed. Thank goodness she could close her office door against it. The headache thumping behind her eyeballs needed no more encouragement. "Morning," she murmured as she passed the reception desk.

"Sarah, wait up," Rebecca raced to her side, "what's going on with you?"

"Nothing." She didn't have it in her to deal with Rebecca today, not after another night without sleep. She picked up pace towards the refuge of her office.

Rebecca stepped in her path and raised an eyebrow. "First

you have two hot men visit within minutes of each other and now this."

She pushed open Sarah's office door and stood aside. All the blood drained from Sarah's head. An enormous bouquet of flowers dominated her desk. Vibrant red and white roses. In a blink, they wilted brown and reeked of death. She grabbed for the door jamb; the flowers came back into focus again.

"Crap you're as white as a ghost. You okay?"

She swept the space for anything amiss then turned to Rebecca. "Were you here when the flowers were delivered? Do you know who they're from?"

Rebecca's face broke into a broad grin "Well, I didn't catch his name, but he had the most gorgeous Irish accent I've ever heard."

"This is important. Was he from a delivery company?"

The young woman bit the side of her lip, her pupils shifted up and right.

"Rebecca!"

"He had no uniform or anything. But he was built, like he totes worked out. Bet his abs—"

"How old?"

"Jeez, Sarah. I don't know. Mid-twenties?"

Not Michael, Daniel or the detective then. Sarah turned her glare on the flowers.

"Was there a card?"

"I might have had a teeny tiny look. There was a sealed envelope. Do you want me to open it?"

"No!" She immediately regretted her sharp tone. "Sorry, I've got it." She closed the office door against Rebecca's curious gaze.

The sweetness of the roses assailed her. She skirted her desk, taking the widest berth possible. A nervous titter bubbled up. *For goodness sake they're a bunch of flowers not a ticking bomb.*

She perched on the edge of her chair and turned the white envelope over in her hands. There were no markings. No clues. Her heel jittered against the floor. Now or never. She unpeeled the seal and pulled out an old-style plane ticket. It was in her name for a flight to Belfast. Next week.

What? What was going on?

Tearing apart the envelope she searched for any other information, but it was empty. She rifled through the mass of stems. Finally, at the very bottom of the bouquet, she found a card. "We need to talk."

She threw the card across the room and reached for her phone.

FIVE

With each squelchy thud of her runners, Sarah strove unsuccessfully for clear thought. Rain bit at her face, coursing off her nose and chin. She had yearned to reach out to someone, anyone, after reading the note, but there was no one to call. No one who would understand her past. So, she'd turned to the one constant in her life. Running.

Following the curving paths of the Botanic Gardens, she passed stretches of green spotted with dripping Moreton Bay fig trees. White capped waves churned up the harbour in the distance. Yet even amongst the wild winds and deserted grounds, Sydney still felt safer than Belfast ever had.

Questions collided inside her brain with the jolt of each step. The ticket had to be from Daniel, but why did he want her back in Northern Ireland? What was he going to do? And why were the flowers delivered to her work? Hadn't he found where she lived? Hope flickered then died. It didn't matter. If he hadn't found her address yet, he would soon. And he'd know about her kids.

Her lungs burnt, screaming for more oxygen. She pushed harder, ignoring the demand. What if he already knew Riley was in Dublin? Then she had to get on that flight to Belfast. Doubling back from Mrs Macquarie's Point, she ran on.

The ticket and flowers could be from Michael. What if, after all these years, he just wanted to talk? But why? Michael wouldn't – wouldn't what? Hurt her? Betray her?

"Enough!"

A couple shrank from her path, huddling closer together under an umbrella. Had she yelled that out loud? She had to get herself under control.

Narrowing her attention to the mechanics of her body, she forced each foot to strike down in time. Next, she overlaid her breath into the beat, dropping her diaphragm to pull the air deep. As she approached the towering white sails of the Opera House, her heartbeat anchored to the solid rhythm of her feet. Only then did she allow herself to process options.

She needed help. And Riley needed protecting until she could sort things out. If she went to Evan, he'd want proof. He might even think the ticket a ploy to get Riley home. Yasmine was out, she had her own family to keep safe.

Sarah continued around the paved shoreline of Sydney Cove, leaping over the water gushing to the drains. Her father? She shook the idea from her head. He'd made it clear he wasn't interested in her problems years ago. She rounded Circular Quay and weaved her way through the tourists awaiting delayed ferries.

That left Detective Stone. She rolled her lips between her

teeth. That man tipped her off kilter. And he was hiding something, something even darker than his aunt's murder. Besides, he'd expect her to testify, which would send Daniel to jail.

Her thoughts skidded to a halt. Wasn't that what she'd always wanted? To see Daniel pay? She accelerated round The Rocks foreshore, the two-storey sandstone buildings of the past dwarfed by the modern-day cruise liner docked at the overseas passenger terminal. She wasn't a naive girl anymore. A man like Daniel never paid. She sprinted by the grey granite and concrete pylons supporting the Harbour Bridge.

There was only one solution. She would ask Detective Stone to organise protection for Riley in Dublin in return for a testimony she would never give. When Riley was safe, she'd meet with Daniel, assure him she could do him no harm, and then she would fly away from Belfast again and leave the lot of them to their manipulations and lies.

Fudge's tail thumped the ground. He'd plopped the ball again at her feet. Sarah threw it, and he scampered across the backyard in pursuit. When she'd finished her run yesterday, she'd been so sure. Had organised to work from home today to do this. She released a sigh and pulled Detective Stone's card from the back of her jeans. She typed the number in three times before she got it right.

"Yes?" a husky voice rumbled down the line.

Her mind went blank.

"This is Detective Inspector Alec Stone. Identify yourself immediately."

"I'm...I'm sorry. I thought you'd be awake. I'll call back

later."

"Ms Calhoun?" His tone was still cool but less menacing.

"Yes?"

"It's 1:00 am in Belfast, but now I'm awake, you may as well continue."

The time difference.

"Ms Calhoun? Sarah?"

"Yes? Sorry. Right." For goodness sake stop it Sarah. You need this man's help, and he won't give it if you keep babbling like an idiot. She raised the piece of paper on which she'd typed what she wanted to say.

"Last time we spoke, I couldn't get past the photos you shared. After thinking on the matter further I realised I do have recollections of the night in question. But I have conditions that need to be met."

"Conditions? Mam do you think this is some sort of joke?" The ice in his voice cut through her bravado.

"No, I know it's not a joke. I just..." She stood, pacing out the space to the back fence while Fudge trotted beside. "I did some research. Ever since 2006, not one case against Daniel has made it to trial. Witnesses recant, two even went missing. Before I agree to help, I have to know my children are safe. They don't deserve to pay for this. Riley is in Dublin. What if Daniel finds him there?" Her voice rose in pitch.

"Sarah," the detective's steady tone settled over her, "I swear your children will come to no harm. If what you know can help put McNaulty away, we will place you and your family under protection. First you need to tell me what you know."

"Not over the phone." She cleared her throat. "I've arranged to come to Belfast next week but won't leave Australia until Riley's under protection."

"I cannot authorise an operation of that magnitude based on your word."

Her voice flattened to a knife's edge. "As it is my word you require in a statement, Detective Stone, you will have to trust me – what I witnessed will be of immense value to your case. If you can't meet my terms, I'm afraid I can't help."

A long pause drew out between them. She held her hand over her mouth praying she hadn't pushed him too far.

"I will organise protection for Riley. For now, your girls should cease all predictable activities. You should discuss the situation with your ex-husband and—"

"No. He is not to be involved. I won't put anyone else in danger."

"That's misguided thinking. I'm sure Mr Barker—"

"Evan Barker will not know of my involvement with the McNaultys. Ever. Are we clear?"

The line stayed silent for a beat, then another.

"We will discuss it further upon your arrival in Belfast. Send me your flight schedule, and I'll organise a protection detail to pick you up from Belfast airport. They'll take you to a safe house."

"No!" Oh God, she'd yelled at him. She had to pull her head in. "Sorry, it's just I'm sure with his resources Daniel will know I've arrived in Belfast, so any kind of special attention would alert him to the fact I'm working with the police."

"Ms Calhoun, have the McNaultys been in contact with you?"

Her face heated. "No." She retraced her steps to the back

fence, taking a deep silent breath. "Look, I will come up with a viable reason for being in Belfast. Please no protection. I will be fine."

"If you are playing some sort of game—"

"Believe me, Detective Stone, I know this is no game. These are my conditions. Riley under protection, Evan kept out of the picture and no detail assigned to me. If you do these things, I will help you put Daniel McNaulty behind bars for life. If we have an agreement, please put it in writing."

"I hope you know what you are doing Ms Calhoun. I will have the agreement drawn up, but we will discuss the terms, in particular your protection, when we meet in person."

"I'll await your email."

She hung up, hoping she knew what she was doing too. Her children's lives depended on it.

Lying back on the wooden deck, Sarah closed her eyes against the sun's glare. Shame prickled. She hated lying to the detective. Making a promise she had no intention of keeping. At least he'd agreed to protect Riley. And work had been happy to assign her long service leave. One obstacle left. She dialled.

"Hi Evan, you got a minute?"

"Only just. A client's about to arrive."

"I have a favour to ask." She could hear him shuffling about papers.

"Go on."

"I've been offered an overseas assignment for a few weeks. I know you've got work, but what would you think about the girls going to stay up at your parents' farm next week?"

"It's mid-term. You never let them miss school."

"I've spoken to their teachers, and they are happy to send some homework along." She'd have to remember to flick an email to the school after this call. "And Sophie's been begging to see your parents for months." Sarah chewed at the flesh of her cheek. The girls would be safe at Doug and Wendy's farm in Tooraweenah. A stranger couldn't buy petrol in that town without it being reported at the pub.

"When would you leave?"

"Next Friday."

"Where to?"

Sarah sat up and scooted her backside to the edge of the deck. "It's for an international housing solutions company."

"I didn't ask who, I asked where."

Sarah picked up Fudge's tennis ball and compressed it between her hands. "Belfast, but it's not what you think."

"And what's that?"

"That I'm going to check on Riley."

"A month ago, Ireland was off limits."

"It's a huge break for me, Evan. The company want to invest in housing for some of the less affluent suburbs of Belfast. Because of the Troubles and everything, they specifically sought an outside community engagement specialist with a working knowledge of the areas, one who holds no allegiances." Thank God she'd practised her cover story before ringing.

"You're telling me you don't plan to visit Riley?"

"Of course I will, but I'll have a lot to do in a short amount of time. It's a big contract." Sarah rolled the ball across the slats of wood next to her, back and forth beneath her palm. "Well, what you think?"

"I'm sure Mum and Dad would be thrilled to have the girls. And Fudge if need be." He paused. "I might even take a week off to go too."

"The girls would love that."

Fudge whined, and she threw the ball in a bounce shot at the back fence. Silence filled the line. Evan cleared his throat. "Will you be okay on your own over there?"

"It's been a long time, a lot has changed."

"Sorry Sarah, someone's knocking at the door." He covered the mouthpiece, muffling his voice. After a small exchange he returned to their call, using a brusque tone she knew well. "My client's here. I have to go, but I'll confirm when I've checked with my parents."

She hung up. Fudge nuzzled into her lap, and she scratched behind his ears. Cockatoos squawked above. She watched the flock fly over and fill the branches of the red gum next door. The next step was flying to Belfast. But once she'd met with Daniel, she could come straight home. She slid her arms around Fudge, burying her face into his neck. Detective Stone would be angry, but what could he do?

Sarah jolted awake with a scream. Sweat soaked her bedclothes. She'd just stood there, her feet cemented to the ground, as Daniel tortured the last breath from the girl. The one from the detective's photos. When the girl's lifeless head had lolled to the side, it had worn Ally's face.

She scrambled to the bathroom sink and splashed water on her face. A shiver rippled through her. She shook her head, knew she was being ridiculous, but tiptoed to Ally's room anyway.

Kneeling next to the bed, she watched the gentle rise and fall of her daughter's chest and inhaled the citrusy scent of Ally's favourite shampoo. She touched a tendril of her daughter's hair, the contact almost bringing her unstuck. What were those other mothers dreaming? The ones whose daughters' beds lay empty. She reached for Ally then stopped. If she clutched her daughter to her chest, as her arms itched to do, she would never let go. Instead she hugged herself and listened to Ally breathe.

She stayed until the pins and needles in her feet became unbearable, then placed a gentle kiss on her daughter's cheek and slipped out of the room.

Re-entering her own space, she stripped out of her damp nightdress, moved to the *en suite* and stepped into the shower. Hot water beat down, her skin tingling as the heat melted the goosebumps away. She leant her forehead against the wall. Snapshots of the girl's lifeless body flashed in her mind. If Daniel was a monster, what did that make her?

She picked up the loofah and scrubbed. Streaks of red appeared on her skin, like the lash marks on the girl's breast. Her chest curled in on itself and water gushed over her head.

Daniel had to be stopped. She couldn't walk away again. But she had to put everything in place first. The girls would be safe with Evan and his family at the farm, but if she actually planned to take on Daniel, someone had to protect Riley twenty-four seven. Detective Stone had organised some kind of surveillance, but the police had limited resources. Riley needed someone whose only mission was to protect him. Someone who could extract him immediately if need be.

Someone like her dad.

The realisation landed like a punch. In the last five years, at Evan's urging, she'd let Max spend time with the kids, but she had not yet seen him herself. Why would she? After the way he treated her back when she'd needed him most…

Sarah lifted her suitcase over the immaculate black marble steps of her childhood home and set it aside. Unbrushed hair swung in her eyes. Taking a band from her wrist, she tied a tight ponytail, pinched colour into her cheeks, and tucked in her skew-whiff shirt. She reached for the brass knocker, and paused. Maybe she should have rung ahead, found time between the misconnected flights and airport delays of the past three days. But then it would have been easier for him to refuse. She rapped twice.

The door opened, and Sarah's mouth dried. Max stood tall before her, shoulders squared. They hadn't seen each other in over a year, and yet his expression registered no change, no welcome. Instead he widened his stance to block the entryway. Sarah smoothed a hand over her hair. His gaze travelled to her feet and back up, but he said not a word. Sarah forced a tight-lipped smile.

"Hi Dad, can I come in?"

"Don't see why."

"Because," making sure her tone remained steady and low, "I'm in a bit of trouble, and I need your help."

"I warned you you'd be out for good if you took that job in Belfast."

Sarah's hands curled into fists. "I only need to stay for a few weeks. *Once I get a job, I'll find my own place. I could back pay you rent.*"

He crossed his arms. "*And that fiancée of yours?*"

"*We broke up. You've no idea what it was like over there.*"

"*No idea? I worked Belfast on secondment with the Brits in the seventies. I said you couldn't handle the likes of it. Knew your do-gooder meddling would be a mistake.*"

"*My God, Dad, I was working.*"

"*Don't you take the lord's name in vain with me, girl.*"

A minor bird's squawking cut into their silence. Max checked his watch. Sarah longed to rub at her scratchy eyes, but it wouldn't do to show more weakness.

"*Please, even one night. I haven't slept in days.*"

"*You made your choice, girl, went against my instructions.*"

"*But—*"

"*You break the rules, you take the consequences.*"

"*I'm your daughter.*"

"*And more's the pity.*"

"*What?*" Sarah registered her shrill tone but couldn't stop the heat flaring up her neck.

"*You can't come back, tail between your legs, because of some fight with your boyfriend. You made your bed.*" He nodded with sharp emphasis and flicked a hand at her. "*I'm just grateful your mother never had to see you like this.*"

Sarah took a step towards him. "*What the hell happened to you when she died?*"

Max's face reddened. He grabbed the side of the door. "*Get out and don't come back.*"

Sarah's palms lifted. "*Dad, I'm—*"

"*You're a disgrace. I'm done with you.*"

The door slammed in her face.

Sarah's hands shook as she reached for her suitcase. He hadn't even asked what trouble she was in. Memories surged of Gerry and Michael and Belfast. She swallowed them away.

Don't come back? What kind of father says that to his only child? She pulled her suitcase in bashing clunks down the stairs. Evan would let her sleep on his couch. At least he always had before. Sarah reset her shoulders and headed for the bus.

She didn't need Max. She'd survive on her own. And when she became a parent, she'd never fail to be there for her child...

Sarah fixated on a crack across the top corner of the wet tile at her feet, refusing to allow the pain from that day to take hold. Instead she racked her brain for another option. Any other option than the father she hadn't seen in seventeen years. She came up empty. After a lifetime in the army, Max had the skills. But this was family asking, not work. Switching off the taps, she seized a towel and wrapped herself tight. She stared at the steamed-up mirror. She could pay him for his time. Make it a job, a contract. He'd honour that.

After dressing in flannelette pyjamas, she slid into the non-sweat-soaked section of the bed and curled on her side. Tomorrow she would contact her father. She'd do it for Riley. And then she could make Daniel pay for what he did to Gerry. For all the pain he'd caused.

SIX

Sarah scanned the shadowy interior of Max's local again. The pub's main lounge, if you could call it that, centred around a metal bar topped with a felt green runner. Numerous beer taps poked out from behind, while eight fixed steel barstools stood empty in front. A television in the corner played greyhound races, muted in deference to a pounding hard rock anthem. Sitting in a booth hugging the wall, fidgeting against its scratchy brown fabric, she wished for the umpteenth time she hadn't arrived early.

A thump sounded outside. Her gaze shot to the door. It banged open, and a booming laugh filled the room, launched from the hulk of a man who entered. A slighter mate trailed behind, their good-natured jostling settling down when they took up a perch at the bar. Her spike of adrenaline dipped away.

She checked her watch. 12:59 pm. What was she even doing? He didn't believe in excuses, didn't forgive mistakes.

"You're a disgrace. I'm done with you."

Sarah gnawed at her thumbnail. His words still stung, even all these years later. A huff escaped her mouth, and she sat on her hands. Enough. You can do this. Present the job to him, then leave. She filled her nose with the musty stink of stale beer. The bar door swung open.

Max Calhoun. He hadn't changed a bit. Not his military grade crew cut, nor his stocky rigid frame. He marched straight over, his stare nailing her to the seat. A flicker passed through his silver eyes. Something? Nothing? She couldn't tell. She'd never been able to read him.

"Sarah." He gave a curt nod and sat down opposite her, his craggy face clean-shaven, back unyielding and eyes assessing. She straightened her spine. It didn't matter what he thought of her. This was for Riley. She looked him straight in the eye. The inner corners of his brows drew in. Concern? A tickle of salty tears threatened from the back of her throat.

"Dad." Instead of rational argument, her voice broke, and she found herself repeating her words from years before. "I need your help."

Max remained still, expression blank.

Dammit. She sniffed and did her best to curb emotion from her voice. "Riley is in Dublin, and he is in danger. I would like to employ you as his bodyguard while I sort things out. I will pay you for your time." She didn't break eye contact. Just waited, unable even to breathe.

"What the hell mess have you got yourself into now, girl? Why is your son on the other side of the world from you if he's in harm's way?" His words were a slap across her face, the judgement rolling off him in waves. He hadn't changed at all. Hard as nails. Her hands clenched into fists. How could she forget Max could reduce her to nothing with just one word or a look?

It hadn't always been like this. They used to build forts together, go camping. One time they'd hired a houseboat and left on a family adventure for a whole term of school. Her dad had spent hours teaching her to fish. He'd been exacting, seeing everything in black and white, but her mum always smudged his edges into grey. When she died, he buried his grief under work. No time or patience or interest left over for a teenage girl. From then on, she dealt with everything alone. Until Michael. She stared into her lap. Her sinuses stung. No, damn it! Damn him. She wasn't going to collapse in a heap. If Max wouldn't help, she'd find someone who would. Snatching up her handbag she pushed along the seat to leave.

"Sarah." Max's hand closed over her forearm.

If she didn't get out of there, she'd lose her composure completely. She'd hoped because of Riley, he might be different. Softer. Kinder. But she was still on her own.

"Forget I asked. I'll sort something else out." Her voice whipped at him as she wrenched from his grip.

"He is my grandson." Max's voice rumbled across the booth.

Her throat constricted so tight she couldn't speak.

"I don't want your money. I want to know what's going on. Why haven't you asked that boy from Belfast to help?"

"That is not an option." She made to leave.

Max raised his hands in a gesture of retreat. "Okay." He stood. "You need to calm down. Sit. I'll get us a drink and then you'll tell me everything."

Sarah's stomach churned, nausea, relief and shame colliding. How could she explain that her relationship with Michael was the cause of all this? That Max had been right all along. She had been a naive fool. Buzzing filled her ears, and the room around her wavered. Michael had never really loved her, or at least not enough to matter...

The whup, whup, whup of a single helicopter pulsated from somewhere near Belfast City centre. An ambulance's wail joined in. Sarah stared at the green numbers of the bedside clock. When they flicked over to 3:00 am the bedroom door scraped against the carpet. The bed dipped next to her and Michael's arm curled around her waist. He buried his face in the back of her hair and a gentle sigh brushed the skin of her shoulder.

Her mouth dried. He reeked of smoke. Where had Daniel taken him? Had they come from where the ambulance was headed? Her head ached with unanswered questions. All the secrets, his sneaking around.

"Michael?"

"It's okay, mo chroí. Go back to sleep." He caressed her hair.

She separated her body from his, sat up and switched on the bedside light. A warm flush filled the room.

"Sarah, sweetheart, I'm just after getting back from a long night. I'm shattered. Could we talk in the morning?"

Indecision coursed through her. She desperately wanted to fold back into his embrace. Maybe she should leave well enough alone. Then she spied the pool of clothes he had discarded on the floor. All black.

"Where did you go tonight with Daniel?"

His eyes shuttered. "He needed my help. Come back to sleep."

A lump lodged in her throat, but she resisted the gentle tug on her arm. "Michael, please. What is Daniel getting you into?"

"He is my brother and needed help. I'm all he's got. Now sleep." He leant across her and flicked off the light, swamping the room in darkness.

Her nose stung. "But that organisation he's in, once they get their hooks into you, they'll never let you go."

"Leave it alone, Sarah. Goodnight." He turned his back on her.

She drew her knees up and hugged them in tight. Tears pooled as she stared at Michael's back, willing him to turn over, wishing he'd take her in his arms and tell her there was nothing to worry about. That nothing had changed. But it had. Michael had travelled deeper into Daniel's world tonight, to a place where she could never follow...

Every nerve across Sarah's skin vibrated with the memory of Michael's touch, the yearning for what they'd had. What she thought they'd had. Max set a glass of red in front of her, its contents swishing to the brim. She took a sip. Her swelling anger devouring any lingering desire. Michael was nothing to her now. No one. She set the glass aside and sat tall.

"I will tell you everything, but you have to promise never to share it with Riley or the girls."

Max crossed his arms and nodded.

She ran through each relevant event, beginning with that night in Belfast. Only once did her focus stray from his, during her confession about Gerry. She couldn't bear to witness the disgust that might pass through his expression. She finished with her decision to return to Belfast and testify. Max's stare burrowed into her, his mouth drawn into a tight line.

"That monster comes near my grandson I'll run a knife through him gut to snout." She let out a strangled laugh. He was going to help, going to protect her boy. "What about the girls?"

"Evan will take them to his parent's farm. It's isolated. They'll be safe there."

"And you? Who will have your back?"

"I'll be fine." She took a drink from her glass, avoiding her father's gaze. "Detective Stone will be there. He'll make sure I'm safe. But I would like to brush up on the self-defence you made me learn as a kid. And," she twisted the glass in a circle by its stem and looked back up, "I want to learn to shoot a gun." Max placed both hands on the table and leant into her face.

"Girl there is no I. We do this together."

Sarah's throat caught. He wasn't turning her away, not like last time. Maybe, just maybe, people were capable of change.

SEVEN

After five days of being tackled, hit, strangled and punched, Sarah's body longed for rest. Bruises spread across her skin in a palette of blue, black and yellow. Her muscles trembled. Even so, she remained determined to master every move Victor threw at her. Victor, Max's buddy from the army, stood almost seven-foot-tall, was agile and strong and showed her no mercy.

And he'd dropped her to the ground, again. She pushed back to standing, positioned her feet hip-width apart, this time remembering to put her right foot forward. She would get this blocking action right if it killed her.

Victor feinted at a kick, and before she had even dodged away, he was behind her, arm hooked about her neck. But he was off balance. She seized his arm with both hands, bent forward, threw him over to the floor with a thud and ran to the gym door. Last time she'd celebrated downing him and he'd swiped her feet from under her. This time he laughed.

"Good," Victor nodded, "we finish for today. Tomorrow's your last, yes? Morning at shooting range, afternoon with me." Victor shook her hand with a firm grip. "You are a quick study."

"I had a great teacher." Sweat slid down the path of her vertebrae. She tugged a towel from her bag and looked up. Her dad stared back with an expression she hadn't seen since she was a kid. He looked pleased. Proud. Warmth spread through her. He looked away to check his watch.

"Time to fetch the girls, Sarah, and say your goodbyes. You want me to drive you?"

"No, I'll be fine, Evan's house is not far from their school. See you tomorrow."

She mopped up the sweat slicked on her face, called out thanks to Victor and headed to the gym's exit. When she glanced back over her shoulder at Max he was absorbed in conversation with Victor, probably planning tomorrow's torture. She shook her head with a smirk, then walked to her car as fast as her wobbly legs would allow.

Sarah turned off the engine and stared unseeing at her dark driveway. Ally's anger hadn't dissipated at all since last week, when she'd learnt of Sarah's "work trip" to Belfast. Her daughter had flared straight up, accusing her of abandoning the girls to be near her favourite, Riley. Even during their goodbye embrace just now, Ally's body had remained stiff and unforgiving. Sophie was the opposite. Evan had to prise her, sobbing, from Sarah's arms. Leaving the two of them had stripped every ounce of energy she had left.

With bed a siren's call, she dragged herself up the front

stairs to the door, dug out her house key and slid it in the keyhole. Prickles spread up the back of her neck. The bolt was already unlocked. She scanned the front yard, her gaze skimming left and right. Nothing. She rolled her shoulders and stared back at the door, trying to recall locking it this morning. Easing the door wide, she allowed it to fully open with a soft clunk against the wall then she checked the alarm panel. Deactivated. She swept the hall for an intruder. Light spilled from the kitchen onto the varnished floor.

Grabbing her mobile phone, she dialled ooo. She toed off her shoes and edged forwards towards the light. Every sense vibrated with awareness. A floorboard creaked under her weight. She froze. She looked back to the door, confirming her escape route, then continued on, legs bent at the knees, poised to run. Before rounding the final doorway, she held her breath, her ears straining to detect any movement or sound. Her shaking finger hovered over the call button.

"What about ye, Sarah?" A hard-edged West Belfast brogue called from the kitchen. Her muscles coiled for flight, her instincts screaming *run!*

"Ach Sarah, come on in. No need to be scared. I've a message to deliver from Daniel, and then I'll be away."

Her body might be demanding she flee, but her brain registered there was no point. Whoever the man was, he'd track her down again. She slipped her phone into her pocket to keep her hands free if she needed them and stepped around the corner. A huge man she'd never met before was seated on her dining chair, his hefty legs planted up on the table. Light bounced off his bald head, the stink of BO and cheap deodorant hovered in a mist. His eyes, almost lost in his muscular bulk, were studying something in his meaty hands. A frame stolen from her mantle, displaying a photo of her three children last summer. Rage surged up from her toes.

"They're good looking bairns, Sarah."

Her limbs trembled with inaction. Her voice came out low. "Get your hands off them and leave, or I'll call the police."

He chuckled. "No need for peelers. Daniel just wants confirmation you'll be on that plane tomorrow."

"What does he want with me?"

"That's nought to do with me, but I would do exactly as he says." He waved the frame in the air. "For their sake. Daniel's not a monster, but sure he has a job to do."

Sarah stared at the photo. Her voice flattened. "I'll be on the plane."

"Grand. Then I'm away."

He discarded the frame. It slid across the table, only just coming to a stop at the edge. Her skin bristled as the man brushed past her, but she stayed perfectly still. When the front door banged shut, she shot forward and rubbed the man's smudges from the glass with her shirt.

You will not touch them, you bastard. I swear I'll kill you myself before you come near my kids.

She marched to the lounge room to return the photo to its place, her fingers unwilling to release their hold once she'd settled the frame in position. She took in each detail of her children's faces; the dusting of freckles from a summer in the sun. Thank God the girls hadn't been home. Or Fudge. What would Daniel's man have done then?

She returned to the kitchen, uncapped the bottle of shiraz she'd opened the night before and took a gulp straight from its neck. The alcohol warmed her but didn't erase the fear snaking up her back. Max wasn't leaving for two days. She pulled out her phone and paced. He answered on the third ring.

"Dad, it's Sarah. I need you on a plane to Dublin tomorrow. I can't leave Riley alone any longer."

"Hold your horses, girl. What's going on?"

She exhaled slowly. She needed to calm down, or Max would want to stay with her. "Look I'm okay, but Daniel sent a messenger to check I'd be on tomorrow's plane."

"What!"

"He was in my kitchen when I came back from dropping the girls off at Evan's. He's gone now."

"Are you hurt?"

"He didn't touch me, just shook me up. Which I think was the point. But if he can get into my home on the other side of the world so easily—"

"Then Riley's a sitting duck."

She lowered to a chair. Her nose scrunched at the lingering stench of the intruder and she stood again. "Please can you leave tomorrow?"

"I'll be on the first plane."

"Thanks." She pulled out pine scented disinfectant from under the sink and sprayed the table and chair.

"What's that detective going to do about this?"

"I haven't told him." She scrubbed every inch of where the man had touched.

"Why the hell not?" The tone of Max's voice stopped her mid wipe. "What are you going to do, arrive in Belfast and offer yourself up like a sacrifice to this psycho? The police need to protect you."

"They will." She moved to the loungeroom and cleaned every remnant of the intruder from the photo of her kids. Fears swirled and collided in her head. "What is Daniel up to, Dad? Why does he want me in Belfast?"

"I don't know, but you've decided to take him down, so let's do it. We've already built your skills. I'll get Victor to organise a gun for you over there. There's no way you'll get one through legal channels fast enough."

"I'm not sure I want one."

"No discussion on this, Sarah. That snake cannot be trusted. No gun, no trip."

A weight landed with a thud on her chest. How much of herself would she have to give up before this was over?

"Look girl, we've trained you well, but to defend against a group a gun may be the most effective protection you'll have. The most important resources are still your brain and your gut. Listen to both before you act, and you'll be right."

"Okay." She put the cleaning gear away and washed her hands. "Let me know your flight details when you have them. And Dad?"

"Yes?"

"Thanks."

She ended the call and stared at the moonlight bouncing off the swing set in her backyard. Her fingers gripped the bench. Daniel McNaulty had made a huge mistake by having that man enter her home, having him physically threaten her kids. Her family would never be safe until Daniel was behind bars. Once she landed in Belfast, she had to find a way to meet with the detective in secret. But first she would find out what Daniel thought he knew about her, and more importantly what he really wanted.

The next morning the firing range was full, people assigned to every cubicle, many using desks to balance longer-range rifles. They squeezed off shots, but she could barely hear them through her earmuffs. She almost hadn't come today, in case the man from her kitchen was tailing her. But she realised Daniel wouldn't care. He was arrogant; would never consider her a true threat. He never had. And that would be his downfall.

Standing up at the firing window, she pictured Daniel's man, the one from her kitchen, and his sneer as he pawed the photo of her children. She edged her right foot ahead of the left, leant forward a touch and slightly bent both knees. Drawing in a breath, she cradled the gun in her left hand, steadied it with her right, released the safety, aimed for the black and white paper target, and on a measured outward sigh, squeezed the trigger. She rolled with the recoil and started the sequence again. It was second nature now, her muscle memory taking charge.

Thoughts of the man in her kitchen and his implied threats returned, then she pictured Daniel. And fired with a cold hatred that stunned her.

Her thumbs and inner elbows ached from her hours of practise. This past week she had pushed her body beyond its limits. But in a few hours, she'd get on a plane to meet a man who would stop at nothing to get what he wanted. She would need every skill and resource she could develop.

At least her visitor had confirmed the flowers were from

Daniel and not Michael. Hopefully, she could avoid her ex-fiancée all together.

She pressed the button calling the paper silhouette target back to her cubicle. Five shots had hit in the torso's target rings, but one, the last one she suspected, had hit the paper human right between the eyes. The perfect kill shot. She flew out tonight, and whatever was waiting at the other end, she'd be ready.

EIGHT

The plane dipped its left wing, and Sarah got her first full view of Belfast. She spotted the River Lagan, and, winding with it, the towpath where she'd trained for marathons. She tracked the canal from the town outskirts through the city centre and out to Belfast Lough. To the north, rising to a peak overlooking the entire city, sat Cave Hill. Her chest tightened. Unwanted memories pushed their way into her thoughts.

Summer rain. Laughter. Bright yellow gorse. Promises. She shuffled about in her seat, her movements sudden and jerky as she slammed her mind shut.

The plane circled to line up with the runway, and she glimpsed the Titanic Quarter, with its new angular building and surrounding apartments. So many buildings had popped up in the city centre since she'd left.

But as she studied the working-class pockets of the city – West Belfast, Crumlin Rd, Sandy Row – the interfaces where most of the deaths and violence had occurred, the post-Troubles regeneration was non-existent. Her gaze caught on Cupar Way, a kilometre long, fourteen-metre-high, two-metre-thick concrete and steel barrier separating the Protestant Shankhill from the Catholic Falls.

Past frustrations flared. That 'peace wall" had been erected for over forty-five years and was only one of a hundred dividing Northern Ireland's tribes. Because that's what they were, tribes who attended segregated schools and used bus stops unofficially designated "safe for our kind". Clans who turned a blind eye to the paramilitaries policing their communities; the commanders doling out punishment beatings, kneecappings and house cleansings by fire – without proof, without trial. Each side's fears, prejudices and suffering a mirror to the other.

The landing gear clunked and whined into place.

She flexed her fingers, curling and uncurling them a few times, then drew her hair back into a ponytail and attempted to tame the frizz thirty hours of travel had caused. She tied a light scarf around her neck and tightened her seatbelt. She had no idea what was down there waiting for her. She had to be prepared for anything.

After the plane touched down, she gathered her belongings and moved towards the exit. The aerobridge awaited like a gangplank. She clutched at her backpack with clammy hands. Last time she'd entered this airport's arrivals hall, she'd been met by army patrols and dogs.

Body searches, tanks, machine guns, explosions, riots, hijackings.

Her knees locked, her legs refused to budge. Fellow passengers stepped around her. A man bumped her shoulder, his muttered frustration dragging her back to the present. She hadn't even considered dealing with Belfast itself, that it alone might rip the lid off all she had buried.

Emerging into the arrivals' hall, she squared her shoulders and scoured the awaiting faces for one of Daniel's men. Not a soul took notice of her. She stood braced, waiting. Minutes passed. Still no one came forward.

Her racing pulse slowed at the reprieve. Only then did she take in the hum of normality surrounding her. Gone was the menacing silence, when soldiers patrolled the hall, machine-guns always at the ready. People were milling about, unhurried, unworried.

In a daze she collected her suitcase from the carousel and rolled it outside. The sun was the next surprise, its morning rays warming her face, not hiding behind a wash of grey. No barbed wire blocked the road. No army checkpoint searched under cars with mirrors. Just blue sky, sunshine and people going about normal activities. Belfast City Terminal was like any other airport in the free world.

She pulled out her phone and tried Max. It went straight to voice message. She typed in Riley's number. When he didn't answer either, she began to pace. She dialled Max again.

"Why aren't you answering your phone? Call me as soon as you get this." She jabbed the end button and dialled Riley.

"Riley, where are you? You need to ring me now."

Had something happened while she'd been in the sky? They both knew her arrival time. She tried each one again. No answer. She tapped the phone against her thigh. The plane had been on time. Where were they? She turned up the ringer as loud as it would go, kept her phone clutched in her palm and rolled her bag to the cab rank. If they hadn't called back by the time she reached the hotel, she would call the detective.

She flagged a black taxi and gave the address for the hotel she'd found online. They turned onto the motorway, and she distracted herself by looking out the window searching for any sign of the Belfast she'd known. She scanned the sky for the helicopters she dreaded, listened for their whirring blades. But as much as she strained her neck and ears, she could neither see nor hear even one. Instead the soundscape of normal city life filled the air: buses and trucks chugging along, cars racing past, horns blaring. A PSNI Land Rover passed by, painted white and trimmed with blue and yellow checks – even the police vehicles had evolved from their militaristic grey.

Her muscles eased, her shoulders dropping back into place. The city had changed. Maybe things would work out easier than she'd thought. The corners of her mouth lifted. Perhaps she could manage this after all.

The taxi entered the suburbs and took a left turn. All oxygen wheezed from her lungs. That corner ahead. Just around that bend. They'd stood there embracing, laughing, kissing. A week later she had fled their home. She was wrong. She couldn't take being here. She pushed the heel of her hands into her eyes, trying to block the memories, to keep them at bay, but failed just as hopelessly in her goal as she had that night...

Sarah braced her left palm against the pub's brick wall and bent in two with laughter. Michael's Groucho Marx-inspired impersonation of the bartender continued, pretend cigar and all. "Young man that is no way to grab at a lady."

The laughter tapered away. It was the right time. As soon as they were home, she'd talk with him, and then they'd deal with Daniel together. When she planted a peck on his mouth, his arms wrapped around her waist and drew her in. She softened against him, parting her lips. For a moment she savoured the taste of whiskey and heat, then ducked from his hold. "Uh, uh, uh, Mr McNaulty, definitely not appropriate behaviour."

Michael laughed again and hooked his arm through hers. They rounded the street corner and stopped dead. A crowd of people had formed towards the end of the road. At their centre, a police Land Rover rocked back and forth. God were the RUC policemen still inside? The attacker's jeers knifed through the warm night air.

Michael turned to her. "There's no way round."

A mass of men, women and children flooded in from all directions. Most wore hoods pulled up over their heads and scarves masking their faces. Her heart sped up. This was no impromptu protest.

Michael seized her hand. "Hold tight."

A rumbling shook the ground behind. Swivelling round, they were confronted by a wall of grey. Armoured Land Rovers now barricaded their exit. Swarms of riot police poured out, dressed in black boiler suits and brandishing batons. The officers joined shields, forming straight lines of defence. The clear masks on their helmets reflected the rioters' animal-like frenzy. The terraced houses of the suburban street loomed overhead, boxing everyone in, them included. More people appeared over fences. Hatred vibrated through the dark. Land Rovers arrived at the other end of the street closing ranks around the lame vehicle, trapping the swelling crowd completely. A metallic taste burst onto Sarah's tongue. "Michael, we have to get out of here."

Crunching sounds came from their left, rubbish bins dragging across gravel. The crowd's own militia was forming, their fury palpable. On a loud roar, a mass of people surged towards the crippled Land Rover, tearing Sarah and Michael apart.

"Michael! Michael!"

Overhead two helicopters arrived and drowned out her cries. The thunderous booming of their beating blades pounded in her chest. The stark beam of the helicopter's searchlights glanced over her and caught on a bottle flying above. When the petrol bomb exploded into the police line a mighty cheer swept through the hordes. Fire flashed, and an orange glow lit the night. The stench of gasoline filled the air. A barrage of rocks and bricks and petrol bombs pummelled the police line.

She scanned the crowd for Michael, but a pack rushed forward again, enveloping her in its rage, pushing her closer to the front line. Plumes of acrid smoke stung her eyes and throat. Shit, Sarah, don't panic. Just think. Think!

The night sky lit up with another lobbed bomb, but the RUC's boiler suits protected them from the flames. Sarah clawed her way to the side, but the crowd drew her back in again, and struck out at the RUC like an attacking snake.

God, there was no way out. The police had the narrow street completely cordoned off. She tasted anticipation, as if the crowd knew something she didn't. An ominous whistling flew over her head, giving her a split second in which to crouch down and cover her face with her hands. An explosion hit behind the RUC line just metres away. A soldier, barely past boyhood, fell to the ground screaming out in pain, his riot gear no defence against the *nail bomb. His anguished screams were muted by jets of water bursting at the crowd from a cannon on top of a Land Rover. Sarah tripped and slipped, trying to get away. All around her people were mowed down, their feet taken out from under them by the sheer force of the spray. The hail of rocks, bottles, petrol bombs and bricks resumed. The crowd chanted: "SS RUC, SS RUC."*

The police moved towards them. A small group broke through their line and climbed a Land Rover. A flash of familiar blond hair raised a brick above his head. He smashed it against the Land Rover's roof. No! What was one of her boys doing there? He was just a kid. Sarah elbowed through the crowd. "Liam, get down. It's not—"

Oomph. A punch of pain slammed into her side. A sharp blast of water knocked her onto her arse. Her torso pulsed, winded by the canon's power. Something whizzed above her, and an ear-splitting cry pierced the night. Liam tumbled from the vehicle, hit by a plastic bullet.

"No! Stop! He's only ten." Sarah scrambled to her feet. She stumbled forward but was pushed back by the riot shields. Flashes of smashing glass burst around her. A sudden sting slashed across her cheek. She reached to her face, and her fingers came back red. Orange flashed again. Petrol fumes overwhelmed her lungs. "Please, I work with that boy. Let me help him."

The officers' faces remained blank.

"He's only a child. I'll take him away."

"You Australian?" barked a commander from behind the line. "What are you doing messed up in this? Get the fuck out of here."

"I'm trying to! Please, let me through." Her eyes watered

from the smoke. Another missile flew over her head and smashed to the ground.

Finally, he broke the line to let her through. "Go!"

She charged over to Liam. "Are you okay?"

His body convulsed with sobs. A flash of fire burst to her left. She had to get them out now.

"Liam sweetie," she heaved him off the ground. "Wrap your arms and legs around me. I have you." Clutching Liam tightly to her body, with her chest burning and water dripping from her clothes, she ran the eight blocks to home, praying Michael would be there when she arrived...

She wound down the cab's window and sucked in the fresh air. The visions were so vivid, so raw. That night had changed Michael. What if she'd managed to keep hold of his hand? Could she have saved him from Daniel? Would they have made it through?

She inhaled deep and exhaled slow. Michael made his choices. She had to concentrate on her own. She moved her attention to outside the cab and frowned. "Excuse me, driver. I said the Cathedral Quarter. You've gone way past. This is heading into The Falls."

"Aye, miss. Daniel McNaulty would like a word first, so he would."

You idiot Sarah, you absolute idiot. The IRA had always run the Black Cabs. Clearly, they had some left. She hid her phone in her pocket and sat ramrod straight. Three blocks later, the driver eased the car to a stop at the kerb, next to a pub. His gaze flicked to hers in the rear-view mirror then slid away. The neighbouring block was a well-kept paved area dedicated to the IRA fallen, their names memorialised in gold on standing granite blocks. Sarah dried her palms down her thighs.

The cabbie unlocked her door, returned his hands to the steering wheel and kept his focus out the front windscreen. Guess she was on her own then. She wrestled her suitcase from the car and barged straight into the rock-like chest of the man from her kitchen. He yanked her case away with ease, grasped her elbow and guided her towards the entry of Murphy's Bar. She glanced around hoping for witnesses, but the street was deserted. When she stumbled on the front step, she threw off his loosened hand.

"I'm perfectly capable of walking alone." She hoped he hadn't noticed her jelly legs. "Who are you anyway?"

"Seamus." He shoved her forward. "Now go." He pointed to a closed door at the end of the bar then settled on a stool between her and the exit. She didn't budge. Instead she allowed her pupils to adjust to the dull light. The space had the traditional ambience of Irish pubs worldwide. A tiled black and white chequerboard floor, ringed by cosy wooden booths upholstered in warm tartan hues. The pub was empty, except for the young barman stocking glasses. When she caught his eye, Seamus snarled something at him, and the barman swiftly turned his back.

Seamus gestured again to the closed room.

Okay, through the door it is. She took a steadying breath, turned the handle and entered. A whisky brown stare pinned her to the spot.

Neither one of them moved, lost in their first sight of each other in seventeen years. Michael had lost none of his appeal.

Thick eyelashes. Dark wavy hair still worn a little long, messy and curling around the collar of his shirt. A white shirt hugged a toned physique, sleeves rolled to the elbows. The tug in her belly almost took her to her knees. Her gaze met his.

Michael's eyes, at first full of surprise and questions, went dead, the sudden cold drowning her like a wave. He stood stiffly, gathered his papers, and headed to the door, his sights set beyond it. The fine hairs on her skin rose to attention as he moved closer. She caught his smell, the same cologne she used to buy him. Before she knew what she was doing, she reached out her hand and touched her fingertips to his bare forearm.

He glared. "Don't."

The bitterness in his voice shredded her. "Michael, please."

The silence swelled until he broke away and opened the door. "I've no clue why you'd deign to come back—"

"What? But Daniel—"

"I don't want to know." The door closed with a sharp bang, leaving her alone.

Her heartbeat drummed in her ears as she fought the desire to chase after him. She had to remember why she was here, what was ahead. Backing up against the wall, she swallowed hard and fortified herself for Daniel's arrival.

Trophies of the man's power and wealth dominated the room. In a glass case an autographed Celtic football uniform sat alongside the championship belt of a famous heavyweight boxer. Next to her head hung a signed original of the 1916 Proclamation of the Republic, worth over a hundred thousand euros. Between two overflowing bookcases was a huge, black, leather-bound chair pushed up to a mahogany desk. Suspended on the wall above was a wooden sign carved into a heart-shaped

Celtic harp. Her gaze swept past a decanter of whisky and fell on a photo on the desk. A short homely woman with bobbed auburn hair stood next to Daniel, surrounded by four children of various ages, from a babe up to a teen. Daniel's family? Surprise washed over her. He actually had kids?

She looked to the open door and listened for footsteps. Hearing nothing, she plucked her phone from her pocket, preparing to take a photo of Daniel's family when a voice from the door slid over her skin.

"Would you look at that? My man Seamus forgot to confiscate your phone. I'll take it for now, shall I?" Daniel sauntered towards her holding out his hand.

She braced. Daniel was short for a man, five foot eight, but his presence filled a room. His suit and shirt were black, matching his dark eyes. He had aged, the hard lines on his face carving away any previous boyish charm. He leaned in. She thrust her phone at him, silently cursing her stupidity at losing her only lifeline.

"Calling Riley in Dublin?" Her gaze locked with his. He'd better not have touched her son. "I'll put your mind at ease." He turned and sat on his chair. "Your son is healthy and safe. Training mighty hard as we speak."

Her hands balled into fists. She imagined slamming one into his self-satisfied grin, his nose bursting in a gush of blood. But he was playing with her, a cat with its prey. And he'd unwittingly given up a card, confirming he did have someone watching Riley. Information she could do something about. Daniel was so smug, trying to bully her into submission again. But she was older now, wiser. He had no idea what she was capable of, how far she'd go to protect her family. Best to keep it that way.

She swallowed down the hatred and anger, boxed it away, then lowered herself to the chair opposite him and remained silent. Daniel pulled out a cigar and cut off its head, struck a match and raised it to the cigar's end. When he finally inhaled, she was ready to explode. *Rein it in, Sarah. This is about power. About control.* He needed to believe he had the upper hand.

"And how was your little reunion with Michael? He left here at quite a pace. I do hope you didn't say anything to upset him."

She bit down on her back teeth. Had Daniel set his brother up? Michael had looked shocked when she'd entered the office, unsure of what was going on. She glared at Daniel's smarmy grin. Of course, he had. He wanted to unsettle her, but he had also tested Michael. Daniel didn't trust his brother.

He had revealed another card. She just had to live long enough to use it. She silenced her whispering fears. If Daniel wanted her dead, she would be. He wanted something else. She crossed her arms. "Michael and I had nothing to say to each other. You're the one who summoned me here. Why?"

"Ach, straight to the point." He puffed at the cigar, enclosing the room in a haze of cloying smoke. "We know about the visit of your man Stone. He's determined to pin that McCann kid's death on me, and for some reason, he believes you can help." The muscles across her back went taut. "What Stone doesn't know is now you work for me."

Her hands balled into fists.

"And as your employer, I'm insisting you give Stone what he wants."

"What?"

"Aye, get me arrested. I don't care how, but I want this to go to court. And when you take the stand in front of the lot of them – the prosecutor, judge, media, and Stone – you'll testify there is no way I could have murdered Gerry because I was with you that night. In your bed. And that's the reason you ran from Belfast."

A sour taste burst on her tongue. "No one would believe I was with you that night. I was leading a camp in Glebe."

"Now, Sarah, you were at the camp, but the other staff swear you drove back to Belfast and never returned."

She gripped the sides of her chair so hard her palms stung. "I can't."

"You can, and you will." Daniel leaned back in his chair. "Think on this very carefully. If you do as I say, you can return to Australia, to your children, and forget about Ireland for good. If, instead, you choose to betray me I will destroy everyone you love, starting with your son."

She didn't move an inch, afraid of what she might do if she did.

"One last thing, Sarah. Have you ever asked yourself why Stone is so intent on hunting me down? He'll tell you it was the Omagh bomb, but he knows that's a lie. Can you trust a liar with your children's lives? Ask Stone about Olivia. He wants to blame and punish me, but Olivia's death was all his fault." Daniel checked his watch and moved to the door. "Right, you best be on yer way. Seamus will see you back to a cab."

Sarah lifted her chin, rose from her seat, and walked from the room without a backward glance. No way she'd let the bastard see her crumble.

NINE

Hunched against the cab's back door, gripping her returned phone tight, Sarah stared at the cabbie's thick hands. His fingers grabbed so hard at the wheel, his knobbly knuckles protruded in angry red. Why should he be nervous? Did Daniel have another surprise in store? She checked outside. It looked like they were driving in the right direction; in fact, if the new bars and eateries were anything to go by, they'd entered the Cathedral Quarter already.

You're okay Sarah. Daniel needs you alive.

The car lurched to a halt, the door lock clicked open. She shot out, suitcase in hand, ready for anything this time, to find herself in front of a white, five-storey building flanked by two stark trees sticking out of the pavement. The Morton, her hotel. The cabbie sped off, forgoing his fare. Sarah watched the tail-lights disappear around the corner, then scanned the faces in the few cars driving by. No one paid her any attention. She had been left alone.

She dialled Riley's number, each unanswered ring a ratchet tightening the clutch on her chest.

"Hi Mum."

The street blurred over. "Riley! Why didn't you answer before? I rang so many times. I told you I'd land at 7:00 am." Her voice came out shrill and strained. Riley took a moment to answer. When he did, there was an edge to his tone she hadn't heard him use before.

"We had an early weights session."

"You could have sent me a text. Put my mind at ease."

"Mum, I'm fine. I made it through the last six weeks on my own."

Her insides twisted. His tone was the impatient one Evan used when he thought she was being unreasonable.

Pull it together, Sarah. Do you want him to know something is wrong?

"Sweetheart, I'm sorry. It was a long flight, and I just needed to hear your voice. How are you?"

"Good," excitement warmed his tone, "actually, great. My team's on top of the ladder, with only two games left to play this round. There's an awards thing and party on Sunday night. Hey, maybe you could come?"

"I'd love to." A beat of silence. Perhaps he hadn't thought she'd say yes. "Riley?"

"Granddad will be there. He's come over for a few weeks to watch me play in the comp." Her shoulders softened. Max. They hadn't shared their reconciliation with Riley. "Sorry, Mum, I can't un-invite him from the ceremony, but you will still come, won't you? I can't wait to see you."

"Of course, I'll be there. In fact, how about I spend the weekend? I could get a hotel, come watch your game."

"Cool." A horn sounded from Riley's end. "Mum, I have to go. We're warming up."

"Okay, honey. I'll see you tomorrow. Love you."

"Love you too."

She hung up. The rapid hammer of her pulse had slowed but not yet settled. She dialled the pre-paid mobile she'd given the girls. When they answered straight away, her knees unlocked, and she sank onto her suitcase. With each story of horses and creeks and chickens, her chest loosened. All her children were safe and happy. For now.

Sarah rolled her bag through the hotel's automatic doors and swept the small brightly lit foyer for signs of anyone watching for her. Whoever had decorated the place had a thing for the Orient. In the corners, artificial palms and bamboo, that would be more at home in a Balinese resort than a three-star Belfast hotel, grew in large white pots.

She paused. A man dressed in an ill-fitting business suit strutted directly towards her from the breakfast buffet. Her muscles tensed, but he walked straight past her to the exit while speaking tersely into his phone. She exhaled and approached the counter to check in.

"Right you are then, Ms Calhoun, Room 315 is ready early so you can go straight up." The full-figured receptionist passed over a credit card-like key, her too-loud voice grating on Sarah. "Oh, and there's this wee package that was hand delivered for you."

Sarah eyed the shoe-sized box wrapped in thick brown paper.

To Sarah Calhoun from Max. Handle with care.

Oh crap. She looked at the receptionist. Did the girl know what was in the box? Had she looked?

"It's not that heavy like, but we could deliver it to your room?"

Did the girl have to yell so everyone could hear?

"No, I've got it." She picked up the box and a familiar weight inside shifted to the left. The gun. It had been sitting behind the desk, unsecured, waiting for her. What had Max been thinking? She glanced over both shoulders. The receptionist lifted her eyebrows.

"Is there anything else I can help you with?"

"No, no thank you. I'll be fine." *Fine. Fine. You won't be fine if you're caught with an illegal firearm.* She swallowed. *Calm down, don't draw more attention to yourself.* She tucked the box to her side, muttered another thank you and made a beeline to the lift. After pressing the button, she scanned the foyer, tension braiding her shoulders. She looked back to the unchanged floor number of the lift and shifted the box up higher on her hip. Sweat beaded along her hairline. *What was taking so long?*

Finally, the lift groaned to a stop in front of her. She rolled her bag in, let the door close and leant against the back wall. She fished her phone from her pocket and sent a one-handed text to Max.

Package received. C u in Dublin tomorrow.

It was cowardly not to ring him, but she couldn't afford to let slip about her detour to Daniel. Not yet. Not until the sludge in her brain cleared enough for her to decide how to handle things.

She found her room at the end of the corridor. Once inside, she left her bag, walked straight to the wardrobe and crouched in front of the safe. She placed the box inside, unopened. The locks clicked into place, and the knot in her solar plexus unfurled. She sat back on her haunches and cast her gaze about the room. A queen bed took up most of the space, its black headboard butted up against an eggplant feature wall. She pushed her sluggish legs to standing, emptied her pockets and fell across the white bedspread. The scent of fresh linen enveloped her. She'd done everything she could cope with for now. Her eyelids drooped in slow blinks. Her muscles melted into the bed and she fell asleep.

Rattling and buzzing dragged her awake. She groped about on the bedside table for her phone while her eyes strained and fluttered against the brightness of the room. A text came into focus. *Where are you? Ring me.* She burrowed back into the pillow. She was nowhere near ready to face Detective Stone. He would have to wait.

She turned onto her back and stared at the opaque light fixture. The morning's events came crashing back. Her mind scoured each word Daniel had spoken, each one Michael hadn't. A sick feeling moved through her gut. What exactly was Daniel up to?

Swinging her legs to the side of the bed, she racked her hands across her face. If she gave the police an alibi for Daniel right now, they wouldn't even charge him. Why was he ordering her to wait until trial? She stood, stretching her arms above her head.

Did it have something to do with Detective Stone? Or with Olivia, whoever she was?

Bending forward, she locked her knees and placed both hands flat on the floor, but her leg muscles resisted the stretch. Her body twitched with edginess. She tried pacing but the space closed in, the stuffy air clogging her lungs. She rubbed her palms on her denim-clad thighs, pressure expanding under her skin like an over-filled balloon.

Tossing open her suitcase, she pulled out workout clothes and threw them on. She needed space right now, fresh air, or she was going to lose it.

Exiting left from the hotel she sprinted along the concrete footpath towards Queens Bridge. She bounced foot-to-foot at a red light, waiting to cross to the Lagan Waterfront. Seagulls squawked above the blaring traffic. Opposite her a new, steel-tubed statue of a woman faced the water, a hoop held above her head. The Beacon of Hope. A huff escaped Sarah's lips.

The second the lights turned green she leapt forward, veered right and pushed on. The once barren route hummed with new life. The lunchtime crowd swelled about her, slowing her movement. Her skin shrank tighter. She darted and dodged forward, concentrating only on the tarmac in front of her.

When she crossed the Ormeau Bridge, the mothers with prams and lunchtime joggers dropped away.

Ten minutes later, concrete gave way to nature. Now she recognised the path. She climbed a steep staircase, and Lagan Meadows spread out before her. Yellow wildflowers and seeded dandelions dotted the grass. Her jammed diaphragm released, and a rush of oxygen filled her chest. She took a moment to revel in the full expansion of her lungs and took off again, noting the position of her feet as they struck the ground, placing her weight evenly across the width of her foot. Her strides developed a steady rhythm. Her mind shifted into gear.

She'd faced off with Michael and his brother this morning and survived. And Daniel had revealed more to her than he'd planned. Even after all these years, he didn't trust his brother. That could be useful. Although Michael had been so cold.

Stretching the back of her head away from her shoulders so each vertebrae of her back stacked as it should, she increased her pace. Daniel had confirmed he had someone spying on Riley; that was her priority. She had to find out who. Only then could she tell the truth on the stand. She accelerated, looping back round to the canal. Once she'd given her evidence, there was no way Daniel would walk free.

Sweat covered her skin, its presence familiar and settling. At least Daniel's plan freed her to meet openly with Detective Stone. She could tell him everything. At least everything about that night. But what about the rest? Could he be trusted?

She flexed her hands and curled them back in, pumping her arms harder. He'd used his own time and money to find her in Australia. This was definitely more than a job to him. Was it about Olivia? Daniel had been so full of triumphant spite when he'd spat out her name. She meant something to the two men.

The well-groomed path narrowed. Sarah passed across a footbridge and into a wooded area, the air filled with the sound of croaking. Her feet thudded faster, and she lengthened her stride. If revenge drove the detective, it made him a dangerous ally. It would colour his decisions, blind him to her family's needs. Stone couldn't learn of her meeting with Daniel. If he did, he would force her into protective custody. She'd lose all control.

Her breathing laboured out of time. She forced her exhale to match every third strike of her foot. She had to figure out Daniel's plan, his motivations and what was going on between him and Michael. She needed to discuss it with someone else, get some perspective. Max? No. He'd insist on coming to Belfast to protect her, leaving Riley exposed. And he'd tell Stone. She had to handle things on her own. She'd figure out the spy in Riley's life and find a way to expunge them.

A high-pitched twittering drew her attention. A flock of swifts swirled and dived across the darkened sky. She shivered. A sheet of cloud had closed over the morning sun, the brisk wind cooling the moisture coating her skin. She turned around and headed back to the hotel. She needed to book her flight to Dublin. Then she'd respond to Detective Stone's text. Put him off until Monday.

When she rounded the final corner to the hotel, her step faltered. Detective Stone glared at her from the entranceway. For a brief moment she considered running by, but instead she slowed to a walk and stared at the ground, attempting to get her heaving breath under control. Her hair was plastered to her face, and sweat pooled under her arms. Must this man always see her at her worst?

His taut stillness drew her gaze. A black leather jacket and jeans accentuated a grittiness she didn't remember. Energy vibrated off him in waves. That she did remember. She smoothed back her hair with both hands.

His mouth compressed, puckering his jagged scar. "Where

have you been? You landed five hours ago. You were supposed to ring as soon as you'd checked in."

Sarah's eyebrows drew in. She strode right past him to the hotel door. A hand wrapped around her forearm, jarring her to a stop.

"Where do you think you're going?"

She glared down at his fingers. Her skin throbbed at their point of connection. "I need a shower."

Breaking from his grip she headed for the lift. He followed right behind her. What was it about him that sent her so off-balance? He was just a man. A rude one at that. The lift doors opened, and she got in. When she turned to face him, Detective Stone stood firm, silent. *What did he want from her?* She jabbed at the third-floor button. Whatever it was he could damn well wait. She would not feel guilty. She was an adult who could do what she wanted and right now she wanted to get away.

His arm blocked the closing doors. "I warned you once already, Sarah. This is not a game. You insisted on no surveillance, and I gave you that. But I am still responsible for you while you are in Northern Ireland."

"Well then, you're off the hook. Tomorrow morning I'm flying to Dublin."

"For how long? You need to give your statement."

"I am not your employee to order about." She halted his objection with a flick of her hand. "My first priority is to see my son, and if that doesn't suit you, you can suck eggs."

She didn't miss the slight raise of his brow. A hot flush flared up her neck, blooming onto her cheeks. *What was she, ten years old?* She hit the close door button and glowered at his arm obstructing the door. But it didn't move.

93

"I'll give you your statement, but only when I've confirmed Riley is safe. If all is well in Dublin, I will meet with you Monday morning."

"We've vetted everyone in Riley's life."

"Do you have someone watching him twenty-four seven?"

"No, but you do. You should have told me your father was here." His expression filled with mistrust.

"Okay detective, you want me to tell you everything, you go first. This obsession with taking Daniel down is more than a job to you."

His gravelly voice turned to cement. "My aunt was killed in an explosion. McNaulty sourced the components for the bomb."

"Is that it?"

"Is that what? What more do you want? Daniel McNaulty murdered my aunt and walked away free as a bird. Just like he did from the murder of Gerry McCann. That psychopath has held this city hostage to his own brand of terror for almost twenty years. Obsession?" He stepped closer. "You bet. I won't rest until Daniel McNaulty is rotting away in a jail cell, and I'll do it with a smile on my face."

"Who's Olivia?"

The fire in his eyes turned cold. "How do you know that name?"

"I. Uh..." *She hadn't thought that through.* "I researched you online."

"We're done here. Be at the station Monday 9:00 am sharp." He turned and marched away.

Sarah's mouth fell open. What was that? Who was Olivia? Once she got back from Dublin she needed to find out.

TEN

Six freshly mown soccer pitches stretched out in a perfectly manicured line, greener than any Sarah had ever seen. Next to them lay a set of futsal courts, the artificial grass pristine. Alongside the grounds ran a gym, its glass front steamed up from the heated pool inside. Milling outside the nearby canteen a rabble of boys and girls, dressed in various soccer kits, called out and chatted in languages from all over the world. Their excitement echoed through the hall.

Sarah paced the facility's foyer. She checked the time again, shoved her hands into her jacket pockets and paced some more. A step thudded behind and before she could turn, two arms curled about her waist and lifted her in the air. A laugh she'd recognise anywhere vibrated against her back.

"Riley, you'll hurt yourself." She wriggled against his hold. "Put me down."

"It's so good to see you, Mum." Riley crushed her ribs one more time and lowered her feet to the ground. He kept his arms resting loosely on her shoulders and when she turned to face him, her heart squeezed. His smile was full and real. She reached up to his cheek. It had a healing cut, the yellow, faded bruising suggesting the injury was old. She traced over the scab with her thumb.

"Hey, no sad face. It's not that bad. What's Dad say? Wounds heal, and chicks dig scars."

The corners of her mouth broadened. He was all light, her boy. No dark corners. No worries, no venom, just joy.

"Have I told you how much I love you?"

Riley laughed. "Only like ten times every single time you ring." He bent down and kissed her on the top of her head.

As she hugged him tight, she noticed a young woman standing to the side watching their every move. Waves of thick blonde hair fell around her sculptured, square face. Was she a teacher? Too young. A coach? Overdressed. There was a look in the woman's pale eyes. Unease branched out across Sarah's back. Riley turned. His gaze locked with the woman's and gentled.

Oh no.

"Mum, I want you to meet Siobhan. Siobhan Dunning, my mum Sarah Calhoun."

Siobhan looked a good five years older than Riley, wore skinny jeans, brown-heeled boots and a fitted burgundy top. Every movement conveyed a sensuality that had Sarah's "mum radar" sounding an alarm. A bright smile now masked whatever Sarah had seen earlier.

"Hiya, Ms Calhoun, I'm well excited to meet you. I've heard so much about you."

Sarah couldn't say the same. She had no idea who this girl-woman was. Neither Riley nor Max had ever mentioned her. Riley made a face, bugging his eyes out at her lack of response. She offered her hand. The girl's dainty manicured fingers were cold in her grasp. "Pleased to meet you, Siobhan. How long have you two known one another?"

Riley crossed to Siobhan and tucked her into his side. "We met my first week." Riley looked down on Siobhan's face, his voice melting into intimacy. "She is the best thing that has happened to me over here."

Tentacles of worry coiled around Sarah's ribs. Had the girl even been vetted? A bell sounded and Riley looked over his shoulder. A group heading for the canteen yelled out his name.

"Sorry, guys, I've got to go to lunch. I'll see you this afternoon when I finish up."

"I had hoped we could eat lunch together?"

"I can't, Mum, camp rules. But Padric and Colleen have invited you home for dinner tonight. Then you can meet my family."

His family? Her mouth drew tight. Exactly how well settled was her son in Ireland?

Riley kissed Siobhan, gave Sarah a peck on the cheek and ran off to jump on a teammate's back.

"Uh, I could give you a lift to your hotel if you're in need, Ms Calhoun."

Sarah swung her attention back to the girl. "Thank you, Siobhan, a lift would be lovely." She would collect her own car later. She needed to learn as much as she could about this girl, and how deeply involved she was with her son.

Siobhan pulled up at an old red Fiat. "The lock is broken that side, so the door should just open."

Sarah slid in the passenger seat and studied Siobhan's profile. A cool shiver fanned across her skin. "So, Siobhan, any chance you are free for lunch?"

Sarah cradled a bunch of yellow roses as she hurried up to the red brick Georgian townhouse. She checked her watch and groaned. Losing track of time at her Dad's had been careless. After Siobhan declined the invitation to lunch, her suspicion about the girl increased. She'd made a detour to see Max, hoping he could shed some light on her, but he'd revealed very little, other than to say Siobhan was "nice", and she should just trust his judgement. Pressing her finger to the O'Leary's doorbell, she moistened her lips while she waited. With a swift motion the door swung inward and a tall man with a Guinness paunch and receding orange hair reached past a grinning Riley and pumped her hand in greeting.

"Welcome, welcome. Och, it's grand to finally meet you. I'm Padric, Riley's host Dad, as your lot call me."

At least she could relax about Riley's safety here. When Detective Stone was vetting the family, his superintendent had personally vouched for them. He had served alongside Padric in an Irish and British peacekeeping force sent to Somalia in 1993 and gave him a glowing reference.

Padric's booming voice called everyone to the cosy lounge room. "This is Colleen, my wife."

A plump brunette holding a swaddled baby accepted Sarah's flowers with a shy smile, and managed a quiet, "Hello" before Padric took over again.

"And these here are Saoirse, Niamh, Fionn, Donal and the wee one in his mother's arms is Colm."

The children all appeared to be under the age of ten. Colleen disappeared with the flowers to what Sarah assumed was the kitchen.

"I'm so happy to meet you all. Can I give Colleen any help with dinner?"

"Not likely, you're our guest."

Riley beamed. Sarah could only assume it was due to bringing his two families together. Following Padric, he led her into a formal room decorated in brocade wallpaper of black and pastel pink. A lace-edged linen cloth set with floral dinnerware sat atop a cherry wood dining table.

The doorbell rang again, and Riley practically ran from the room. Sarah's smile tapered away; clearly her son had another priority.

Padric settled at the head of the table, half-finished glass of beer in his hand. He gestured for her to sit. "So, you're aways from home. Riley tells us you've work in Belfast."

"I'm running focus groups for an international firm interested in investing in new housing." Another day, another lie.

Footsteps came down the hall, along with a girl's throaty laugh. Riley entered with a flushed face, a smudge of lipstick at the corner of his mouth and Siobhan locked to his side. Sarah's leg jittered against the floor. She wished now she hadn't discouraged other girls from her son's life. First love held so much power. Siobhan greeted each O'Leary with polite warmth but turned a guarded smile to Sarah.

The girl might have avoided lunch earlier, but she couldn't

slip away now. Sarah arranged her face into what she hoped was a friendly countenance.

"Siobhan, why don't you grab a seat by me." There was a pause in the activity of the room. Sarah realised she'd overstepped the mark of a guest, telling someone where to sit, but she had to find out more about the girl.

Colleen returned, put Colm into a highchair, and left again. Riley took a seat the other side of Siobhan and the kids filled the other places.

Sarah turned to Siobhan. "So how did you and Riley meet?"

"I serve food in the soccer camp kitchen."

"Oh, I thought Riley told me you were in your final year of school."

"The money's to help out my Granny."

Riley bent forward. "It's lucky she got the job. Camp had already started, but another worker had to leave."

"So, coach said you scored two goals today, Riley," Padric cut in.

Riley's chest puffed up. "You should have seen the last one. I was up against the—"

"What about your parents, Siobhan?"

"I live with Gran now. I'm new to Dublin too."

"Where did you move from?"

"My mum's unwell, so I moved to complete school."

That didn't answer the question. "What about—"

"Dinner." Colleen returned with plates of roast beef, carrots, parsnips, Colcannon mash and gravy. Padric said grace, then it was all hands in. Colleen's bottom barely touched the seat before she stood again, helping to serve the children's food.

Normally Sarah would have stepped in to help, but she

couldn't waste the opportunity to grill Siobhan. "Do you have siblings?"

"Colleen love, while you're up, would you grab me another ale?" Padric turned to Sarah, as Colleen left the room. "You must be so proud of Riley. He's quite the star at the camp."

"It's fabulous to see him succeeding in what he loves. What about you Siobhan? What do you want to do?"

"I've not figured that out yet."

Colleen returned with a beer in one hand and a wipe in the other. She cleaned Colm's face and finally ate her own luke-warm dinner. Sarah finished what she could from her plate and placed her knife and fork together. The girl didn't want to talk about her family. Time to find out why.

"So, Siobhan, what do your parents do?"

"Mum's a nurse."

"What about your Dad?"

Riley glared at her. "Mum. Leave it, okay."

Each time she tried to draw Siobhan out, someone changed the subject. She forced a smile to her face. "It's okay, Riley, we're just getting to know each other, aren't we Siobhan?"

The girl had stopped eating, her plate still half full. Riley rubbed Siobhan's back, and the girl stared at her lap.

Colleen left again and re-entered the room with dessert. "Me Ma's rhubarb tart."

Sarah took in Siobhan's curled shoulders. Guilt if ever she'd seen it. She spoke over the kids' excited squeals. "So, Siobhan, you were telling me about your Dad."

"He's away with work."

"Your Mum's on her own?"

Siobhan pushed back her chair and fled from the table, her

stuttering sobs echoing down the hall. The front door banged shut, and the room faded into an embarrassed silence. Colleen cleared her children from the table.

Riley stood, his mouth set hard. His newly deep voice resonated with anger. "You always do this, Mum. Couldn't we have a nice dinner without the Spanish Inquisition?"

A rush of heat flared up her neck. She had pushed it, but the tears were a total over-reaction. Surely that proved Siobhan was hiding something.

Riley turned to their hosts. "I'm sorry, Padric, I have to go after her. Thank you, Colleen, for a lovely dinner." His gaze cut to Sarah. "I'll walk you out."

The burning sensation rose to her face. She turned to her hosts. "Colleen, Padric, thank you for a delicious dinner. I'm terribly sorry for my son's rudeness. Siobhan's his first girlfriend and he's—"

"Mum!" Riley snapped from the hall.

Sarah stiffened, gave an apologetic smile to her hosts and headed to the front garden. "Riley James Barker, don't you dare talk to me like that again. I had no idea taking an interest in Siobhan's life would upset her that much."

"You never do. Couldn't you have just left her alone?"

"What's the big secret? I asked about her family."

"You cross-examine everyone in my life. All my friends at home joke about it, you know. How you must have a degree in interrogation. It's embarrassing and unfair." Riley thrust his hands in his pockets and sat on the front step. "I really like Siobhan. You better not have wrecked it."

"I was trying to get to know her. They were questions anyone would ask."

"No, Mum, not anyone. Just you. When she didn't want to talk about herself, you should have stopped." Riley exhaled loudly. "Siobhan is missing her parents a lot, okay. She feels bad for leaving them. That's why we hit it off so well and why she burst into tears. Happy?"

His last question doused her anger with doubt. Had she been too harsh? The embers of instinct flickered. She recognised manipulation, and that girl was a master. She would have to go about unearthing Siobhan's secrets in a different way.

"Riley," she gentled her tone, "enough. I am your mother and you will treat me with respect. That said I am sorry I upset Siobhan, she seems – nice – and if it would make things better, I'll come with you now and apologise."

He looked at her, unblinking.

"Honey, she won't blame you for my insensitivity."

Relief swept his face. "You sure? I don't want her to think anything but good of me."

Sarah's shoulders relaxed. Her boy may have flared up protecting his girlfriend, but his mum's opinion still mattered. She slid her hand around Riley's bicep and let him lead her to Siobhan's front door where she smoothed everything over, using the meeting to take in every detail of the girl and her home. Siobhan Dunning was definitely hiding something.

The following night excited chattering and energy filled the soccer camp's auditorium – staff, students and guests alike awaiting the beginning of the awards ceremony. Sarah sat slumped in her seat. Riley had saved her a chair on the aisle, but she was in the row behind Max and Siobhan. Had he placed them like this on purpose so she couldn't question Siobhan again while he sat up front with his teammates. Sarah stared at the perfect messy updo revealing Siobhan's neck. Max cracked a joke and a sultry laugh burst from the girl's mouth.

Sarah bent forward, elbows to knees, her index fingers rubbing in circles at her temples. Why was she the only one suspicious of Siobhan? When she opened her eyes, she spotted a white PVC bag sitting under Siobhan's chair.

Could she? She looked up. Siobhan and Max's heads were angled close, fingers pointing to something on the stage. Their shoulders bobbed again in laughter. Sarah's lips pinched together. The girl had everyone fooled. Her focus snapped back to the bag. After scanning the people around her one last time, she reached for her own handbag, leant forward and slipped Siobhan's inside.

She gave Max's shoulder blade a glancing touch. "I'm just going to the bathroom." She held her bag tight against her ribs and walked directly to the restroom.

Darting into a stall, she shut the door and sat on the closed lid. Her fingers inched at the press-stud holding Siobhan's bag shut. Her pulse quickened. Riley would never speak to her again if he found out. But he'd given her no choice. It was the only way she could think of to get information. Last night's internet search had produced no results for Siobhan Dunning. Nothing at all. It wasn't possible in this day and age.

Prising open the stud, she turned the bag left and right, allowing the bluish hue of the overhead fluorescent bulbs to light up the contents. Wallet, phone, sunglasses, perfume, tissues, lipstick. Nothing out of the ordinary.

She sighed. Maybe there was something wrong with her,

always assuming the worst. She gently shook the bag to jostle the contents around. Something jangled. She reached in and pulled out Siobhan's key ring - a brushed metal tag with a harp stamped on one side. It was familiar. She turned the tag over, nothing on the other side.

The door to the ladies' room banged open against the wall. She jumped. Footsteps clattered across the tiled floor, coming her way. She stilled. A cubicle door shut. She exhaled, just someone using the loo.

Polite applause filtered in from the auditorium, and an older male voice spoke. Pulling out her own phone, she snapped a photo of the tag and dropped the key ring back in the bag. Next, she picked up Siobhan's bright orange Burberry wallet and turned it over. Not a copy, a real Burberry purse. Expensive taste for a student and kitchen hand. Opening it she found nothing unusual – student ID, money, store cards, a little cash. Her attention moved to Siobhan's phone. She swiped it on. The screen was locked.

A huge cheer roared from the club's auditorium. A coach congratulated his team on their winning streak. They would be playing in the finals, the European Junior Champion of Champions, in two weeks' time. Applause rumbled.

She scrutinised Siobhan's phone. The code was sure to be something simple, a number sequence easy to remember. She combed the wallet and found Siobhan's date of birth on her driver's license. What? Wait a minute. She checked it again. And again. Siobhan was eighteen years old. What was she doing dating a sixteen-year-old?

Thunderous applause swelled from next door, but this time Riley's unmistakable voice came over the loudspeaker.

"Thank you so much. Everyone on this team has worked so hard. I'd be honoured to captain you all through the Champion of Champions tournament. You rock!"

Captain. Sarah smiled. Riley was getting everything he'd dreamed of. As the cheering and hollering faded, the sounds of chairs being dragged and stacked took over. Music started. She'd stayed too long. She stuffed everything back in, careful to do up the press-stud, and hid Siobhan's bag inside her own. She'd have to find a way to slip the bag back. Hopefully its disappearance hadn't been noticed.

A driving base beat escaped from the auditorium's side door, booming out across the deserted soccer pitches as Sarah and Max slipped outside. The night air bit at her cheeks but she paid it no notice. She led Max into the dark of the fields and divulged her discovery.

"... and on her license was her birthdate. Dad, Siobhan is eighteen years old!"

"For Christ's sake, you stole Siobhan's bag and searched it? What is wrong with you?"

She whirled to face him.

"Didn't you hear me? Siobhan is eighteen. What would she see in Riley? He's just a boy. What could she be getting out of it unless she is up to something?"

Max took hold of her upper arms and looked her dead in the eye. "Can you hear yourself, girl? Your boy is bright, a looker and one hell of a sportsman. He was just named team captain, for Christ sake! Every girl in that room wants him."

Max's thunderous voice rattled through her. Pulling from

106

his hands she stormed further into the dark. Max's low taut voice slowed her steps.

"But you weren't there, were you? You weren't in the crowd cheering as Riley's name was announced. You," and he jabbed his index finger at her, his voice growing in volume, "were hidden in a toilet cubicle snooping through his girlfriend's handbag. Riley will never forgive you if he finds out."

"He'll never know."

"What going on, Sarah? You're seeing enemies that aren't even there. I get you're under stress, that this court case is raising demons, but you've got to wise up. Riley is fine. He's more than fine. He's the king of this soccer camp and has a gorgeous girl on his arm. If you're not careful, you'll ruin it all for him. Stand down."

Blood hammered at her temples. She wanted to scream that Daniel had a spy, that he'd confirmed it himself. But she couldn't, not without revealing how simple it had been for Daniel to capture her. For Max to do his job of protecting Riley, he needed to believe she was safe. But she also had to get him to listen.

"Dad, you told me to follow my gut."

"Did you not listen to a word I said? You'll lose your boy. He'll never trust you again."

"You don't know Daniel like I do. We have to stay a step ahead." She could no longer look into his disbelieving stare. She brushed past, stalking back towards the hall.

"Sarah!" She jerked to a halt. "I stuck to my guns with you and we lost years. Don't make the same mistake."

"I'm not."

"No? Riley said you'd overreact to him having a girlfriend."

A beat passed. "Unless there's more going on. Has McNaulty done something? Should I be guarding you instead?"

"No!" Her shout rang out into the dark. Her lungs wheezed in and out. "Nothing's happened. It's just hard to trust Riley is safe."

"Trust is a two-way street. You asked me to take care of him, and I am. I've spent time with Siobhan. She's just a schoolgirl, missing her parents and smitten with your son. The O'Leary's like her too. So what if she's a bit older. In your eyes, no girl will ever be good enough. Stop the hysterics for a moment, and you'll know I'm right. You have to let Riley grow up sometime."

"This is not about letting him grow up. There's something not right about her. I know it."

"Stone is a trained detective. If he believed Riley was in any danger, he'd move him. And I'd give my life before letting anyone harm that boy." Max moved towards her, concern etched in the lines of his face. "You have to leave Siobhan alone. No more bullshit. If it'll make you feel better, I'll have another word with Stone."

Max didn't believe her about Siobhan. The detective wouldn't either if Max got to him first.

Sarah softened her voice. "You don't need to talk to anyone, Dad. You're right. It's this court case. It has me twisted in knots. Once I testify, I'll be able to relax." Reaching over, she placed an awkward peck on his cheek. "Sorry for dragging you out here. I think I just need sleep. I might go back to my hotel, yeah? I'm flying to Belfast early tomorrow anyway."

"You want a ride?"

"No, I've got my rental here. I better go in and say goodbye to Riley. I'll call soon. Night, Dad." She turned from Max and trudged back to the side door.

Re-entering the hall, her lips pressed hard together. Riley's arms were locked around Siobhan, his gaze lost in hers as they swayed to a slow song on the dance floor. Heat spiked from the roots of Sarah's hair. She was right about Siobhan, but like Michael with Daniel, Max wouldn't listen. So, she would find proof of the girl's duplicity, then remove her from Riley's life before she could do harm.

ELEVEN

S he'd walked into the police station that morning determined to keep it together. To give her official statement in as clinical a manner as possible. But ten minutes in, the grey walls of the interview room were swimming. Sarah hugged herself tight and let her chin sink, unable to meet Detective Stone's gaze.

Another crack of a fist against cheekbone. A spray of blood.

The detective continued. "After the beating, what happened next?"

The stench of shit and piss. A gun being drawn. Oh God. No. No!

"Sarah, I need you to answer the question."

Her hands tented over her mouth and nose.

"You can do this."

"Daniel placed the barrel of the gun to Gerry's temple."

"And then?"

She shook her head.

Gerry's screams, pleading, begging.

"I know this is hard, but I have to hear you say it."

"Daniel shot him."

Ears ringing, biting her cheek to silence her scream, gagging on the taste of blood.

She was roasting from inside.

"Sarah," Detective Stone called her name but she couldn't latch on.

Michael and Daniel wrapping Gerry's lifeless body in the throw rug from her lounge.

White spots whirled in her vision.

A red trail of blood smeared along the wood of her hallway.

She closed her eyes to stop the spinning.

He moved his chair right next to her, his hand touching her left shoulder.

"I didn't stop them. God forgive me. He was just a boy, and I did nothing to stop them." She gulped in air, but it wouldn't go deep enough.

"It's over now." Stone's voice softened. His palm rubbed up and down her spine.

The sips of air were getting faster. Her hand grasped at her throat.

"You're okay." He spoke softly in her ear. "Slow it down, and you'll be okay."

She rocked back and forth. The long soothing strokes on her back continued. "Just concentrate on my voice. I've got you. You're okay."

Gradually, the convulsing quieted, leaving her hollow inside. Her voice scratched against her throat. "What kind of monster just walks away?"

"If you had intervened in any way, McNulty would have killed you too."

Fever rushed to her head. Her hand flew to her mouth. "I think I'm going to be sick."

He pushed her head between her legs. Her lungs heaved in and out against the rush of bile up her throat.

"You did what you had to, Sarah. You survived. Now we'll give Gerry his justice. Together, okay? We'll make McNulty pay for that night, and the rest. I give you my word I'll keep you safe."

Every muscle ached with the weight of her shame. She didn't deserve his understanding. What she'd done, her cowardice, was unforgivable. She stared at the black scuffmarks smudged across the grey flooring. There was only one way forward, one way to redeem herself. She pushed her shoulders back and met the detective's sympathetic gaze.

"Daniel has to pay. No matter what. Promise me he'll pay."

A sigh escaped Detective Stone's mouth. "There she is." He tucked a stray piece of hair behind her ear. "We'll get him, Sarah. I promise. Together we'll take him down for good."

The detective drove her straight from Antrim Police Station to Maggie Mays. No discussion. No choice. He insisted she had to eat.

Maggie Mays was a university student institution. The cafe's warren of small rooms and home cooking had seen customers through thirty years of exams, break ups, hangovers and flirtations. Many years ago, it had been her home away from home.

Sarah pushed through the cafe's door and found herself enveloped in the earthy scent of coffee. She sagged into a wooden booth in the far corner, limbs heavy, pupils scratchy. Inside though, her shame hardened into determination. Daniel's time had run out.

Detective Stone left to place their order at the counter. He had surprised her this morning. The gentle strength he offered as he guided her back from the edge. She'd been able to lean on him, almost believe she was safe.

When the detective returned to their booth, he kept the banter light, teasing her for supporting Manchester United. Fifteen minutes later a young waitress plonked two full fry breakfasts on the table. Sarah had told him she could only manage a coffee, but, when the plates piled high with bacon, beans, sausages and tomatoes arrived, her stomach growled in disagreement. She dug in.

The humming chatter of other patrons and the gurgle of the coffee grinder filled the lulls in their conversation. But he continued to watch her. Wary, like he was ready to catch her if she crumbled. His protectiveness cut through every defence she had left. She needed that look to go away. Pushing her empty plate aside she forced herself to look up at him.

"You okay?"

His voice hit her chest with warmth that travelled to her belly. She held his stare. "Thank you, Detective Stone." Such a small phrase for all he had given that morning.

"I think we're beyond the formalities, don't you? Call me Alec."

"Thank you, Alec." His Christian name sat intimately on her tongue.

He leant forward, fingertips reaching her side of the table. She resisted the urge to grab on, instead snatching up her coffee mug and downing the remaining liquid.

"This comes back to bite at you, you talk to me, okay? Any time of day. Anything I can do."

She stared into the mug. Tiredness dragged at her. She'd had a fitful night, worrying about her statement, about failing to get the words out. And what would happen if she did. She'd tried distracting herself by adding Siobhan's birthdate to her online search but had come up empty. That only intensified the anxiety. *Anything I can do.*

"Actually, there is something. Riley has a girlfriend, Siobhan Dunning. Have you looked into her at all?"

"We vetted his host family, teachers, coaches and team members, but I don't remember her."

"Could you check her out for me?"

"Why? What's the problem?"

"I don't know, but something is off. She's older than him, and I can't find anything on her. I mean nothing at all. I need to be sure Riley is safe from Daniel before we move forward."

"Riley is safe. Even your Dad has found no signs of Daniel in his life."

A lump formed in her throat. The desire to blurt out everything pushed against it. She wanted to yell that Daniel had admitted placing a spy near Riley. But how could she explain? She'd have to tell Alec about the cab ride, her meeting with Daniel, the threats. Alec would put her under protection. And she still didn't know his true motives. No, trust was a risk she couldn't afford to take. Instead she dug out a pen and paper and wrote down Siobhan's name and birthdate.

"Please just check her out for me. I didn't trust my instincts when things were falling apart with Michael and that got Gerry killed. If you come up with nothing, I promise I'll let it go."

Alec's gaze bored into her. When it dropped to the paper in her hand her stomach did a nervous somersault.

"I'll run her through the police database." He took the note from her and launched into a withering commentary on the failures of the current Australian cricket team. He was lightening the mood. After the trauma of this morning, he'd given her exactly what she needed; a full belly, help with Siobhan and a laugh. There was a whole lot more to the man than she'd given him credit for.

Sarah sat up in her bed, a banging sound knocked around in her skull. She blinked fast, trying to differentiate between reality and the dream world she'd just left. The bedside clock glowed 11:30 pm. She was in her hotel. Had gone straight to bed after Alec dropped her back here.

The pounding sounded again. She froze, adrenaline pulsing through her body. A fist bashed on her door. She slid out of bed and moved towards the entry, carefully, quietly. Holding her breath, she checked the peephole. Her shoulders dropped back in place. She unlatched the chain and pulled the door open.

Alec barged past her, his body rigid as he scanned the room. Sarah closed the door. "Well hello to you too."

He didn't answer but instead went to her wardrobe and pulled out her empty suitcase.

She folded her arms. "What do you think you're doing?"

His focus didn't waver. He removed her clothes from their

hangers and threw them in the case. She took a step towards him. "Alec! What is going on?"

"At five o'clock tomorrow morning, the Armed Response Unit will raid Daniel McNaulty's home with an arrest warrant."

Sarah recoiled from the punch of his words. *No, no, not yet.* She wasn't ready. Riley wasn't safe. "But you told me we had weeks."

"The Chief fast tracked it, against my recommendation." Alec continued packing. "They'll suppress your name as a witness, but I'm taking no risks. You have to move to a safe house tonight."

She couldn't go to a safe house. How could she get Siobhan away from Riley if someone watched over her every second of the day?

Alec tugged out another set of hangers and emptied them. She moved forward, touching her palm to his arm. His head snapped up, and he looked at her for the first time since entering the room. His gaze travelled the length of her body, searing every exposed inch of her skin. Her cheeks flamed. She hadn't considered her clothing when she answered the door, she'd just been so relieved it was him. She seized a long cardigan from her half-packed case threw her arms into the sleeves and closed it tight. When she turned back, he hadn't moved. Her mouth dried. A shadow crossed his face, and he twisted back to the packing.

Sarah slammed the case shut. "Alec!"

"You need to get dressed and leave for the safe house now."

"I'm not going anywhere."

He swung around, the swell of his anger pushing her back a

step. However safe she'd felt with him earlier, the man before her now was dangerous. Thank God she hadn't shared Daniel's threats and plans. He would have taken complete control. She turned away and steadied her breath. She had to get him to leave her situation as it was. Riley needed her.

"Hear me out," she soothed, her palms surrendered to him. "With Daniel's connections, he already knows I'm in Belfast. If I disappear, he'll know I'm the witness. It'll leave Riley exposed. I can't do that."

"Are you insane? You return to Belfast after seventeen years, and all of sudden McNaulty is arrested for murder. You don't think he'll put two and two together?"

"Daniel thought I was working in Glebe that weekend. And this is not his first arrest. I'll reconnect with old friends; let it be known I'm here to catch up and see how Belfast has changed. If I suddenly disappear, he'll know it's me. Riley would be in danger."

She pressed her hands flat against one other, raised their tips to her mouth. She had to get him to agree. She had to be free to protect her son. But with his arms solid across his chest and a black look in his eyes, it was obvious she was getting nowhere. She had to compromise.

"You said they could suppress my name until I testify. Give me that. As soon as I appear in court I'll move to your safe house. Just give me time to be sure about Riley, and I'll move into protective custody. I promise." She held his stare, her insides knotting with the lie.

"This won't happen quietly. The media will be all over it. If they find out it was you—"

"They won't."

"You'll have to carry a panic button."

"A what?"

"A panic button. You press it, and half the police force of Belfast will descend on your location. I won't agree to your plan without it."

"Okay." She pulled her cardigan tighter.

"We're going to get him this time, Sarah." Then Alec smiled, the crinkle of his eyes softening his scar. "Get some sleep. I'd say I was sorry for waking you, but my liking of that nightdress proves me a liar."

Her cheeks heated again. She ducked her head and skirted past him to the door. "Goodnight Alec."

He closed the distance between them and paused, expression serious again. He reached into his shirt pocket and handed her a single piece of white paper. "I was going to give you this when we got to the safe house." Typed in black was the heading Siobhan Dunning.

"You were right. Siobhan is a little off. I'll follow up tomorrow to see what I can do, but to be honest, unless she does something illegal, our hands are tied. If I were you, I'd show this sheet to Riley and get him to break contact with her himself."

His advice hit her like a jab. It wouldn't matter what she showed Riley now. After her last visit he wouldn't listen.

"Sarah," Alec stopped right in front of her, his minty breath brushing her face. "I will be back tomorrow with the panic button. In the meantime, if anything happens to make you feel unsafe in this hotel, go straight to my house." He scribbled down an address on the back of a business card and handed it to her. "Do not go to the station. McNaulty's entourage will have invaded the place."

"I'll be fine."

"And I'll be checking in with you. You must answer my call every time." Before she could argue, he placed his finger across her mouth. She went rigid. Every nerve in her lips woke up. "Agree or I'll change my mind."

She managed to nod in agreement. "Good. Now lock the door behind me. The chain too."

She relocked the door, then leant into it, her lips still tingling from his touch.

Whatever that was, Sarah, shut it down. Now.

She exhaled, pushed her half-packed suitcase from the bed and pored through the information he'd given her.

TWELVE

L ying tangled in the white sheets of the hotel bed, Sarah
stared at the slanting shadows on the ceiling. She'd tried
coaxing her body into sleep, but the noise in her head wouldn't
quit. Questions and conclusions clamoured for attention. She
reached over and snapped on the reading light, then picked up
the paper Alec had given her and reread it for the hundredth
time.

Siobhan Dunning
Born: 10/08/1996
Graduated St Louis Convent Secondary School Dublin
2014 - (6A1's, 505 points)
Juvenile record (sealed) - 2x Possession of controlled
substance (cannabis). Fines applied
Mother - Fiona Dunning from Dublin.
Occupation: Nurse
Father - Aidan O'Halloran (senior) from Crossmaglen.

Occupation: Builder. Currently serving 5 -10 years in Port-laoise Prison for armed robbery.

Portlaoise Prison. Righteous anger flooded her. Only the most serious of offenders were sent there - prisoners convicted of terrorism or organised crime. She leapt to her feet and walked the length of the room. No one had believed her, not even Max. But she had been right. Siobhan was off. Her father had ties to organised crime and Crossmaglen. Daniel was organised crime in Crossmaglen. The girl had been clever, hiding behind her mother's maiden name, fabricating a need to re-sit her senior year in Dublin. Siobhan had to be Daniel's spy.

But was this enough proof? Max would say the evidence was circumstantial. Maybe Alec could talk to him. But what if Max triggered Alec to doubt her again? She'd only just gained his trust. Best to keep the two men apart.

The wail of a siren cut into her thoughts. She checked the time. 4:30 am. A wave of nerves surged through her. In thirty minutes, the Armed Response Unit would burst into Daniel's home. No doubt he would be waiting fully dressed, confident everything was going according to his plan. Once Daniel was arrested, she'd have forty-eight hours before he was charged or released. She had to get Siobhan away from Riley before then. But how? She couldn't show her son the sheet of paper. How could she explain why and how she'd got it? Revealing the truth, her real reason for being in Ireland. would put him in even more danger.

She found a hair tie, shoved her hair into a bun, and switched on her laptop. Beaming out at her were her son's gorgeous honey-brown eyes as he pressed his cheek intimately against Siobhan's – the latest posting to his Facebook page. Sarah pushed the screen away. Riley looked so happy, but that girl didn't care about him. He was being played.

Sarah's jaw went slack. She'd been approaching this all wrong. Riley didn't need to break up with Siobhan. The girl could leave him. She rested against the headboard. How much would it take to get the girl to walk away? If her clothes and Burberry wallet were anything to go by, Siobhan liked her labels. Daniel must be paying her a lot. He always knew where to strike. Siobhan would need to leave Ireland, so the amount would have to be considerable. Only the kid's university account had that kind of money. She looked back at Riley's face in the photo. Getting him safe took priority. She'd get a bank cheque in the morning and deal with the consequences later.

She checked the account and withdrawal limits, ignoring the apprehension prickling up her spine. This plan could save both Riley and Siobhan. The girl was young and probably had no idea what she was being sucked into. Just like Sarah all those years ago. She had to get Siobhan to agree to leave, and fast. Tomorrow she'd go straight from the bank to the airport and be sitting outside Siobhan's school when she'd finished for the day. Siobhan could be on a flight that night, gone from Riley's life for good, before Daniel suspected a thing.

New knots of tension twisted across her shoulders. She massaged the ones jamming her neck. This plan could work. It had to. She was running out of time.

Sarah scanned each girl exiting St Brigidine's wrought iron gates. The girls looked almost identical in their forest green school uniforms, skirts past their knees and tartan ribbons in their ponytails. A flash of a blonde walking alone captured her attention. The girl's head was down, absorbed in her phone. Sarah pushed off the bonnet of the car and zeroed in. With thumbs flying over the keys of her phone, the girl didn't notice her approach. "Hello Siobhan."

The girl's head whipped up. Her initial wince transformed into a smile, but Sarah hadn't missed it. Not at all.

"Ms Calhoun, Riley will be well-pleased you're here."

"Actually, Siobhan, I was hoping you'd have time for a chat?" She fell into step with Siobhan and ever so subtly guided her towards her silver Peugeot rental.

Siobhan looked back at her phone. "Um, sure, just let me send this." After a flurry across the keys, Siobhan tucked the phone in her pocket and followed Sarah to her car.

"Would you like to go for a coffee somewhere?" Sarah climbed in the driver's side and indicated for Siobhan to join her in the car.

"I better not. I've to be home by 4:00 pm, or Nan will worry."

"Okay, we'll talk in here."

A trill of laughter filled the air, and a group of girls bustled by. Sarah watched them through the windscreen, taking a moment to exhale. Then she angled her body towards Siobhan and used the most measured voice she could.

"The thing is, Siobhan, I know who you are, who you really are, and why you're in Dublin. And I'm going to help you get out."

Siobhan's hand slipped to the door handle, but Sarah was ready with her finger on the override button.

"Ms Calhoun, let me out. I'm not comfortable talking with you like this."

"Well, Miss O'Halloran, I'm not comfortable with you using my son to get to me." Siobhan's body stiffened. "That's right Siobhan, I know everything about you. Your real name, your juvenile record, your father's incarceration and his connection to Daniel McNaulty."

Siobhan's white knuckled fist grasped the door handle again. She'd scored a hit with that. Daniel was definitely involved. "But my juvey record, it was, it was sealed."

Siobhan's stammering caused hope to flood Sarah's body. This was going to work.

"You came to Dublin, not to sit your final school year, but to connect to my son. That ends today."

Siobhan's face paled. "But you don't understand, if I didn't come—"

"Stop! I don't care why you agreed to sell out a beautiful young man. What I know is from this moment forth, you will disappear from Riley's life for good. Forever. We are going to get you out of Dublin."

"I can't!"

"Siobhan, you have to. Do you honestly think Daniel will ever release his hold on you? I met him seventeen years ago, and he is still trying to control me."

Siobhan's eyes welled with tears. Bitterness spread on Sarah's tongue. The poor girl was terrified, another victim in Daniel's game. Oh, she would enjoy bringing him down. She sat taller. She was doing the right thing helping Siobhan get free. She reached into her handbag and offered up the bank cheque.

"Let me help you. If you take this, you can escape for good.

It's enough money to get yourself set up in London, to start afresh."

Siobhan focused on the cheque for a moment. Sarah's heart stopped beating as prayer replaced her breath. The girl shook her head and melted into a mess of tears. Through the sobs she choked out, "But I love him."

"You don't know what love is!" Sarah's voice lowered, her words vibrating with rage. "If you don't leave today, I will tell Riley everything."

A shadow fell over the passenger side. Fury blazed from the face at the window as her son's fist bashed on the glass.

"What's going on? Open this door now!" He shook the locked handle.

Sarah straightened to her full height before letting Siobhan's window down.

"Riley, this is nothing to do with you. Siobhan and I are sorting something out."

"Is that why my girl is crying? You are something else, Mum. Something else." Riley reached through and unlocked Siobhan's door, his glare pinning Sarah down. "Siobhan, get out of the car." Riley wrenched the door open and pulled a sobbing Siobhan into his embrace.

Sarah's insides churned. How had he even found them? Then she remembered Siobhan's last-minute text. Her mouth twisted and she jumped out of the car. "How did you know I was here?"

"Are you kidding me, Mum? That's all you have to say?"

"Riley!"

"Okay." Sarcasm dripped from his voice. "Siobhan texted she had a surprise for me. I don't know, I suppose she believed seeing you again would make me happy." He placed Siobhan behind his back. "Now you answer my question. What are you doing here?"

Blood roared through Sarah's body, pumping so hard her head hurt. Riley didn't understand she was trying to protect him. But how could he? There was so much he didn't know.

"Honey." She reached out a hand to him. He flinched as if she were contaminated. The muscles in her back hardened. "Riley, that girl, I know you have feelings for her, but she is not who you think she is."

"I told you, Riley," Siobhan said, "I told you she hated me. She even offered me money to leave Dublin."

"You manipulative bitch!" Sarah took a step towards Siobhan.

Riley widened his stance. His beautiful eyes were cold and hard. "Don't you dare."

"But she —"

"No. You get in that car now, Mother. Drive back to Belfast and don't come back."

The indignant outrage in his voice sliced her open. She clutched his arm.

"Riley, honey, you have to—"

"I don't have to do anything. I can't even look at you right now. Just go." Then her loving, kind and generous son shrugged her off, wrapped his arms around Siobhan and walked away, without even one glance back her way.

Sarah sank onto the car bonnet. This couldn't be happening. Everything she had done was to protect her son. To ensure she wouldn't lose him. And now he'd walked away. No one had taken him. He'd left of his own free will. She shuffled to the car door and collapsed into the seat. Resting her head on the steering wheel, her mind filled with Riley's face, replaying the scene again and again, like a track on loop.

Knuckles rapped on her window, a rush of hope surged through her and her gaze shot up. But the hand was attached to a middle-aged woman dressed in workout gear. Sarah slumped back in her seat.

"You all right there?" Concern lined the lady's face.

Sarah let down her window. "Just a long day."

"You sure love?"

Sarah nodded. "I was about to leave." She turned the engine over and guided the car from the kerb. Before she knew it, she was in the O'Leary family's street. Up ahead, outside their red brick townhouse, sat Siobhan's empty car. Sarah pulled over a few houses before, but left the engine running. A sick feeling wormed low into her belly. *Don't come back.* Her hands clenched the wheel tight. Talking to Riley now would be a mistake, especially with that girl around. He needed time and space to calm down.

She switched her foot from brake to accelerator, passed the house and drove away. Numbness closed over her. When she reached Dublin airport, she had no memory of the journey there. She returned the hire car, boarded the plane to Belfast and curled into her seat. How on earth could she protect Riley now?

THIRTEEN

By early evening Sarah had arrived back at her hotel and was swiping her room key at her door. The entry light flashed green, but her hand hesitated on the handle. What would she do in the room? Stare at the four walls? She certainly wouldn't sleep. Not with Riley's words repeating over and over in her head. She swayed back onto her heels. Maybe she should ring him? Her eyes closed and her chin sank. He'd hang up. She couldn't take that, not yet.

She needed to divert the smothering pressure of failure, needed to escape. She turned and rode the elevator back down.

The lift doors opened, and dance music spilled from the hotel bar. Too many people, too much noise. She trudged to the hotel exit and onto the street. A frenzied wind whipped open her coat. She snatched it closed, fastened the buttons and turned up its collar. Swinging right, she buried her hands in her pockets and started walking. Coming to Belfast all those years ago, she'd been so sure she would make a difference. Instead she got lost, became unmoored from everything she believed in. Looking up from the ground, a bar over the road caught her attention. The Blackout. Black material lined its windows, curtaining out the world. No music or noise pumped from its door. Perfect.

She crossed over and leant her weight into the solid door to enter. A flint-coloured bar stretched the length of the softly-lit, narrow space. Behind the bar ran a mirrored wall. Funky, old-style posters, memorabilia from World War Two, hung against exposed brick walls. In the far corner a small after-work crowd chattered, but the front end of the bar remained empty. She climbed onto a lone stool and waited for the bartender to turn so she could catch his eye. Alcohol wouldn't solve the mess she'd made, but she had to stop the pain.

A creeping sensation tightened her scalp. She looked to the mirror. A middle-aged man stood behind her, a smirk on his doughy face. She gripped her handbag strap. Had Siobhan already reported to Daniel? Moving her weight to the right, she edged off the chair. The man's meaty arm slipped to the bar, blocking her in. His gaze rested on her breasts. "And what do we 'ave here?"

"Glen, move on, yer git, or you'll have to leave," the bartender called from the other end of the room. Glen took one last look at Sarah's bosom and weaved away.

"Sorry about that. He's no more harmful than a blowfly."

Sarah scoffed. She was a total mess. Couldn't even recognise a drunken sleaze as a nuisance not a threat.

"What can I get you?"

The bottle of Smirnoff vodka caught her eye. At least drunk she might be able to sleep.

"Double vodka neat, please." She turned to the bartender, to thank him for his help. Recognition stirred. Spiked red hair covered the man's head and the point of his chin. A smile lit his face, revealing a chipped front tooth and deep-set dimples. "Well, if it isn't Miss Sarah? What about yer?"

"Quinn Maguire. Look at you. You're so grown up."

"Ach, and you've not changed a bit." He leant in. "You know I had quite the crush on you when I was a lad. We all did."

Her cheeks warmed. Quinn's impish grin broadened and the leaden weight on her chest lifted a touch. "How are you, Quinn? Last I knew, you and Liam were ten years old leaving chaos in your wake. How is he? What's he up to?"

A cloud passed over Quinn's face. He picked up a glass, suddenly intent on pouring her drink. Stiffness entered his voice. "We grew apart, so we did. Liam's still in the life."

The weight resettled, forcing Sarah to sigh. So Liam hadn't got out. Another boy she'd left. Another one she'd failed.

"It's not all bad like. Do you want to see me boys?" He pulled out his wallet and flipped it open. Three carrot-topped boys grinned out with their father's cheeky smile.

"Quinn, they're precious."

"Yeah, precious wee terrors, but they're my world, so they are. What about you, any littlins?"

"Two girls and a boy. They are everything." Her voice caught. She downed the vodka in one gulp, the liquid burning a path of fire down her oesophagus.

"So what brought you back to our town?"

"Work. I run focus groups for a housing company."

His eyebrows lifted. "Aways to come to ask a bunch of questions."

"Hmmm." Sarah stared into the empty glass in her hand. She hated this, the lies pouring from her mouth. But Belfast was more village than city. You never knew who knew whom. She cleared her throat. "They're an international firm and wanted someone with experience living in Belfast but not a local." She placed her glass on the bar and looked back up at him.

"Another?"

She nodded. When he reached for her glass, she touched her fingers to his.

"What happened to Liam?"

Quinn scanned the bar then met her gaze and bent closer. "After the riot, getting shot and all, he couldn't let go." His voice dropped to a whisper. "He's a lieutenant for the 'RA now. Selling their drugs and shite."

A glass banged on the bar and they shot apart.

"Oi, Quinny, stop your flirting. A man's not a camel, you know."

Quinn poured Sarah's drink and moved to Glen at the far end of the bar. Sarah finished her vodka and had to swallow again to keep it down. She slumped onto her elbows and stared into the empty glass. First Michael, then Gerry, then Liam. She'd failed each one. Now she couldn't even hold on to her son. Couldn't make him listen. Just like Gerry that last time. She hadn't got through to him and look how that had ended...

Sarah bit her cheek, fighting the impulse to gnaw at her nails. Gerry stalked back and forth across the tiled floor, his anger bouncing off the hospital's mustard walls. The waiting room would test anyone's patience. The noise of the harried medical staff bustling down the corridors; the ammonia stench; the pinging of machines every time the operating theatre doors swung open; and the not knowing. The helplessness of not knowing what was going on.

She tried to think of something to say, anything that would diffuse Gerry's growing rage, but there were no words. Nothing to make sense of the reality that somewhere beyond those doors, his fourteen-year-old brother was fighting for life after grown men had smashed metal poles against every bone in his body, then shot out his knees.

"I'm going to fix those feckin' IRA bastards. Every single one of them. Kieran's fourteen for fuck's sake! He's a kid!"

"I know, honey, it's awful," Sarah touched her hand to his arm, "but Kieran will need you when he comes round. It's not going to help if you can't rein your anger in."

Gerry jerked away. "Do you know what they said when they rang for me Da to collect him? That Kieran's been dealing. That's bollocks. He smoked one joint with his mates. Only it wasn't IRA weed. They told me Da if I'd joined up, they wouldn't have had to make an example of Kieran. That it could have been dealt with on the quiet like. Can you fucking believe that? They blamed me! Now me Da won't look me in the eye, me ma's in tears, and Kieran's on an operating table. So no, I won't rein it in. I'm going to kick their fucks in."

Sarah linked her hands behind her head and released her breath in a rush of air. Gerry had done it. He'd beaten the odds and got out of the life. But this attack on his brother would drag him right back in. She stepped into his space, and gently grasped *his upper arms. His tobacco-scented breaths huffed across her face.*

"It's not your fault Gerry. All you did was follow your own dream."

Every word sounded trite. His body didn't soften under her touch. Instead his cold hard voice sliced right through her. "I'm done. We're done. It's time someone ended them for good." Gerry yanked out of her hold and stomped towards the hospital's exit.

Her heart twisted in pain for the boy. He was way too young to have to deal with all this. She paused. What exactly was he planning to do? To end them he'd have to bring down the whole organisation. Her pulse rate accelerated. Surely he wouldn't risk it? Touts were fair game, their executions guaranteed if they were discovered.

She hooked one arm through her backpack and ran for the door...

Would she have been able to save him if she'd found him that night? Sarah pushed the torn remnants of a Harp beer coaster from her lap, then tipped her glass upside down to her mouth. Empty again. She squinted, searched for Quinn, and found him, somewhat blurry, at the far end of the bar.

"Quinn," she called out, waving and pointing to the glass. She lost balance and had to grab hold of the bar. Quinn frowned and gestured she'd need to wait while he finished on the phone.

A sickly sweetness puddled on her tongue. She should stop drinking. But her failures hadn't quieted yet. She rested her forehead on the bar and cleared her lungs of air. When she drew in her next breath, a woody scent hit her nostrils. A thrill of awareness shot through her.

"Is this what you call staying safe? Really, Sarah, you have to use your head."

"Alec." She sat back, blinking to gain focus on the whirling room. "I'm having a drink." Her sticky tongue forced her to enunciate each word precisely.

He leant in. "I'd say you've had more than one." His breath caressed her ear, raising bumps across the surface of her skin. He raised an eyebrow.

Uh uh. She twirled around on her stool and leapt off, but her legs tangled, and she fell forward. He caught her on his chest. She looked up. His mouth skewed slightly to the right in a smile and his lips parted. She couldn't tear her gaze away. Perhaps that's what she needed. To lose herself in whatever it was that heated inside her when he was nearby.

When his head dipped, she surged up to meet him halfway, but large hands pressed her gently back. He stared into her face, the silence lasting a beat too long. "As much as I'd like a taste, Sarah, it's a bad idea."

Heat burnt a trail to the tip of her ears. What was he playing at? Hadn't he leant in first? She snatched up her bag and took a wide berth around him as she stumbled to the door.

"Wait. I'll drive you back."

"Leave me alone."

He grasped her elbow. "I said, I'll drive you." His fingertips brushed the lower side of her breast and her nipples hardened. *What was wrong with her?* The man had just pushed her away. She wrenched her arm back, but he held firm. His other hand pressed into the small of her back, and he guided her outside.

His closeness befuddled her ability to think. She needed to pull her treasonous body into line.

A bleep sounded and she found herself being folded into a car. She tapped the back of her head against the head rest. God, when she'd parted her mouth, she must have looked like some panting puppy. Why couldn't he just leave her alone?

When he sat in the driver's seat, she cringed into her door, letting her hair fall in a curtain around her face. The back of her head burnt with his stare. Then the engine rumbled to life, and they pulled away from the kerb.

She swallowed, trying to settle the swirly nausea caused by the car's movements. She shouldn't have had that last drink. Maybe if she just closed her eyes... When she did, she re-lived leaning into him. Her lids flew open. What was he doing in that bar anyway? Had he followed her there? He pulled the car up outside her hotel.

"How did you find me tonight, Alec?"

"Belfast is a small town."

His condescending smile flared the fire in her belly. "You never answered my other question, you know."

"What question?"

"About Olivia."

His stillness consumed the car's air.

"Olivia is none of your business. If you mention her again, we are done. Are we clear? I will walk away from you, from Riley, from everything." The set of his chin, the outrage tightening his mouth told her he was angry, but for the first time she heeded the emotion underneath it all. Pain. She reached over to place her palm on his forearm.

He jerked away. "Clear?"

"I didn't mean to upset you."

"No?"

"No! God. I..." She slumped. Her head pounded. She'd never fix this with alcohol blurring her brain. She unlatched the car door. "Thank you for seeing me home."

She had barely closed the door when the car pulled out and roared away. Sarah swayed on the spot. How had she not seen the pain in him before? She tucked her hands in her pockets and walked as straight a line as possible into the hotel, wishing with all she had that she'd never left her room.

FOURTEEN

Sarah grasped at the security chain attached to the wall and squinted. She concentrated on slotting the pin into the slide on the back of her room's door. When the two finally locked together, her body sagged against the wall.

First Riley, then Alec? Are you determined to make a mess of everything today?

She heaved herself upright and shrugged her coat to the floor. With the ground unsteady under her feet, she weaved towards the bathroom, catching her shoulder on the door jamb as she entered. She rubbed at the bruise and switched the shower on.

Peeling off her clothes, she studied her naked body in the mirror. Her eyes fluttered closed. She hadn't longed for a man's touch like this since Michael. Heat flushed her face. Alec hadn't wanted her though. How would she ever face him again?

The drubbing in her head got louder. She guzzled two glasses of water at the sink, and another with a pain killer.

Steam filled the room. She pulled her hair into a bun and went to fetch the hair tie she'd left beside the bed. A square of yellow lay on the white bedspread. An A4 envelope. She snatched a pillow to her naked front and backed up fast against the wall.

Where the hell had that come from?

Her gaze cut to the open doors of her closet and the safe. It remained locked. Was there still an intruder in the room? She held her breath, her ears scouring for any rustle, any noise. Nothing.

She dropped to her knees and peered under the bed, then at the foot of the drapes. No one. The room was clear.

Had the envelope been on the bed when she first came in?

Christ Sarah, are you going mad?

With shaky hands she drew her dressing gown around her body and tied it at her waist. She turned off the taps and returned to the envelope.

With her forefinger and thumb she pulled out a single piece of paper. Riley's birth certificate. What? Blood pounded against her eardrums, almost splitting her head in two. Why would someone send her that?

Squinting her fuzzy eyes, she scoured the document, but everything was listed exactly as it should be.

Her body swayed against the whirling room. She sank to her knees and curled into a ball. Her eyes squeezed shut. She couldn't take anymore. What if everything she'd done had been for nothing...

"We've asked for an orderly to transfer you to the maternity ward, but it could be a while." The midwife rolled the newly made-up

crib to the side of Sarah's bed. "I'm off now, but the dayshift staff will check in on you after handover."

After gathering up the used nappy and dirty wrap the nurse bustled out the door.

Sarah relaxed into the pile of pillows propping her up and stared at the bundle in her arms. His little fists had escaped the pastel swaddling and were pushed up against his chin. She traced a finger across his flushed cheek and down his button nose. His tiny tongue pushed at his bottom lip. She bent and inhaled the sweet scent of his head. He gurgled softly, and Sarah pulled him tighter to her breast. "Just you and me now, mister."

She closed her eyes. Every part of her body ached, the adrenalin rush of birth fading away.

A minute later, a new midwife poked her head into the room. "There's a very excited dad out here. Is he allowed in yet?"

Sarah bristled at the tinge of judgement she'd dealt with all night. "Of course."

She winced as she shuffled her bottom back into a more upright position, while trying not to disturb Riley.

When an uncharacteristically rumpled and bleary-eyed Evan entered the birthing suite, she almost laughed out loud. "You look how I feel."

He placed a takeaway cup on the side table as his gaze searched her face. "How're you holding up?"

"Surprisingly good, although I wouldn't say no to a sip of your coffee."

"It's hot chocolate, I bought it for you." He gestured to the edge of the bed. "Okay if I sit?"

Sarah nodded.

He settled in and reached across and stroked a thumb across Riley's forehead. "Hey there."

His gentle voice filled Sarah with warmth. She'd turned up at Evan's door last year, a bedraggled crying mess following Max's rejection, full of secrets she refused to share, but he'd taken her in anyway. A month later, when he leant in for their first kiss, she hadn't been sure, but their years of friendship led to a partnership that was so easy, so safe.

Not fiery and all-consuming like with Michael.

Evan's attention shifted to her again. "You really okay? I wish you'd let me be here for you."

"You were. I knew all along you were just outside."

"That's not what I meant."

Sarah placed her hand on his forearm. "I needed to do it on my own."

"I know," Evan reached into his jacket pocket and removed a small black box, "but that's the last time." He knelt at the side of the bed, and Sarah's head shook side to side.

"Evan —"

"I mean it. We've been living together all year. It's time to make it official, to become a family."

"But—"

"No more buts. Sarah Calhoun, will you marry me?"

Beholding the solid, dependable man kneeling before her, taking in the loving expression on his face, she knew she'd never meet a better partner. Surely, over time she could learn to match his feelings. Build a family for Riley's sake.

She looked down at her son's chubby face. Enough selfishness, enough mistakes. Everything she did moving forward would be for him.

She met her lover's hopeful stare.
"Yes, Evan Barker, I will marry you."

The shivering woke Sarah. The hotel room was sideways, the nylon carpet scratching her cheek. She shifted to sitting, her blurry focus resting on the birth certificate.

Oh God. Her vision sharpened. She had to figure out who sent it.

A shudder shook her, and her teeth began to chatter. She stumbled to the shower, prepared the water and climbed in. Her skin prickled under the hot spray.

It had to be Daniel. Leaving the certificate on her bed, invading her space, stank of him. She pumped shower gel into her palm and lathered it over her skin. Perhaps when Siobhan reported Sarah's visit yesterday, he decided to remind her what was at stake. Rinsing off, she watched the foam spiral down the drain.

Or Alec could have left it to scare her. He certainly wasn't being straight with her, seemed to like catching her unawares. Resting her forearms against the tiles she directed the spray to the crick in her neck. Her drunken lurch for him flashed in memory. She groaned and turned off the water.

The last option was Michael. She stared at the taps. But surely he wouldn't go about things that way.

Grabbing a towel, she dried off, dressed, then searched the envelope and certificate for clues. Nothing. Not a name or mark. Not even a crease or smudge. She threw them on the bed and paced.

This new threat, even if the person who sent it had no idea, raised the stakes too high. Riley had to leave Ireland as soon as possible.

Her fingers pinched the bridge of her nose. How could she make that happen when he wasn't even talking to her?

A buzzing noise cut into her thoughts. She checked the phone's caller ID. Max. It was barely dawn, what now?

"What's wrong?"

"What the hell, Sarah?"

"What?"

"That stunt you pulled yesterday, you should have come to me first."

"I did, and you wouldn't listen. You told me to back off."

"You'll be lucky if Riley ever talks to you again."

Yesterday seemed so long ago, but she had to fix things there too. Her thoughts tangled. The only way Max could understand the true danger was to tell him everything. Should she risk it?

"I'm going to say this straight, girl. You are failing your boy, with all your suspicions and accusations. You need to start acting like an adult, like a parent."

A febrile heat rushed to her head.

A parent! Was he fucking kidding? When she'd needed him to be a parent, he'd deserted her. Hadn't protected her against anything.

"Don't you dare. You have no idea what parenting is."

Silence.

"Sarah," the strained timbre of Max's voice lowered in pitch, "if you keep on this way you are going to lose your son. You need help. Maybe you should talk to someone."

"I did what I had to do to protect my son. Like I asked you to do."

"I am. I just didn't realise I'd have to protect him from you."

She hung up on him and threw the phone on the bed. Her hands shook. How dare he? He was only in Riley's life now because she'd asked him to help. And he doubted her judgement? Couldn't anyone have her back?

A roar surged from her toes. She screamed it out, tearing her throat raw. But it didn't help. Her body needed to run. Still shaking, she threw on her shoes and charged out the room.

A red hue tinged the dawn sky. Sarah's runners hit the pavement, her lingering hangover loading weight to each step. For the first two kilometres she concentrated only on maintaining form, taking care to strike the pavement evenly across the soles of her feet. She passed the Cupar Way walls and its murals of martyrs and slogans with a glance.

Finally, the burn in her lungs eased, and she found her rhythm. She needed a new plan, one that would force Riley to leave Ireland. But she'd made such a mess of things. No way would Alec or Max help.

Passing an open corner store, her gaze flicked over the day's newspaper headlines: *"Data reveals increase in bombings - 69 in the past year." "Great British Bake-Off new series premiering tonight." "Drugs Gang chief linked to loyalist and republican factions."*

The putrid stench of rotting garbage hit her nostrils; a truck emptying bins crawled the street ahead of her. She turned down a side street, running by a shuttered bar. Snapshots of Alec's face filled her mind. His brief smile as he rebuffed her. The anger in his glare as he threatened to abandon her.

She picked up the pace, edging towards race speed.

Back to Riley, Sarah. She lengthened her stride. The first step to getting him out of Ireland safely was getting rid of Siobhan. In a flash it all came together. The Blackout. Quinn. Liam. She could set Siobhan up using Liam's drugs.

Her breath caught. That was crazy. She'd have to find a place to plant the drugs and get the police to search Siobhan. What if Riley was with the girl when they did? Her pace eased off. He'd be booted out of camp, lose his scholarship. He'd have to leave Ireland.

A steep incline rose before her. She rocked her weight forward to her toes and sprinted hard, her calf muscles screaming in rebellion. Pain was something you had to push through. Everyone lost dreams, had to endure disappointment. Riley was strong. He would rise above it.

At the top she bent over, unable to run further until she regained her breath. She stretched out her calves against the kerb. If she was serious about this plan, no one could ever find out, or she'd lose everything. Her ears registered thumping foot strikes approaching from behind. She turned to see a large man with a baseball cap pulled low over his eyes, running straight at her.

Her instincts screamed.

She didn't think, didn't look back again, just sprinted as fast as her body would allow towards Grosvenor Street and the closest police station she could think of.

The gates of the station were closed and barricaded like a fortress. Barbed wire and broken glass topped the building. Bullet dents pockmarked its concrete walls. Sarah's gaze shot to the watchtowers. Surely if the man in the cap wanted to hurt her, he wouldn't do it here in full view of armed guards and cameras. She crouched in front of the gates, making a point of retying her shoelace.

Approaching thuds sent tremors along the path. She resisted looking up. Hopefully if she ignored the man, he'd run on.

A large sports shoe slapped to a stop in line with her knees.

"For God's sake Sarah, don't hover in front of a police station. They'll think your scouting for an attack."

Her head jerked up. Alec loomed above her, cap in his hand, sucking in air. His arm muscles were thrown into definition as he held his sides. The sweat soaked t-shirt clung to every contour of his chest. Despite everything, desire tugged low in her belly. Her face flushed with memories of the previous night and she stood. "What are you doing here, Alec?"

"I'll give you this, you sure can run. I've been trying to catch you for the last five minutes."

Her focus snagged on his mouth then darted away. "Look, I'm sorry about last night. But I've bigger things to worry about now."

His expression sharpened. "What's going on?"

She studied the lines and nuances of his face. Did he know about the envelope? She desperately wanted to ask, but if he knew nothing, alerting him would only complicate things further. She altered position to stretch out her quads.

"Nothing. Family stuff." *Couldn't he just give her some space after last night. Stop turning up wherever she was?* Unease lodged in her chest. "How did you know where I was this morning?"

He gestured back in the direction of her hotel, clearly

wanting to move, but her feet stayed firmly planted. He ran his hand over his head. "You run first thing every morning, so I waited outside. I wanted to apologise for what I said last night. You'd had too much to drink and weren't thinking clearly. I should have let it slide."

Her gaze shifted from his. "Let's just forget everything from last night."

"Everything?" His mouth spread into a smile, like always twisting to the right. Warmth flared across her cheeks. "I was surprised to see you up so early."

He was teasing, trying to move them to comfortable ground. "Running cures many ills," she shrugged and set off walking in the direction he had indicated earlier.

Alec caught up, matching his steps to hers. They walked in silence, her stare to the ground, but she was completely attuned to him. His palm hovered just off her waist when they crossed the road, and her skin lit up beneath his touch. Each time his head angled her way, her pulse leapt. So, when his upper body straightened, she was immediately on guard.

"There is one thing more. You'll receive your summons today. The whole thing's been fast tracked through the special court. You're to take the stand next Wednesday."

Sarah's stomach slid to her feet. It was all happening too fast. Riley was running out of time.

"Hey, it's okay." His hand brushed across her back. "I'm keeping watch on you. I promise you'll be safe."

She sped up her steps. One week. She had to put her plan into motion today.

They reached the lobby of her hotel, and she immediately

turned to go in. "Thanks for letting me know. I guess I'll see you then."

His hand settled on her upper arm. "You would tell me if something was going on?"

"Of course." She gently eased from his hold, and the twin lines between his brows deepened.

"Sarah, you know I'm on your side?"

For a moment she wanted to lean into him. But unless she was straight about everything, he couldn't help. Alec would do anything to bring Daniel down. She couldn't risk Riley getting caught in the crossfire.

"All's fine, Alec. Don't forget to stretch." She slipped through the hotel's front door and jogged straight for the stairs, betting the five flights would put him off following.

She entered her room and reached straight for her laptop to check Irish law. She'd been right. Riley would get cautioned but, being her third drug arrest, Siobhan would be charged. Next, she booked a second hire car, using an old credit card in her married name. The only place she could think of to plant the drugs was in Siobhan's car, as long as the passenger door lock hadn't been fixed. Timing was going to be everything. She'd hide the drugs during school hours, and, upon her return to Belfast, call in an anonymous tip to the Dublin police. Riley could head home over the weekend with Max. Just in time for Sarah to take the stand.

Her insides knotted in apprehension. So much could go wrong. She pressed her hands into her eye sockets. The whole thing was wrong. But she had to stop the McNaultys from getting their hands on her son. It was the only plan she had.

FIFTEEN

Cupping both hands to her mouth, Sarah blew warm air on her fingers, wishing for the hundredth time she'd brought gloves. Her stare remained fixed on the shuttered Blackout Bar. Surely Quinn would open up soon. Movement drew her attention to the corner. She sighed with relief and jogged over the road. "Morning Quinn."

"Well what about ya, Miss Sarah. Two visits in two days. People will start to talk." He slid the mesh security door up and unlocked the front door.

"Actually, I've come to apologise. I left without paying last night. I didn't even say goodbye."

"Ach, no need. Your man, he left me a fifty-pound note that more than covered things. I hope you were okay. You looked a might ticked off as you left."

"Uh, you could say that." She shifted foot to foot. "Look, there is something else. Do you have a minute to talk?"

He gestured for her to enter the bar. When her runners

suctioned noisily to the floor, he laughed. "Looks like it'll need an extra good mop today. Cuppa first? We've a machine now. It's the real thing."

She pulled up a stool and sat. "Sounds perfect."

As he made their coffees, she glanced around the space, halting on the spot where she'd made such a fool of herself the night before. Had Quinn seen it? God, she hoped not.

"There you go." Quinn pushed a steaming mug towards her and sat. Bringing the coffee to her lips, she couldn't help a sigh of pleasure.

"Good?"

She nodded, her fingers thawing from the cup's heat. Quinn checked his phone. She put her drink down.

"Sorry, I'm sure you have a thousand things to do. I just, I want to go and see Liam. Do you have his address?"

"Leave him be. Trust me, I tried."

"Maybe I could get through to him." She ducked her gaze from his. "I always could before."

"You don't understand."

"I do."

"No. Things have changed." He dragged a stool from end of the bar and sat facing her, coffee in hand. "Most of us in the North, we want to leave the past behind and get on with living normal lives. We've no army, no searches, no curfews. No need to be Catholic or Protestant. We can just be ourselves."

"I know, and Liam can—"

"No. A few can't let go. They thrived on the thrills, the power. It made them who they were. But with decommissioning, they became nobodies. An embarrassment even. Who has a use for armed robbers and bombmakers in peacetime?"

"Quinn, I know all this. But surely there's hope. Liam was different."

Sighing, he unlatched the dishwasher under the bar. "After you left, Liam got himself lost. He'd trouble with his leg, ended up with a permanent limp." He stood and as he talked, he unloaded glasses, placing them in neat rows on the shelves behind him. "Then his Ma scarpered to Scotland with a fella, leaving Liam in the council flat to fend for himself. He was four-teen and alone. The men of the IRA stepped in, became his family. When peace was declared, a radical section broke away, including Liam's division. They continued the drug running that had funded their war."

He closed the emptied dishwater and turned to her. "A group of us tried to get Liam out; someone even set up a mechanical apprenticeship for him. But Liam wouldn't listen. Now his section has aligned with the Russian bratva and traffic anything they can - guns, drugs, fuel, people. The gang they are now, they've no true cause, no soul. All they care about is power. And they will go to any lengths to hold onto it."

He grabbed a bucket and started filling it in the sink. Sarah sipped at her coffee. Quinn was trying to protect her. If he only knew... She threaded her fingers together and leant her elbows on the bar. "Is Liam still in his mum's old house?" The muscles of his back flexed, but he didn't shift. "Quinn."

His shoulders sagged and he turned. "He's still there, but please don't go. You've no idea what you're walking into."

"I'll be careful, I promise." She climbed down from her stool and pushed forward her empty mug. "Thanks for the coffee and your help. Take care." She scurried out of the bar, before what

Quinn said could sink in. She couldn't afford to be cautious. She only had one week.

Sarah checked her watch: two hours until dark. Waiting was doing her head in, but she couldn't visit Liam's house in daylight. There'd be too many people about. She reached for the novel on her bedside table. On her third reading of the same paragraph she let the book fall to her lap. Her plan was insane; there were so many holes.

A knock sounded at her door. She wasn't sure if she could swallow the club sandwich she'd ordered from room service, but she'd eaten so little in the last two days. She had to try.

"Coming."

She opened the door and froze. *Michael*. She had no idea how to move, what to say. She needed another twenty-four hours. "Go away, Michael."

"We need to talk." He pushed past her, the scent of sandal-wood and orange trailing him into the room. "Daniel's ragein'. They've denied him bail. I'll appeal, but everything is moving too fast." He rubbed the back of his neck. "Sarah, I don't under-stand what's going on, but you need to be careful. If you don't do as he says, he'll crush you and yours."

Was this a trick to distract her until Daniel could blindside her with something else? She crossed her arms. "If you don't leave, I'll call the police."

"You mean Stone?" He moved towards the open room door, but instead of leaving, he shut the door with a bang and turned to face her. "I've watched you with him, you know. Seen him leaving your room late at night. You screwing him?"

"That is absolutely none of your business. Get out."

Michael glared, his gaze tracking her as she circled away from him, He racked his palms across his face. "I'm sorry. I didn't mean to..." His hands dropped to his sides. "Jesus, I just don't understand."

"There's nothing to understand. You need to leave."

"No." He stepped towards her.

She backed away, both palms up to halt his advance. "I'm not doing this, Michael."

He kept coming. When her heels hit the wall, his hands landed either side of her head. "Why did you leave? We were grand until that riot and then you left without a word. I know you weren't happy about Daniel but —"

"Not happy?" Her voice turned shrill. "Daniel destroyed every chance we had." She tried to duck under his arms, but he seized her shoulders, his fingers digging into her flesh.

"No, you did, when you left. You got married less than a year after leaving Belfast. How Sarah? How after everything we shared?"

He leant in closer. It was too much. The familiar heat of him, the scent of his cologne. She turned her head to the side and closed her eyes but couldn't escape the memories crowding her brain...

Stroking Liam's head she prayed he would stay asleep after the trauma of the riot. The smell of smoke and petrol wafted from her damp hair, turning her stomach. She shuddered, reliving the moment when the fist-sized plastic bullet hit his leg. Watching helplessly as he fell. Her eyes welled. What happened tonight was madness. She could never raise a family here.

Another chopper flew low overhead making the windows rattle violently in their frames. The trouble wasn't abating. Was Michael still caught up in that mess? The front door slammed downstairs.

"Sarah? Sarah!"

She raced down the stairs and threw herself into Michael's arms, wrapping every limb around him, burying her head into his neck.

"You're here." He held her tight. "I watched you break through the line, then couldn't see you anywhere. I'm so sorry." Michael pulled back to look at her and saw the gash on her cheek.

"What did those bastards do to you?"

"I'm okay. A glass smashed up and caught my face."

"If they touched you—"

"It wasn't the police. It was a bottle." She slid her legs from his hips until her feet touched the floor. "I've got Liam Breen upstairs in bed. A plastic bullet hit his leg. It's badly bruised, but his mum didn't want him outside, even to go to hospital. She'll get him in the morning."

Michael's fingers brushed down her face. "When you ran to him..." He shook his head. "What was he doing on top of that Land Rover?"

"He's ten years old; just got caught up in it all."

"The bastards shouldn't have shot him. He's a kid." Michael removed his coat and jammed it on its hook. "They're mongrels, Sarah. You should see some of the others. The RUC were out of control."

"They were all out of control. Everyone. I don't understand,

Michael. How could we ever raise a family here? It's not a place for children."

"We're fighting for our families, for our children. And after the news coverage tonight of the RUC violence, of Liam getting shot, the world will see. The Brits won't be able to shove us under the rug anymore. Daniel says we'll be free."

With each word he spoke, the chasm between them deepened. "Michael," she hugged herself, "what about us? This is no place to build our lives."

"Don't you see? We just have to make it through this last hurdle. We've only to wait a little while longer."

She closed her eyes and drew in a long breath to steady her shaking body. Why couldn't he see there was no end to the hate and violence? No simple solution. She had to make him understand. Closing the space between them she rested her palms on his chest.

"You've worked so hard, getting your degree, passing the bar exam. We could move away and still fight. Use legal means. Play to your strengths. You could petition the politicians. I would help."

"This is my home."

The vice-like grip on her ribcage tightened. He had to understand what he risked by staying. One of them was going to get hurt or arrested or killed.

"We don't have a little while, Michael." Taking his face in her hands she looked into his honey-coloured eyes. "This isn't how I wanted to—"

Daniel burst through the front door. "Where the fuck are you at, Michael? We need you! Dermot Malone has been shot dead. It's all gone to shite! We need you out there. Now!"

Sarah grasped Michael's shirt with both hands. "Michael, please! Please don't go. We need to finish this."

"I have to go and see what I can do." He brought her palms up and pressed his mouth to each one. "I'll be back as soon as I can." He grabbed his discarded jacket and ran outside, slamming the door behind him.

Sarah snagged her own coat from the hook. She had to chase him down. Had to stop him before it was too late.

A howl from upstairs pierced the silence, then she heard loud sobbing.

"Dammit!" She couldn't leave. She re-hung her coat and took the stairs back to Liam, hoping beyond hope that Michael would return to her soon, free of Daniel and ready to talk...

Michael's breath grazed Sarah's cheek and she opened her eyes. So many images vying for attention, so many emotions. She stared into his gaze. Every night, from that one forth, she'd slept alone, while Daniel demanded all of Michael's time.

He leant in and a heated exhale travelled down her neck. "You haven't answered my question, Sarah. How could you leave me after all we shared?"

She tried to push him away, to get space, but he wouldn't budge. "You shared nothing with me. Even when I needed you, you chose him."

"He needed me too."

"You changed."

"I changed when you left me. You took every bit of goodness and hope I had and disappeared." His gaze slid down her face to her lips.

He lunged in, crushing his mouth on hers, aggressive and pained. There was wetness, but no fire, no heat. Her heart sat empty. He groaned and pushed her lips apart with his tongue. His teeth clashed against hers. Desperate. He threaded his hands in her hair and wrenched their lips apart, his breath coming fast and hard. "Did you ever love me?"

"I never really knew you."

His forehead dropped to hers. "You were the only one that did."

Compassion stirred for the broken man before her. She wanted to reach out and ease his pain. To comfort him. But the threats against her kids repeated inside her head.

"No. The man I thought I loved had strength. He'd never have let Daniel tear us apart, never let him threaten my family." Ice encased her voice. "And never, ever, would the man I thought I loved have made a living off the slavery and torture of children." She turned her face from his touch. "Go away Michael. I don't want you here."

He slammed her body back, her head cracking against the wall. Pain seared through her skull. Who was this man? He'd only ever laid a hand on her with love. Was he going to beat her now? Is that who he'd become? Looking directly into his eyes, she searched for the man she once thought she'd share her life with.

Michael released her quickly, as if his hands had been scorched. He paced the room. Had this violence always been at his core? How had she not seen it? She glanced to the door, weighing up her ability to escape.

Suddenly the air in the room changed. Her gaze whirled back to Michael. His expression was hard. She slid her left foot forward, bent her knees and braced, ready to defend against whatever he had planned. He stalked towards the door, looked back at her with dead eyes.

"Daniel was right. You're nothing but a cold, judgemental bitch."

He was right. Cold contempt was all she had left for this man who'd promised her the world. He'd given in. Become weak. Betrayed everything he once believed in. Everything they'd worked for.

"I've one last message for you. From Daniel. You're to stay put in Belfast. No more trips to Dublin to visit your lad. You're to fall into line, or Daniel will make sure you do."

He yanked open the door and left.

Sarah stood motionless, waiting for the axe to fall. But there was nothing. No rush of emotions, not even fear. She closed the door, moved to the bed and lowered herself down. She exhaled every bit of air from her lungs. A smile curved her mouth. She still had time to save her son.

SIXTEEN

F rom the driver's seat, Sarah scrutinised Liam's unlit street. Republican martyrs loomed from a faded wall mural, their painted AK47s aimed at her heart, as if they knew her intent. Air erupted from her mouth in a huff. *Well it's your damn lot selling the crap.*

She reached for the door handle and paused. Was she really going to do this? Buy drugs from the IRA? She sagged back into the seat. There had to be another way.

Staring across the road at Liam's front door she couldn't think of a single one. Court started in less than a week. She had to stick to the plan. Easy. What could possibly go wrong?

She groaned. This was insane. Resting her head on the steering wheel she closed her eyes. What would she say when he opened the door? *Hi Liam. Remember me, your trusted youth worker? Got any weed?* She scoffed. As if he'd care about anything but the sale.

Siobhan would though. What if the girl was innocent, like

Max insisted? Sarah wiped clammy hands down her jeans. She was going to hell for this, but Riley was all that mattered. She scanned the deserted street one more time, then slipped on her backpack, pulled the hood of her jacket up as far over her head as possible and darted to Liam's front door.

His townhouse looked like any other along the row – white-washed with shared sidewalls and a barren front yard hemmed in by a brick fence – except for the heavy metal grills securing both the front door and the downstairs windows. Sarah fingered the one-hundred-pound note in her pocket and rang the bell. Uneven footsteps clomped inside, heading her way. She checked over her shoulder one more time.

When the front door opened, she was enveloped in a cloud of sweet smoke. A tall lanky man with a buzz cut, sunken eyes and a pockmarked complexion looked up through long eyelashes with a sneer. "What about ye?"

She was taken aback. Liam was so different. Words evaporated on her tongue. *What was she thinking coming here?*

"Uh I wanted to, that is I'd like to…"

Liam's expression shifted, confusion rippling across his face, and for a brief moment, she recognised the boy she'd cradled after the riot. "Miss Sarah?"

Tension locked her shoulders back. "Hi Liam. Long time, no see."

"Aye it has been a long while." He scanned the street outside, looked her up and down and unlocked the heavy grill. "You wanna come in?"

"That would be lovely." *Lovely? You idiot, Sarah, you're not in some Austen novel calling for tea.*

She stepped over the threshold. Liam shut the grill door

with a clunk, shifted the deadlock into place and banged the front door closed. The keys jingled in his pocket as he led her through the lurking haze and into his front room. The largest flat screen TV she'd ever seen hung on a wall above a glass table littered with half-full ashtrays and a pile of pizza boxes.

He limped slightly as he cleared room for her to sit on the stained couch. Quinn was right. The plastic bullet had caused damage to his left leg. She should have taken him to hospital that night.

"Would you like a drink? I've only beer or milk."

"No, thanks. I'm good."

He sat on the arm of a well-loved lounge chair, its cushions carrying the permanent indentation of his body. "Well, what can I do you for?"

She swallowed the extra saliva in her mouth and met his hazel gaze. "I was hoping to buy one hundred pounds worth of marijuana."

Liam leapt to his feet, his movements sharp and jerky. "Up. Now. Hands out to the side."

She stood as directed and before she knew it, his rough hands were patting down every single part of her body.

"You with the peelers?"

"No! I want to make a purchase." *Christ Sarah, a purchase? Is that the best you can do?*

"And what would someone like you want with drugs?" Liam stepped back, arms crossed over his chest, eyes like slits.

She forced herself to keep eye contact. "I get back pain. It's the only thing that works."

A pause stretched out, then the tension in his body disappeared. "Ach, I know exactly how you feel." He slouched into the seat this time and reached for a tin. "Sorry about that. Never can be too careful." He pulled out a bag of marijuana and some rolling papers. "So, whatcha doing back in Belfast?"

Sarah shifted in her chair. "Just on a short work assignment. Running community surveys on housing for an international company."

"Sounds naff."

Sarah gave a hollow laugh. "Kind of is."

Liam placed the rolled joint onto the ashtray and stood. "One hundred pounds is a fair whack of weed. I can do you seven and a half grams. That be enough to cover you?"

She nodded.

"You want it all in one bag or measured out?"

She hadn't thought this part through. Surely you were more likely to get arrested for intent to sell if you had separately packed bags? "Separate bags would be helpful thanks, Liam."

When he left the room, she exhaled slowly. He seemed to have bought her story. Now she just had to hope he didn't mention her visit to anyone. She looked around. Liam's world consisted of his television, a play station and his drugs, all kept in the confines of his lounge room. Judging by the pallor of his skin, she guessed he didn't get out much. Which was good news for her.

"So, how have you been Liam?" she called out.

"I'm grand. There's a peace and all, ya know."

"So I've heard. Did you ever do mechanics like you planned?"

"Ach, no, biggest waste of time, so it was. I'm doing cracker. Don't worry 'bout me." He moved back into the room, his uneven gait more pronounced now he wasn't concentrating on masking it.

"All done." He held up a package wrapped in layers of newspaper. She handed over the money and took the package in her hands. Its heaviness surprised her. Then the scent from Liam's newly lit joint closed around her. She stood. "Thanks, Liam, I better be off."

"You don't want to stay for a puff? On the house like?"

Loneliness coloured his eyes. Her heart cramped remembering the spirited boy he had once been.

"Sorry, I have to drive. Maybe another time."

She walked to the front door. While he unlocked the grill, she pushed the package into the rear pocket of the backpack and zipped it closed. "Take care of yourself, Liam."

"You too, Miss Sarah. Come visit anytime."

She gave him a brief smile then pulled her hood over her head, clutched the bag to her chest and ran for her car. No longer just a coward and a liar, but a criminal, no better than the paramilitaries she claimed to hate.

In the short dash from Liam's front door to her car, she kept her head down against the blasting arctic air. She opened the car door and dived in.

"What the hell do you think you're doing?"

Her entire body sprang back against the door. "Dammit, Alec, what are you doing in my car?" She held tighter to her bag.

"What's in that?" He indicated the backpack.

Her pulse hammered. "Nothing."

When he reached for it, she knocked his arm away, then unzipped the larger front pocket and presented the contents –

her wallet, gloves and computer – praying that he wouldn't ask to see the pocket behind.

"See?" She re-zipped it as soon as his gaze lifted back up to her face and tucked the bag down her right side. "Now you tell me what you're doing here?"

He stared at her for what seemed like minutes.

"Well?"

"I told you I'd watch over you."

Sarah folded her arms. "Well it's getting a little much, detective, you appearing wherever I am."

"What are you up to, Sarah? Liam Breen is a known drug dealer. What business do you have with him?"

"That is none of your concern."

"Are you fucking kidding me? My prime witness willingly enters an IRA controlled house, and it's none of my concern?" His face flushed red. "Do you have a death wish? Or any idea what being arrested there would do to the case against Daniel? Did you even use your brain?"

"Don't you dare talk to me like that. You're not my father."

"If I were, you'd be over my knee."

She bit down on her cheek. She had to calm this down. Had to get him out of the car before he grew even more suspicious. She softened her tone and turned her face to him.

"Liam was one of my case kids in '97. His leg has nerve damage because I didn't take him to hospital after he was hit with a plastic bullet. I owed him an apology." She shut out the voice on her shoulder screaming at her to fess up. To beg Alec for help. Instead she watched him in her peripheral vision, assessing if her story had worked.

He remained unchanged, his anger billowing. "You are the

only way we can take Daniel down. If you screw this up, we lose years of work. He'll walk free and destroy countless more lives. Don't you care? Don't you fucking care he'll be out there, free to go after your kids?"

"I'm sorry. I didn't think it through."

"Well it's high time you did think, and hard. Your secrecy and games are putting everyone at risk. If you love your kids, you'll stop now, or all three will pay the price for your stupidity." He wrenched open the door and stormed from her car, his parting words ringing in the air, the slamming of the door an exclamation mark on his fury.

The only muscles that moved in Sarah's body were her eyes, tracking Alec until he disappeared around the corner. She remained still. Waiting. She let another minute pass.

Her fingers unfurled from their grip on her pants. He wasn't coming back. She removed the marijuana packages from her backpack and placed them into a hollowed-out book she'd prepared earlier. It wouldn't stand up to a thorough search, but at a glance it would get overlooked.

His parting words replayed in her head. She gritted her teeth. Of course she damn well loved her kids. She'd do anything to protect them. He was the one who couldn't help with Siobhan, who'd promised her she had plenty of time before the matter went to court. It was his fault she had to take these measures to protect her son. Her head pulsed with sharp stabs. And he'd never answered her question about how he found her at Liam's, or the bar last night, or on her run this morning. Her forefingers rolled in circles at her temples. She'd have to make extra sure no one followed her to Dublin tomorrow.

SEVENTEEN

Carousel music burst into her dream. Too loud. Sarah willed back the crash of the waves, the house at Forster, the salty scent of a younger Riley's hair as he cuddled about her waist. Another round of the melody played, dragging her further away. The vision melted to nothing, and she woke to a dark hotel room. Disappointment surged. Belfast. She looked at the green numbers of the alarm clock. 3:12 am. The carousel tune began again. Her ringtone for Evan. She sat upright and answered her phone. "Evan, what's wrong?"

"Sarah? It's Gladys."

Evan's secretary? Sarah flicked on the light. Why was she calling from her boss's phone?

"Where's Evan? Are the girls okay?"

"Ally and Sophie are fine. They're still away with their grandparents." Brittleness filled the silence, and Gladys's breath hitched.

Sarah threw off the bedcovers and swung her legs over the side of the bed. "What's going on, Gladys?"

"I'm at the hospital. Evan's in intensive care. He had to return to Sydney for a client meeting, but was attacked on his way in. He's in a bad way. Felicity would have called, but she won't leave his side, and they don't allow mobiles in ICU."

Who would hurt Evan? A chill settled beneath her skin. "What happened?"

"No one knows. Evan was in and out of consciousness. But he fought the doctors, wouldn't let them sedate him until we agreed to get a message to you." Gladys's voice was clipped, like she was struggling with what came next.

Sarah's fingers dug into her thigh.

"Before I tell you, you need to understand Evan was barely conscious. Wasn't making a lot of sense."

"Okay."

"He kept saying, 'The girls are safe. I didn't tell them. Tell Sarah I didn't tell them.'"

Sarah's hand pressed at her mouth. Daniel had sent someone after her girls. She should have warned Evan. It was her fault he was lying in ICU. She pushed through the ache in her throat. "Is he going to be okay?"

"There's a bad contusion on his head. They have to wait for the swelling to go down, but they're hopeful."

"Can I speak to him?"

"The doctors have him sedated. They want to keep him under for at least another forty-eight hours."

Forty-eight hours. Two days. She couldn't wait that long. This attack changed everything. Perhaps she should stay in Belfast, obey Daniel. But how could she leave Riley to deal with

Siobhan alone? *Riley.* Sarah's heart wailed against her breast-bone. *Oh God. Riley. What if Daniel had gotten to him too?*

"Gladys. I have to go. I'll call again tonight."

With each unanswered ring Sarah's grip tightened on the phone. She drew her knees into her chest. By the fourth ring, her lungs screamed for air.

"Hello?" his croaky voice answered.

Sarah's head dropped to meet her knees. She had to swallow the stone-like lump in her throat before her voice would work. "It's me, Riley. I needed to make sure you were safe."

"I was asleep."

"Sorry, honey, but it couldn't wait."

"Mum, this isn't okay. I've got a big game tomorrow. I think you might need to see someone."

Sarah unfolded her body. "Honey, it's not—"

"No, Mum. No more. I'll call when I'm ready to talk."

She stared at the beeping phone. He'd hung up. Hadn't heard her out. She rang back, but it went straight to voicemail. She hadn't had a chance to tell him about Evan or warn him to be careful. How could she keep him safe when he wouldn't even talk to her?

She speed-dialled Max. It went straight to voicemail. Tried again. No answer. She left him a message about Evan and fell back on the bed, an arm flung over her eyes. A massive hole opened at the centre of her chest. Evan was a good man. She might have blamed him for putting Riley in danger, but it wasn't his fault. It was her. All her. She was so stupid, so weak, always one step behind Daniel. Would this ever end?

She swatted away the useless tears tracking down her cheeks and sat up. She needed to check on her girls. Looking at her mobile, her gaze narrowed. Could Daniel trace her calls? Is that how he found Evan? Well, she wasn't giving up contact. Daniel had taken too much from her already. She pulled on jeans and a coat over her nightie and slipped into ballet flats. There was a twenty-four-hour Spar on the corner where she could buy a disposable phone. He couldn't trace that. She pocketed her room key and raced down the fire stairs into the quiet of the night.

She arrived back at her room twenty minutes later with the new phone and a bunch of flowers that she laid in the bathroom sink. She dialled the girls and waited.

"Hello, Sophie Barker speaking."

Sarah's heart swelled. She climbed under the bedclothes. "Hi, honey, it's Mummy."

Shuffling sounded; Sophie had pulled the receiver away from her ear. "Ally, come quick. It's Mummy!" Her voice returned to the line. "Hey Mum, what goes zzub zzub zzub?"

"I've no idea. What?"

"A bee going backwards." Gleeful giggles filled the line. "Get it? Zzub is buzz backwards."

"It's a good one, gorgeous. You having a good time at the farm?"

"It's the best! But I miss you."

Sarah rubbed her chest. "I miss you too."

"When are you coming home?"

"As soon as I can. I promise I'm doing everything I can to finish this job."

"Daddy went back to Sydney yesterday so he's at work now too."

Sarah braced against the surge of emotion.

"I'm sure he misses you already."

"Okay."

Sarah wasn't sure if Sophie's okay was for her or someone else. Voices murmured in the background.

"Mum, Gramps wants to talk with you, so I better go. I love you."

"Love you too."

"Love you the mostest!" Then Sophie was gone.

"Hello?" The strain in Doug's deep gravelly voice hollowed her out. Doug loved his son as much as she loved hers.

Sarah cleared her throat. "I just got off the phone to Gladys, Doug. How are you?"

"We're waiting for news, trying to keep it quiet here. Have you spoken with him yet?"

"No, they're keeping him sedated for another two days. Doug, I'm so sorry."

"You've got nothing to be sorry for."

Guilt twined up her neck, clogging her vocal cords.

"Sarah, Evan's tougher than he looks."

"Of course he is. He comes from strong stock." She swallowed. She had to get a grip, leave the guilt for later. "Did Gladys or Felicity give you any idea why Evan was attacked? Did anything unusual happen before he left the farm?"

"No. Why?"

"Before the doctors put him out, he seemed to think the girls were in some kind of danger."

"What? No, he didn't say a thing. Anyone comes near those girls, I'll take their head off."

"I know you'll protect them. It's just..." She dragged her hand through her hair. "Look, I'm not sure what this is about. Until Evan is conscious again would you please keep the girls at the farm? Don't take them out. And don't let them answer your phone. After what's happened to Evan, and me being on the other side of the world, I'd rather be cautious. At least until we know what he was talking about."

"Agreed." Silence filled a pause. "You okay, love?"

She bit her cheek. Evan's parents had always treated her like a daughter. She should have stayed in better contact.

"I'm okay. Just wishing I was there."

"All right. Well, you look after yourself. Ally's here waiting."

"Thanks for everything, Doug. I'll ring again soon."

"Hi Mum," Ally sounded out of breath.

"Hi beautiful, you been out with the horses?"

"Yep, Gramps is teaching me how to herd cattle. It's so cool! And you should see my new jumps."

Sarah's throat thickened. Ally sounded so pleased with herself, so happy. "I can't wait to, Al."

"Mum, is everything okay? You sound funny."

Her eldest girl had a sixth sense. Sarah needed to raise her guard. "I'm good. Just missing you a lot."

"Miss you too, Mum." Sarah heard a distant shout from Ally's end. "Sophie's calling, I promised to help with an easy jump. I should go before she tries it without me."

"Okay. Love you to infinity, Miss Moo."

"Love you too, to infinity plus one."

"See you soon okay?"

"Yep. Bye."

Sarah pressed the off button and knew what she needed to do. Daniel might have taken a shot and landed a serious blow, but he wasn't going to win.

EIGHTEEN

S arah threw clothes into an overnight bag, packing them around the book concealing the drugs. She focused only on the steps of her plan, on what she needed to do next, not allowing Evan's suffering or the debris of her relationship with Riley to gain traction. Riley could dislike her, he could hate her if he had to, but no harm would come to him.

Not the way it had to Gerry or Evan.

She moved to the safe and reached in. Her fingers clasped around the grip of the pistol Max had arranged for her. Her pulse tripped. Sitting on the bed, she slid the Smith and Wesson M&P Shield from its moulded plastic holster. She turned it over in her palm, testing its weight. Light, compact, and easy to fire. Too easy.

Apprehension spread up her back. Maybe she shouldn't take it with her? She'd only ever shot at paper targets, not real flesh and blood. Her lips pressed together. It might be more dangerous to have it. Then she pictured Evan unconscious in intensive care.

She re-holstered the weapon and put it in her handbag. If she had to, she'd use it.

In the corner of her vision she clocked the flowers, where she'd left them in the sink. Visiting Gerry's grave had been a stupid idea last night and made even less sense today.

She checked her watch. 5:00 am. There was time. She looked again at the bathroom sink. Paying her respects was one failure she could address, and it would give her a chance to check she wasn't being followed. She grabbed the bunch of flowers and her bag and left the room.

With the thick mist of dawn as her only companion, Sarah pushed through a wrought iron gate and stepped under the high sandstone archway of Milltown Cemetery. She cradled the flowers, making her way along the uneven grey roadway, its surface shiny and slippery underfoot. Her hand clutched the stems as more and more plots rose out from the thick white air. There were so many. Headstone after headstone, the dates of death getting more recent the further she walked in. Her elbows hugged her body as she moved through the scents of lilies and roses left at the gravesides.

She turned down a small aisle and damp grass squelched under her feet. Scanning each headstone in earnest now, she searched for one name.

At the end of the row she found it. A two-metre-high granite Gaelic cross watched over a plot of well-tended grass.

Gerry McCann
1979 – 1997
Beloved Son and Brother
Honourable until the end

Her eyes flinched closed. *Honourable until the end.* She forced a breath to the bottom of her lungs, released it and took another. When she looked back at Gerry's headstone the sun had broken through the mist, bathing sections of the graveyard in light.

She laid the bouquet of seventeen white chrysanthemums, one for each year since she'd run, against Gerry's tombstone. Tears burnt the back of her eyes. She should have stopped him trying to avenge his brother. She should have stepped in when Daniel raised the gun. She knelt, placing her palms flat on his grave.

"I'm so sorry, Gerry. I won't fail you this time. I promise I will not stop until Daniel pays for what he did." Her throat closed up. She pushed a fist against the ache below her ribs and her breath hitched.

A shadow fell upon her back and someone knelt at her side, but she didn't brace or recoil. Alec's scent wrapped around her like a blanket. He pressed a palm between her shoulders. She turned to a face lined with concern and his arms enveloped her. A sob racked through her, and another, and another, until the hiccupping spasms stifled her breath. She held onto him as tight as she could, while her body all but vomited out the fear and guilt and pain she'd buried for years.

When she lifted her face from Alec's chest her surroundings came into view, as did an uncomfortable awareness of his arms embracing her. She'd totally lost it, clung to him as if she were drowning.

"Sorry." She sat back, bottom to heels. Her shoulders curled over and she stared at the flattened blades of grass between them.

"Sarah, look at me."

A knot twisted in her belly, but she did as he asked. The expression on his face stripped her bare. His gold-flecked irises had thinned around dilated pupils filled with compassion she didn't deserve. Her gaze fell from his. How could he give her that when she was so weak, such a coward?

His long fingers threaded through hers, and he led her to a bench to sit. The leather of his jacket slid across her neck and he curled his arm around her shoulders. She steeped herself in his calm. Alec was the closest thing she'd found to solid ground since coming back to Belfast. She couldn't let go. Not yet. They sat in the quiet. The morning mist cleared, revealing Divis Mountain in the distance.

Minutes passed. Alec's breath and body tensed. He removed his arm, readjusted his jacket and clamped his palms together between his thighs. "The other day, you asked about Olivia."

"It's okay, it's none of my—"

"Olivia was my daughter. She was three years old the last time I held her."

Sarah's breath stalled.

He cleared his throat. "The next time I saw her was months later, her little body laid out on a gurney in the morgue."

A hand flew to cover her mouth. Even for Daniel this was

too much. He'd raised Olivia's name so casually. She was just a little girl, a baby.

"Afterwards, I tore at myself for failing her. I drank. I raged. Brawled with anyone who'd fight me." His flat voice faded out.

She reached over to cover his hand with hers. "I'm so sorry."

His mouth twisted. "My ex, Chloe, was so drugged up she didn't remember smothering her own daughter with a pillow. When she sobered the next day and learnt what she'd done, she killed herself."

"Oh God, Alec, please, you don't need to—"

"I do. You need to know." Hardness coloured his voice. "Our marriage was a mess. I was away, working undercover. Each time I came home, things got worse. Chloe grew more distant. Cold. I followed her to a house in Bangor Street. I'd put its owner, a mid-level IRA man, in jail for arms possession."

She gripped his hand tighter. "Daniel."

He gave one sharp nod. "That night, I challenged her. We fought. I slept in the spare room. The next morning she'd gone and taken Olivia. I never saw them alive again. Daniel got Chloe hooked on smack, then sold her to a brothel. God knows what those final months were like for my daughter. And it was my fault. All of it. My girl died because of me."

"Alec, it wasn't you. Daniel is the monster. A psychopath." Now she understood his obsession with taking Daniel down. He knew exactly what she was going through. He had lived it. She couldn't imagine how he'd survived. Searching his face, she found it vacant, still lost in the past. She knelt on the ground between his legs and cupped his face with her hands.

"Listen to me, Alec. You are not to blame." Stroking her

thumbs across his cheekbones, she wished she could erase his pain.

He squeezed her forearms. "Neither are you."

His stare bore into her. He meant it. The pressure of her palms gentled on his cheek. She studied his scar, brushed the pad of a finger across it. "One of the fights?"

He gave a slow nod. "Beer bottle."

Her thumb followed the path of the faded welt down to the corner of his mouth. She leant in and kissed the scar. He went still beneath her and the air around them shifted. She pulled back, and his stare fixed on her mouth. Her lips parted and the next thing she was crushed against him, their mouths joining, their tongues meeting and stroking and tasting. Fingers of heat curled in her belly. Her head spun. It was too much, too intense. She was losing control.

She dragged her mouth from his, heart pumping hard as she recovered her breath. The intensity coursing through her eased, and her awareness grew to the cemetery around them. She looked up and met eyes she couldn't read.

My God. What had she done? Alec had shared his deepest pain and she had jumped him like a dog in heat. Her face flamed.

"That was so wrong. I'm..." Her throat seized up. No words could fix it. She turned and fled, bolting for the car park. Horror and embarrassment powering every step.

She reached her car and rummaged through her bag for the car key. She had to get away.

Footsteps pounded towards her. Her fingers fumbled, dropping the key to the ground. When she reached down to get it, Alec plucked it up.

"Sarah?"

Her hand clutched the base of her neck, the other wrapped about her middle. "I'm so sorry. I'm... I'm horrified."

He offered the key and she took it from him, wincing when even that brief touch shot heat across her skin. "I have to go."

He clasped her shoulders. "Will you give me a chance to talk?"

She shook her head. "You needed me to listen and I—"

His arms folded around her, encasing her in the now familiar smell of leather. "You did nothing I didn't want you to."

Want. That's what the kiss had been all about. Want and lust and desire. Could she not make one good decision? He shouldn't be wasting his time wanting her. She needed all his attention and energy on protecting her kids.

She pushed away and bleeped the car open. "It was a mistake, Alec. And it won't happen again."

Slipping into the driver's seat, she started the engine and drove towards the parking garage where she'd hidden her second car. When she glanced in the rear-view mirror a heaviness moved onto her chest. Alec's head was bent forward, his hands clasped behind his neck.

Sitting in her rental, staring at the rear fender of Siobhan's Fiat, Sarah's eyes glazed over. The pad of her index finger traced her lip. What would have happened if she hadn't pulled away?

With a shake of her head she shut down that train of thought. She couldn't get distracted. Especially by a man who deserved so much better than her. Shouts and laughter sang through the car's open window, drawing her attention to the school's lawn and the girls heading to their next classes. If Siobhan crossed by, would she seem so carefree? Sarah's lips pinched together. Unlikely. That girl's innocence was long gone, another one of Daniel's victims.

He'd always had the skill to pinpoint weakness and vulnerability. Like Alec's crumbling marriage. Daniel had totally exploited Chloe's isolation.

Sarah shifted in her seat and glanced at her bag, the drugs still concealed inside the book. Planting them on Siobhan would destroy the girl's life. Was she behaving just like Daniel?

Her fingers dragged through her hair. Chloe had fallen for Daniel's manipulations and lost everything. So had Michael. Right now she was allowing Daniel to use her fears against her. But what if she chose to share the lot? Like Alec had. He'd revealed his deepest regrets and pain, and she hadn't judged him. If he knew the whole story, he'd understand the danger her son was in.

She could trust him.

Her jaw loosened on a sigh. It was time to stop being ruled by fear. It was time to ask for help.

She pulled out the disposable phone she'd brought from Belfast, and dialled. The line rang unanswered, but her focus didn't stray. She would keep on calling until he heard her out. Just when she expected his voice message to activate, the line clicked open.

"Alec, it's—"

"Where are you?"

"I'm sorry I ran. I—"

"My question was where?"

"I'm in Dublin. I came to...God, I don't know. I don't know what I'm doing. I'm a mess."

"That you are."

Her pulse spiked, the urge to blurt everything down the phone all but taking over. But she snapped her mouth shut. Phones could be hacked. She had to use her smarts.

"What do you want, Sarah?"

Her fingers lifted to the base of her neck. "There's things, things you don't know."

"I'm done. If there are things I should know, tell me. Stop playing me for a fool."

"I don't trust the phone."

"Then come back to Belfast."

"I have to stay here, to sort things out with Riley and Dad."

"Sarah."

The heel of her hand massaged her sternum. "Alec, would you please come here? Neither of them trusts me at the moment, but they'll listen to you."

"You've earned the mistrust."

The sharp truth of his statement cut through her. She took a moment to settle her breath. "I promise I'll tell you everything."

"Where exactly are you?"

"Do you know St Stephen's Park, where the bridge is?"

"I'll be two hours."

"Thank you."

"This better not be another game."

A surge of shameful heat seared her neck. "This morning wasn't a game. You'll understand when you get here, okay?"

"I better. And Sarah?"

"Yes?"

"We are not done."

The line cut out, and she held the phone to her chest. His accent had sharpened with his anger. But he had said yes and was dropping everything to come to her.

Perched on a stone bench in St Stephen's Park, near the cobble-stone bridge where she'd arranged to meet Alec, Sarah leant back and revelled in the sun's heat tingling across her skin. She turned her face to the sky, closed her eyes and inhaled, relishing the ease of her breath. She'd already freed herself of the drugs, flushing them down a public toilet minutes after her call to Alec. If she could have, she'd have dumped the gun too; she couldn't wait to hand it over to him. She checked her watch: ten minutes to go.

She pushed off the seat and walked through dappled light into a wooded area. Ducks splashed in the lake as she approached the bridge. She savoured another deep breath, this one filled with the scent of damp earth and oak. She loosened her scarf from around her neck and smiled. Things were going to be okay. She hadn't been so sure of anything in a long time. Alec would help protect those she loved. Together they would beat Daniel. For the first time in months she was free of the suffocating grip on her throat.

Leaves crackled to the side of the track. She glanced over and caught a brief glimpse of a furry tail disappearing into the underbrush. She ambled on, the bridge now in sight.

Leaves crunched right behind her. She turned, but an arm wrapped around her waist, trapping her arms to her sides. A cloth clamped over her face, cutting off her nostrils and mouth.

She held her breath and fought, twisting and jerking. She kicked and stamped at the person holding her. She was lifted off her feet. Her burning lungs demanded air. She took one last swing with her foot then gulped in a breath. A cloying sweetness invaded her mouth. Her muscles gave way, softening out of her control. She couldn't scream or bite or cry. Silence muffled all sound. Her vision narrowed. She should have told Alec everything on the phone. Now he'd never know.

NINETEEN

Her head lolled forward, and pain shot through her neck. Eyes opening to black, her lashes scratched against material. She attempted to stand but found herself bound to the chair she sat on. She twisted and turned, struggling to pull her hands from behind her back. Pain stung her wrists. A gag muffled the sound of her screams. She tried closing her spread knees, but the ties wouldn't give. She jerked and pulled again and again against the restraints, ignoring the sawing sensation on her skin. Who had her? What did they want? Her belly lurched, acid flooded her mouth. She needed to calm down. If she threw up, she'd choke.

Exhale. Inhale. Concentrate.

Through a foggy headache, she reached for her last memory. Waiting in the park for Alec, looking forward to seeing him, and then a cloth covering her mouth, no air, fighting. After that, nothing. They must have drugged her. Whoever they were. It had to be Daniel, didn't it? God for once she hoped so because if this was just some bog-standard psycho, she was screwed.

Her ears scanned the quiet. How long had she been out? Had it been an hour, a day, a week? She'd only been ten minutes off meeting Alec. Surely, he'd be searching for her. She screamed again.

A whoosh of air pushed into the room. Sarah froze. Footsteps. Coming towards her. She couldn't move, couldn't see. What were they going to do?

A rough hand pulled at her shirt neckline. She tried pulling away but couldn't. Tears stung her nose. Tobacco-laden breath rushed in her nostrils, making her stomach roll. Then a sting in her shoulder. A rush of cold through her flesh. Her muscles sagged. Her body collapsed into the chair. And black crawled over her.

When she came to, her tongue was stuck to the roof of her mouth. She opened and closed her jaw, moving it side to side. She was still bound and blindfolded, but they must have removed the gag while she was unconscious. A whisper of sound. She stiffened. The even breaths of someone else in the room. Fear and hope entwined in her belly.

"Hello?"

Nothing.

"Hello, I can hear you."

Nothing except breath.

"Please. If you let me go, I'll get you money, whatever you want. I won't go to the police. I just want to get back to my kids."

Her ears strained to find him in the room. It had to be a him.

The roughness and size of the hand, it had to be. The floor creaked. There. To her left and behind. Her head twisted to the sound. Steps, moving in a circle around her. His feet and breath were all she could hear. He wasn't going to help. Wasn't even going to speak.

Fine. She'd get out another way.

"Help!!!"

A sharp crack slapped across her left cheek, and her head snapped to the right. Tears sprang from the stinging pain, and her chin quivered. He snickered.

"You bastard! You gutless bastard!" Rage surged through her veins. She fought against the restraints. Adrenalin lit her every fibre and muscle, but there was nothing she could do. His legs moved between hers. Hot breath fell on her left ear. She couldn't pull further away. But he couldn't control her mind. She began silently reciting a Mary Elizabeth Frye poem, the one she'd spoken at her mother's funeral.

> Do not stand at my grave and weep
> I am not there. I do not sleep.
> I am a thousand winds that blow.
> I am the diamond glints on snow.
> I am the sunlight on ripened grain.
> I am the gentle autumn rain.

The man's hand closed over her throat, but she blocked him out. If she was going to die, she'd do it without fear.

> When you awaken in the morning's hush
> I am the swift uplifting rush

Of quiet birds in circled flight.
I am the soft stars that shine at night.
Do not stand at my grave and cry;
I am not there. I did not die.

At least it was her being punished. Her in pain. Not her kids. Not Alec. If she died now, it would all be over.

Something slid through her lips. She shook her head side to side. A tube, hard and cold. What was he doing now? A thumb pressed hard on her windpipe to stop her moving and a gush squirted into her mouth. She couldn't bring herself to spit out the flavourless liquid. Her mouth too desperate for moisture. Footsteps retreated. A door banged shut.

None of this makes sense.

"Help me! Someone help me!" She shredded her throat raw shouting and screaming over and over. Then it came again. Drowsiness, her muscles giving way. *No!* She tried to fight it, reaching for the poem she could no longer remember. Her vision blurred. Her head dropped forward, and she passed out.

A splash of cold water startled Sarah awake. Her eyes snapped open and blinked against the bright light. Liquid dripped off her lashes, her nose. The gag was back, digging into the sides of her mouth. But for the first time in this nightmare she could see. A heavyset man wearing faded jeans and a black leather jacket towered over her. He'd pulled a dark wool balaclava over his face; unfamiliar pale irises were his only distinguishing feature.

Her gaze darted away from him to scan the room while she could. The walls were a dirty shade of pink. The one window had been boarded up with wood. No furniture. No easy way out. A blue plastic drop sheet covered a section of the beige laminate floor. It was centred under her chair. She sucked in a breath.

Footsteps shuffled behind her. Someone else was in the room. She twisted to see but couldn't.

Metal rasped against metal. The distinctive ca-chunk of a gun slide shifting. Sarah's gaze shot to the man in front. He crossed his thick arms and nodded.

Cold metal pressed against her temple. Her body tensed. Her eyes screwed shut.

Please let my kids be okay without me.

The barrel dug into her head. Click! She recoiled then looked around. Tears filled her eyes. Nothing had happened.

The racking of the slide sounded again. She trembled, sweat breaking out at her hairline. Pressure again at her temple. Click! Nothing. Her body slumped, the trembling turned to shudders.

A rough voice she didn't recognise grated in her ear. "Aye bitch, now you're getting it. If Daniel wants to beat you, shoot you, or shove his dick up your arse, there ain't nothing you can do to stop it. Do you get that now? You can't beat him. Learn to obey orders, or Riley will sit in that there chair, only next time the chamber will be full."

"No!" She wrenched and tugged against the restraints. Her face contorted with rage. Hot tears poured down her cheeks. The men laughed at her.

A burst of white-hot magma flared through her veins. She screamed at them through her gag. The man behind seized her hair and slammed her head back into the chair. Her vision blurred and spotted with pain.

"Shut yer bake, whore, and listen up. Be back in Belfast by five Sunday eve and stay put, or you'll never see your son again."

Her body convulsed. Gorge rose up her throat. She fought to gain control. To breathe.

Pull yourself together. They're not going to kill you. You just have to get back to Belfast.

The pale eyed man turned away and sauntered to the door. A hand pulled back the neck of her shirt. Another sting shot through her shoulder.

How could she get to Belfast if they kept drugging her? She struggled against the drowning sensation, resisting the lethargy swamping her body and mind. But in the end, the drugs triumphed.

Her last desperate thoughts were of Riley.

Sarah prised opened her eyes. The dirty floor stretched out before her. Excruciating pain jackhammered into her head. She winced, clamping her eyes shut. The man's words hit her memory hard. *"Be back in Belfast by five Sunday eve and stay put, or you'll never see your son again."*

She reared to sitting. Pain tore through her, the room spiralled, and she couldn't stop the sudden onset of violent, dry retching. She lay back down to let the nausea subside and scanned her aching body for damage. She was unbound, no ties, no gag. Her skin stung from the restraints, her face smarted, and her shoulder pulsed with pain at the needle site. But she had survived.

Remembering his words again, she shoved through the fog, reaching for complete consciousness. Time. She needed to know the time. She looked down at her empty wrist then around. Her bag, her wallet and her phone were nowhere to be seen. All that lay on the floor was her passport. She tucked it in her back pocket.

Crawling to the wall on her hands and knees, she dragged herself to standing and paused, allowing her woozy head to settle. Her legs were marshmallow, but they held. She shuffled around using the wall for support until she reached the closed door. She placed her ear against it. No voices or sounds of movement came from the other side. Nothing. She tested the door handle. It turned with ease. Was it a trick? She pushed open the door and braced for attack.

Nothing again. The door led to an old kitchen whose counters were covered in a layer of dust and grime. She zeroed in on the dregs of a soft drink bottle and gulped them down, the warm flat sweetness making her gag. She stumbled forward to the open back door. Her eyes watered from the bright sunlight.

Veiling her face with her hands, she scanned the area through a squint. An unfamiliar suburban lane spread behind the edge of the backyard. Riley needed her to think straight. She closed her eyes. The hum of loud traffic rumbled close by. A main road? She forced her ruined body to move in that direction, concentrating on each stride. Like the end of a marathon. Step by step. Ignoring pain. Ignoring thirst. She had to get to Belfast. To keep Riley safe.

She began to run.

TWENTY

From a side street, Sarah limped to the concrete barrier blocking the motorway. She bent in two. The ground spun. Her hands clasped her thighs. She had to keep going. Had to push through. She unfolded and looked up the road. That intersection ahead. It looked like the one near Max's rental property. She closed her eyes and tried to remember driving there. After stumbling another hundred metres, she checked again. She knew exactly where she was. If she could get to Max, he'd give her money and then she could get a flight back to Belfast. Taking the next left, she dragged her feet onwards, scarcely lifting them from the asphalt.

Five minutes later, she hauled her body up the crumbling sandstone steps to Max's front door. Her tongue a fat slug in her mouth. *Please be home, Dad. Please.* The pounding in her head rose to a crescendo. She leant one hand against the red brick-work while her other banged on the door. Flakes of olive paint fell and floated to the floor.

Footsteps thudded towards her. She held herself up through pure will until the door swung open.

"Sarah!"

Her legs gave way. Max caught her before she hit the ground. He carried her in and laid her on the lounge.

Her croaky voice slashed at her throat. "Riley."

A line of wrinkles bunched between Max's brows. He inhaled as if to talk but turned to walk away instead. She grabbed him. "Is Riley safe?"

"He's fine." Max's gaze rested on her red raw wrists. His lips thinned. "You need water." He eased from her grip and stalked towards the kitchen. "Then you'll explain exactly where you've been for the last two days."

Two days? God, that meant it was Sunday. No! What time? She pushed up on an elbow. Her head reeled. She focused hard on the old-fashioned clock on the mantle. 12:08 pm. She lay back flat with relief. She still had time to get back to Belfast before five o'clock. Her eyelids were so heavy. She'd close them a minute. Just a minute.

Strong fingers dug in her arms and shook.

"No! Get off me!" She scrambled back into the corner of the lounge.

"Sarah, it's Max! You're okay, girl, you're okay." His deep bass voice washed through her. When the rise and fall of her chest slowed, he passed her a glass of water. "Sips only."

She was desperate to guzzle the lot but did as her Dad said, savouring the cool wetness of the water's slide down her throat. Then she remembered. *How much time had she lost?* She reached out for her Dad's wrist to check. 1:47 pm. She had to get to the airport. When she made to stand, her father pressed her back onto the lounge and crossed his arms. "Talk, Sarah. Where have you been? When Alec was shot—"

"Shot?" The bottom dropped out of her stomach.

He scanned her face. "You don't know?"

She shook her head, the clutch of fear strangling all ability to speak.

"He called from the emergency room, warning me to be vigilant, asking me to tell you the same."

"Dad! Is Alec okay?"

He shrugged. "The bullet only grazed his arm."

"Who shot him? Have they been caught?"

"No."

It couldn't be a coincidence. The timing was too calculated. It was a warning. To show her what they could do to the people in her life. Daniel was everywhere. If she had just been honest with Alec this never would have happened. The weight of her Dad's hand rested on her shoulder.

"Hey, this is not on you."

"I'm not so sure."

She slouched back into the sofa and closed her eyes. Events still shifted, so muddled in her brain, but she shared the best she could. About her kidnapping. The drugging. And Daniel's demands. By the end Max had sunk to the lounge next to her.

"I'm going to kill McNaulty. When I'm done, there will be nothing left of him."

"Dad, I need you to concentrate on Riley. As long as I get back to Belfast, I'll be fine. We have to come up with a way to get Riley out of Dublin. It's too dangerous for him to stay."

"I'll get on it. What about you? Does Stone know any of it?"

"Not yet." She pulled her sleeves down over her wrists. "Dad, I need to get to the airport. To buy a ticket. I don't have any money."

"Leave it to me. First you need to eat."

A few minutes later, the smell of toast wafted in. He returned and handed her a slice spread with black. A mass of emotion swelled in her chest; Vegemite toast had been her mum's remedy for all ills. Max must have brought a jar from home.

"Thanks." She placed the plate in her lap and looked at him, making sure she had his gaze. "Love you, Dad."

Max cleared his throat and turned. Then he swivelled back, bent down and held his lips to her hair for a beat. When he moved away, his voice had thickened. "I'll get paracetamol. You look like hell."

As she fastened her seatbelt on the plane, Max's question lurked. *Does Stone know any of it?* She tented her hands over her mouth and sighed. She almost got him killed. No more secrets. No more half-truths. Alec needed to know the whole story. But she had to be on guard. No way she'd lead Daniel to his door. She leant her head back against the seat. She'd get a cab to the hotel to prove she was in Belfast by the deadline, rest 'til dark, and then go to Alec.

Sarah paced her hotel room. Exactly eight steps from one side to the other. She went to the window, parted the curtain a few inches and blew out a frustrated breath. At least the streetlights were finally on. She checked her watch. 9:30 pm. It had to get dark soon. She scanned the street in both directions. The white van from across the road had left but the red Fiat was still parked too far up the street to see if anyone was inside. She grabbed the half empty bottle of sports drink and finished it. She couldn't allow anyone to see her leave, or even worse, to follow.

The knot in her stomach twisted. Max said Alec was okay, that the bullet had just grazed his arm, and the hospital had already released him. But what if her Dad was wrong? Against her every intention Alec had slipped into the carefully guarded circle of people she cared about. With his quiet strength and honesty. His intense focus and tender touch. She didn't know what that meant, in amongst every else going on, but she couldn't bear to think about what could have happened to him, what that bullet could have taken from her.

She threw the empty bottle into the bin and snatched up the black sweatshirt she'd borrowed from Max, hooked it over her head and slipped her arms in the sleeves. Alec had to be okay. She wouldn't entertain any other option.

Moving to the mirror, she slid on a baseball cap and secured every wisp of her hair underneath it. She stood back and took in her image. The sweatshirt fell just above her knees; the low-positioned, dark-blue cap shadowed her face. At first glance she might pass for a man. Turning on the TV, she selected the old movies channel and increased the volume so it could be heard by anyone outside her door. She hid her passport in the safe and turned out all her pockets to make sure she carried no identification of any kind.

What had she forgotten? She counted off the completed preparations on her fingers. She scanned the room, spotting the hotel room phone. But she dismissed the idea. If he wasn't home, she'd just wait.

She peeked outside again. A couple passed under the street-light below then became shadows moving into the dark. It was time. She checked the peephole and re-set her cap. After unlatching the locks as quietly as possible, she edged the door open, listened for signs of any presence, then darted to the stairs. When she reached ground level, she kept her head down, turned from the hotel foyer and strode to the back exit for staff and deliveries. She levered the long metal bar down, nudged the door out a touch and scanned the side street.

Coming towards her were a group of men and women, making the most of the last of the weekend. She waited until they passed the door and fell in behind them, doing her best to look part of their raucous party. She stayed close until they veered into the pub 300 metres up the street. After the last of them entered, she let the wooden door close in front of her, dulling the fiddles of a traditional Irish jig.

She flattened her body against the side of the alcove, listening for approaching footsteps. When she heard none, she checked the road. All clear.

Crossing to the unlit side of the street, she forced her body to maintain an ambling pace until she'd passed the illuminated city hall. She searched behind one last time and broke into a run. Being a Sunday, the office area was deserted. Hustling along the flat stretch of road, she took a wide berth around dark doorways, slowing and checking when a truck obstructing her view.

Pounding along the concrete path, her thoughts turned to Alec. So much had happened since the cemetery. Could he forgive her? For leaving in the first place, and worse, for staying away. He had to know she would've gone straight to him when he was hurt, if she'd been able.

The road widened and Sarah crossed, passing the deserted green of the Gothic-style Queen's University. Taking the next left, she raced up the incline. The road lit up with headlights approaching from behind. The space between Sarah's shoulder blades itched. She dashed up a one-way road and hid behind a parked car. A red Fiat slowed on the road she'd left, paused at the no entry sign, then sped off. That was no coincidence.

She leapt up and sprinted round the next corner, ducking into an alley behind a set of shops. She dived behind one of the dumpsters. Beams of light approached perpendicular to the other end of the lane. She hugged the wall tighter. Tried to regulate and quieten her breathing. The car stopped, engine running, blocking the passageway. In the dark, she couldn't make out its colour. If it was the Fiat, they could send another car to seal off the end she'd entered and trap her. Or just wait for her to funnel out.

She shuddered, then shook away the images of that gun and blue tarp in Dublin.

Maintaining her crouch, she crab-walked until she could reach the handle of the closest door. It should lead into the back of a shop. Locked. The rear door of the hair salon was secure too. When she crawled up to the back of the Chinese restaurant, she almost let out a shaky laugh. A brick propped open the door. She slipped inside the dark hall and toed the brick away.

The lock clicked into place. Pulling her cap lower she stole toward the sounds of sizzling food and chatter.

"No pay, no toilet!"

Sarah swivelled round. A waiter ran at her from the bar, his arms waving in the air, shooing her to the restaurant's glass front. She backed up, lowering her chin to her chest to hide her face. "I'm sorry, I didn't mean—"

"Out, out, or I call police!"

She looked from the man to the street outside and back again. His palms were almost slapping her now. She barged out the door, charged across the road, and didn't stop running until two blocks over when she slid into a thin space between an oak tree and a fence. Her breath came hard. Her senses narrowed, aware of every noise, every shadow. But the red Fiat was nowhere in sight. She gave her pumping pulse a moment to settle and took off on the final 500 metre stretch to Alec's house.

TWENTY-ONE

Gravel crunched under her feet as she ran up Alec's unkempt driveway. With her heart kicking against her ribs, Sarah removed her baseball cap and climbed the stairs of his Georgian-style home. She lifted her knuckles to knock but the white panelled front door swung open. Words dissolved in her mouth.

Alec stood before her, bare-chested, the defined muscles of his stomach disappearing below the waistband of black running shorts. At his side, he held a Glock pistol. Was he still in danger?

Her gaze lifted, drawn to a large patch of white gauze taped to his left tricep. She blinked, looked up to his face. Her heart squeezed. Dark shadows smudged his eyes. His cheeks were hollow. She ached to touch him, to reassure herself he was fine. Her hand twitched up, but the expression on his face froze it in place. "I'm so sorry, Alec."

His mouth thinned, his cool eyes studying the bruise on her cheek. The silence stretched out.

Finally, he stepped aside. The hallway lengthened before her, its plain white walls throwing the wide, dark wooden floorboards and trims to the fore. She hesitated a few steps in, turning when the front door lock clicked.

Alec circled past her and entered the front room, leaving her in the doorway, her bodyweight pushing on her toes but still unable to move. *He was so cold, so closed. Did he really think she didn't care?*

Alec lowered into an oversized chestnut-coloured chair. He discarded the gun on the table to his right. Next to it sat an opened tube of topical ointment, tape and fresh bandages. He flinched as he reached for a dressing. Sarah's feet took her forward.

He let the bandage drop into her outstretched palm. She knelt, and his legs parted but his focus remained fixed over her shoulder. She edged closer, her hips grazing his thighs. She slid the dressing between his ribs and arm. The brush of his chest hair against her inner wrists sent a spray of goosebumps across her skin. She swallowed and carried on, curling her fingers around his arm to hold the start of the bandage in place. Skin touching skin.

Alec's elbow pulled sharp against his torso.

Gently, slowly, she prised through the closed space to wrap the bandage around his arm. When she leant in to secure the end, a stream of whisky-scented breath burnt down her cheek. She tensed against the urge to turn her face to his. Suspicion and anger pulsed from him. The last time they'd been this close,

Alec had bared his soul to her, and she'd run away. She was lucky he'd even opened the door to her today.

Easing back, she met his stare. "I shouldn't have left."

A beat passed.

Alec's hand lifted and the pad of his thumb dragged gently across her lips. Every nerve ending rose to his touch.

She held his gaze but didn't move. She had to show him she could trust, that she could give over control.

The back of his hand trailed down her neck, her side, then slipped under her shirt - his callused fingertips skimming the skin of her stomach.

Her focus dropped to his mouth. When he leant in, she closed her eyes. But his lips grazed her cheek. The kiss too tender, too raw. She wanted to lunge at him; she wanted to run. But she forced herself to be still.

His lips ran across her jaw down to her neck. He paused, lingered. When he sucked at the sensitive skin, fire shot to her groin and a faint breath left her mouth. He brushed his lips across hers, left to right. Almost reverent in their touch. She parted her mouth and his tongue swept in, sharing an earthy, spicy hint of whiskey.

As his hand slid up her ribs and over her bra, her fingers flexed. She vibrated with the need to reach for him.

His thumb circled the tip of her breast, teasing her nipple to a point. He pinched it gently between his forefinger and thumb, and her world shrank to one of pure sensation. His gaze held hers.

She couldn't wait any longer. She arched into him, taking his mouth. He lifted her to her feet and buried his fingers at the back of her hair, tilting her head and sinking deeper into their kiss. He steered her down the hall, teeth grazing her neck, hands raking her skin. She was ablaze and dizzy; holding on tight as he backed her up the stairs. With each step they threw off clothes until he guided them naked into his room. His hands untangled from her hair, his mouth pulled away and she was left standing bare.

He stepped back and sat on his bed. The blue of night streamed through the window illuminating the rise and fall of his chest in shadows. His stare locked with hers. An invitation. Giving her one last chance to back out.

"I'm not running." She pressed him back onto the mattress, blanketing his body and taking his mouth.

Aching for more, she straddled his hips, and lowered. The exquisite intensity of being filled by him took her breath away. With each stroke she held his gaze. She would never run from him again.

She lay stretched out across Alec's right side, her breathing back to normal. His fingers painted abstract pictures on her back. She held her hand over his wounded shoulder. "Is it okay?"

His warm laugh buzzed against her cheek. "It's better than okay."

'You know, I only came here to talk."

"Any time you want to converse like that, I'll make myself available."

She jabbed his side. She wanted to let the ease they'd found be enough. But she'd made a promise. She owed him the truth. "I can't imagine what you must have thought, me disappearing right when you were shot."

"Your text made it pretty clear you were done."

"What text?"

"Cancelling our meeting in Dublin. Saying you couldn't trust me with your family when I'd failed my own."

She sat up. "I never sent that!"

"It came from your phone."

"I spent the weekend drugged and tied to a chair," she presented her wrists. "If I'd had access to a mobile phone, I wouldn't have used it to send that."

"What?" He pulled back and flicked on the light.

"I was waiting in the park for you when they took me."

Alec's hands cupped her wrists, his thumbs stroking gently down the sides. He looked back to her face, taking in the bruising. "I didn't even ask. I—"

"I'm okay."

His gaze roamed her body, searching out each and every injury. His mouth twisted, as if he were suppressing his words. He pulled her to his side, pressing his lips to her hair. "Tell me."

She spent the next fifteen minutes giving him every detail of her abduction, answering every question. By the end Alec had shifted them to sitting. Now he swung to face her. His body rigid with simmering tension.

"You have to trust me, Sarah. We need to get Riley away from Ireland before you testify, without Daniel getting wind of it."

"I agree, but I don't know how."

"We need help from someone McNaulty won't suspect." Quiet settled as they both considered options. "The superintendent vouched for Riley's host dad, Padric. He's ex-Irish defence, and Daniel won't suspect him." He took her hand in his. "Why doesn't Max act the bodyguard and we'll get Padric to smuggle them both out the morning of the court case. I know it's last minute, but then there will be nothing Daniel can do to them or you."

"Padric's a good idea." She stared at the large, strong hand encasing hers, tracking the white scar running knuckle to wrist. "I'm also worried for Evan. The girls are safe with Doug, far away from Sydney, but what if Daniel's men visit Evan's hospital room? He can't protect himself in there."

"I'll call NSW Police in the morning to request they put him under protection. They'll take it seriously when I mention his bashing is linked to organised crime. Okay?"

She nodded.

He traced his fingers across the injection site bruise on her shoulder. "You should have gone straight to hospital."

"What for? They wouldn't have found the drugs, I'm sure of it. And I had to be back in Belfast."

He cupped her cheek. "Daniel's men, they didn't?"

"No."

Alec brushed her mouth with his, switched off the light and pulled her down, tucking her back against his front. She stared at the shadows on the wall, emotions unfurling and swelling in her chest.

"When they held the gun to my head, before they pulled the trigger..." she released a careful breath. "You, this, it means something to me."

For a moment it seemed he hadn't heard her, that he might already be asleep. Then he tucked his face into her neck, and the arm banding her waist tightened.

"When I met you, I would have done anything to get you to

testify against Daniel." He laced his fingers through hers. "Now I wish I'd left you in peace. I won't let anyone hurt you again." He kissed her shoulder. "I promise."

He pulled her in closer, and, still entwined, they drifted off to sleep.

A loud banging roused them. Alec leapt from bed and dragged on jeans. More thumps sounded against the front door. He removed his Glock from the gun safe and nodded to his mobile.

"Take my phone. The code is 6198. Any sign of trouble, ring the station immediately."

Sarah clutched the phone, attuned to every sound. The pad of his feet on the stairs, a car grumbling to life down the street, muffled male voices coming from the front door. Had Daniel's men found them? She glanced about the room, seeing it for the first time in daylight. Nowhere to hide but under the bed.

Alec's laugh rumbled up the stairwell, and her taut muscles relaxed. She climbed from the bed, retrieved her underwear from beside the door and scanned the floor for the rest of her clothes. The previous night came into focus. Alec had dropped each item of her clothing on the floor, like breadcrumbs, in a trail from the lounge to the bedroom. Her face flushed. Whoever was at the door would have no doubts about events at the end of the line.

Alec's voice cut through the air, yelling now. Sarah froze. He didn't sound in trouble. He sounded pissed.

"On whose authority?" She couldn't hear the answer, just Alec again in a voice of barely contained fury. "Stay. That's an order."

Sarah looked down at her near naked form. Oh no. She wasn't meeting whatever this was in underwear. She spied a dark blue sweatshirt on a chair and threw it on. Footsteps thumped up the stairs. What now?

Alec's face was ashen. He wouldn't meet her gaze. Instead he looked over the top she wore. "Keep it. But you better put these on."

She put on the bra, pants and shoes she'd worn to his house yesterday. "Who was it? Is everything okay?"

He sat them both on the edge of the bed and threaded his fingers through hers. The expression of pure hell on his face caused a shudder to roll through her.

"Alec, what's wrong?"

"The police are here."

"Oh God, Riley!"

"No. No." He turned to her, his tight expression sending dread into her gut. "Look, I don't know these two, but it's not like the old days. Coppers want to get to the truth now. Everything is going to be all right, okay? But for now, you need to go with them to the station."

"What? What for? I've shared everything I know about Daniel."

"It's not about him. It's...Sarah, they have a warrant for your arrest."

"What are they accusing me of?"

He held her face with firm palms. "The shooting attempt on me."

Every ounce of air left her lungs. "But I didn't. I couldn't. I wasn't even in Belfast."

"I know," his thumbs caressed her cheeks, "but they insist there's evidence against you. I promise it'll be okay."

Boots thudded up the stairs. Alec raised them both to their feet and held her hand. Two men dressed in plain clothes and police flak jackets entered the room. The shorter and younger of the two held back, his gaze skating about the room, never meeting hers. The older officer swaggered forward, his jacket stretched to its limit across a round belly, his small eyes fixed only on her. "Time to go."

She looked at Alec. Numb. Lost.

"It's best if you go with them, Sarah." He gave her hand a squeeze then let go. "I'll follow right behind."

The larger officer pulled her arms behind her back while he cautioned her. He locked cuffs over her wrists. She flinched when the metal dug into her already tender and bruised skin.

"Sergeant," Alec moved in on the man, "take it fucking easy."

"Just following orders. Sir."

Alec cupped her face, his pupils tracking side-to-side, checking hers. "We'll sort it out. Just hang on."

Her head sagged, and she stared at the ground as she was escorted from the house, unsure she had anything left to hang on with.

TWENTY-TWO

Fluorescent tubes projected a harsh blue light across the police interview room. Voices murmured outside the door. Sarah strained to hear who was saying what, but it was pointless.

She shifted her sitting bones against the hard, plastic chair in which she'd been placed. On the opposite side of the table, closer to the door, were two perfectly good, cushioned chairs. She shook her head. At least they'd removed the handcuffs.

A mirror stretching the length of the room loomed to the left of her peripheral vision. She wedged her hands under her thighs. Who watched from the other side? Anyone? No one?

Her head fell back with a sigh. She'd been sitting, alone, for so long. Waiting. Thinking. Which was obviously the point. She rolled her neck. Maybe she should have asked for a lawyer. But wouldn't that indicate guilt? If only the officers would come in, she could explain. She pictured the large sergeant with the bird-like eyes. He was probably observing from behind the mirror, profiling her every move. She sat taller.

Her fingers drummed on the side of her seat. How could they have any evidence to arrest her? It made no sense. She'd been in Dublin when Alec was shot, bound to a chair in that room. Cold shuddered through her. She pulled her hands inside the sleeves of Alec's sweatshirt, lifted them to her nose and inhaled. A hint of him lingered on the borrowed top.

Keep the faith, Sarah. He promised he'd sort this out.

Whatever this was.

She had to stay calm. It would all work out. Bending forward, she folded her arms on the table, and rested her forehead on them. Alec wouldn't let her down. She just had to hang on a little longer.

The handle twitched. It turned. The door opened an inch and closed again. Come back she wanted to scream.

As soon as she slumped back in her seat, the door swung wide, and the sergeant who'd handcuffed her earlier entered. He placed a chair to her left and squeezed himself between it and the table, essentially trapping her in the corner of the room. She straightened and brushed her hands along her thighs.

The Sergeant opened an orange manila folder, her name typed in capital letters on one corner. His bushy eyebrows drew together. Minutes ticked away. Clamping her lips together, she suppressed the urge to talk.

What was he waiting for?

She checked the hallway, glanced back to the bald spot at the top of the sergeant's head. Ignoring her was tactical, a ploy to tilt her off balance. Her right leg hammered against the floor. Alec said police these days wanted the truth. So really, they were on the same side. Any minute now, they'd realise the mistake they'd made.

The younger officer from her arrest entered. Sarah looked around him expecting Alec, but the hall remained empty. The officer closed the door and pulled a chair up to the opposite side of the table. Sarah smiled and tried to establish eye contact. He looked up briefly through long blond lashes.

"Sorry to keep you waiting, Miss."

"Oi, lad. Recorder."

At the snarly tone in his superior's voice the constable aimed a remote at a camera in the corner of the ceiling. Sarah twisted her fingers together in her lap.

"This is Detective Sergeant Kevin Fairview, badge number 650367, and the time is 11:09 am on Monday August eleven. Also present is...." Fairview gave a chin jerk to the younger man.

"Detective Constable Simon Milton, badge number 651996.

"Mam, recite your name, address and date of birth for the recording."

She swallowed. *They're on the same side. The same side.* "Sarah Grace Calhoun, 7 Gardyne St, Bronte, Australia, first of March 1975."

"Ms Calhoun, we have reason to believe that on Friday August eight, you fired three shots at Detective Inspector Alec Stone in a drive-by at the corner of Ormeau Rd and Essex Grove."

She shook her head. "I tried to tell you in the car, I was in

Dublin on Friday, waiting to meet with Alec. I was attacked too, then kidnapped."

"Kidnapped, you say?" He looked her up and down. "Any evidence to prove it?"

She pushed back her sleeves and held out her wrists. Fairview squinted. "Let the recording note Ms Calhoun has bondage marks on her wrists." His face twisted. "Of course, there is no evidence the markings are not the result of consensual play."

Sarah recoiled. A patchy flush flared across Milton's face. Something wasn't right here. The sergeant was choosing not to listen. And Milton had spent more time studying the table than delving for the truth. She licked her lips, trying to encourage moisture back into her mouth. She'd just have to try harder.

Fairview shifted his chair, so he faced her. "What is the state of your relationship with Inspector Stone?"

Heat sprawled up her face. "I don't see how that is any of your business, Sergeant."

Fairview's expression narrowed. "Detective Sergeant."

She concentrated on slowing the rise and fall of her chest. She had to rein it in. Resist the urge to flare up. She stared back at him in silence.

"Okay, Ms Calhoun, we'll play it your way. Let's say, for argument's sake, you were kidnapped. I'm after wondering who would want to take someone like you?"

"There were two men in balaclavas. I never got a look at their faces, but Daniel McNaulty—"

"Mr McNaulty has an airtight alibi for Friday night. Does he not Milton?"

The younger man pulled at his collar. "I believe so, sir."

A chill crept up Sarah's back. "I don't mean Daniel himself."

"Aye I don't suppose you do." Fairview leant back in his chair, hands clasped behind his head. "And just as well, seeing as it was me who shared a pint and game of darts with Mr McNaulty last Friday night."

What! How could a policeman who drank with Daniel be allowed to interview her? Sarah's gaze darted to Milton. "You can't let him do this. It has to be against procedure."

"Sir, I—"

"Shut it, lad."

Milton stared back at the table. Adrenalin stormed Sarah's body. "Where's Alec?"

"Detective Inspector Stone is busy. Now let's return to the facts at hand, shall we?"

What was going on? Alec wouldn't leave her with a man in Daniel's pocket. But Fairview clearly had an agenda, and it wasn't getting to the truth. He had to be dirty. Now what did she do?

"The only suspect without a believable alibi is you, Ms Calhoun. If you were kidnapped, why did you not file a police report once you escaped? And then there's the question of your fingerprints being the only ones on the unregistered gun used to shoot Inspector Stone."

It wasn't possible; she'd had her gun in Dublin. In her bag, the one taken by Daniel's men. Her heart beat faster.

"We also have a witness ready to testify that you fired from a red Ford Fiesta, licence plate XAZ 5623. A car you rented that Friday and dumped in Co. Tyrone afterwards. So, Mam, you'll have to excuse me if I don't believe your farfetched gobshite about being kidnapped."

Her ribs locked.

Fairview folded his arms. "Well?"

She looked back to the door. Alec would come. She had to trust him. Any minute he would come through the door and get her out of here. She had to buy herself time until then. "The witness can't have got a good look at a driver speeding by. They made a mistake."

"That's unlikely, so it is. Young Liam Breen was distraught when he came to the station to report your crime. He couldn't believe an ex-youth worker had done such a thing."

"Liam? Liam Breen said it was me?" Sarah's chin dropped.

Daniel must have planned the whole thing the minute she left for Dublin. She bit her bottom lip between her teeth. Court was only two days away. This was Daniel's way of tainting any testimony she gave. And she'd walked right into it. All along he'd planned to murder Alec and have her jailed for it. Is that why Alec wasn't here? Had they convinced him of her guilt?

A knock sounded.

Thank God. Her gaze shot to the door and met a whisky-coloured stare. She flinched back, confused.

Michael filled the doorway. "Don't say another word."

TWENTY-THREE

"Detective Sergeant Fairview, Ms Calhoun is my client. I insist you end this interview immediately."

Fairview's mouth pursed as he pushed himself up. "Interview terminated at 11:18 am for Michael McNaulty to consult with his client."

Both officers exited the room, clicking the door shut behind them. Sarah's glare never left Michael.

"You've sure got yourself into a spot of bother here, *mo chroi*."

"Don't call me that, Michael, don't you dare."

"As you wish." He undid the buttons of his suit jacket and eased into the chair opposite her. "I've been through the evidence. They have a solid case against you. Fingerprints, a witness, your car, no alibi."

"Give it a rest. I know you and Daniel are behind this. I did what was asked of me." She crossed her arms tight. "What are you up to now?"

"What are you up to, Sarah? Your children are under threat, and you're out spreading your legs for some peeler?"

"Who I sleep with is none of your business."

"That's where you're wrong. Daniel sent me here to tell you to break it off with Stone."

"So, you're his little messenger boy?"

Michael's palm slapped against the table. "No more shite. You've to listen well if you want to survive this. Family should be all that matters. Stay away from Stone."

"How? I'm his main witness."

When he relaxed back into his seat, unease fanned across her shoulder blades. "Aye, have you ever put thought to that fact? How Daniel discovered you were the witness against him? Or how he found where you were living?"

"I don't know. He tracked my computer somehow."

"He didn't have to, not when Stone taunted him with my ex-fiancée's testimony."

Her hand moved to the base of her throat. "I don't believe you. Alec wouldn't do that."

Michael leant in. "When did you decide to testify? When Stone asked, or when Daniel sent you a convincing invitation?"

"Alec would never help Daniel, not in any way."

"Stone is obsessed with taking Daniel down. It's all that drives him. He knew the only way you'd testify was to protect your family. He as good as led Daniel to your door. You don't believe me, ask the man himself."

She stared at a gouge in the table leg. Had Alec betrayed her from the start? Used her to take revenge on the McNaultys?

When I first met you, I would have done anything to get you to testify against Daniel.

Acid curdled her stomach. It made sense. How suddenly after all these years Daniel had found her? Had Alec ever cared for her, even a little?

"There's no need for further contact with Stone. You've given him your statement. You're the Prosecutor's witness now." He tapped the table in front of her and waited until she looked up before continuing. "If you agree to get shot of Stone, I can get you out of here."

She searched Michael's expression. He wasn't lying. Her mouth clenched. She was done being manipulated. Done. She'd break things off with Alec, and she'd testify. But when she did, Daniel McNaulty would go to jail, Michael would get charged as an accomplice, and Alec could go to hell.

"You can tell Daniel I'm done with Detective Stone."

"It's the right decision, so it is."

"Don't you even pretend to know what is right, Michael. Just go."

He stood. His mouth opened then he exhaled, did up his jacket and left without speaking another word.

Sarah leant back in her seat. Was Alec really capable of such betrayal? She thought back to when they first met. The ruthlessness with which he pursued her testimony. The threats, the photos. Yes, he had been capable of that and more. Alec's need for revenge had driven his every move. But what about now? After last night?

She rocked forward, elbows to knees, hands cradling her cheeks. He hadn't been to see her yet. But even if he didn't want her anymore, he'd want her testimony. A testimony she could hardly give from inside a jail cell. She pushed to her feet and paced the small room. They needed to talk, but she was in no position to make that happen. Alec had promised to coordinate Riley's escape with Padric and Max. Could she even trust him to do that?

For a moment, when Michael had leant in, she'd been tempted to tell him everything. But Michael's loyalty had always lain with Daniel. She couldn't risk it. She had to put her trust in Alec to protect Riley. But first she had to break things off with him. Sarah sank into the chair. How on earth could she make that work?

Finally, after another thirty minutes Alec stalked into the interrogation room.

Sarah met his glare. "So much for your new force."

"Your lawyer got all charges against you dropped. They're processing the paperwork then you'll be free to go."

She blinked at him. Dark circles stained his eyes, his voice hummed with distrust. "Alec, I didn't do anything."

His anger hovered like another person in the room, filling the corners, ready to strike. "Why is Michael helping you?"

She tipped her head slightly to the side. He doubted her motives? Heat seared up her chest and neck.

"What? Didn't he share?" Her hands spread flat on the table, her voice deepened. "Or is it just Daniel you trade witness information with?"

Shock fired in his eyes. Shock, but not denial. Sarah surged to her feet. "How could you? How could you risk my life, the lives of my children? Sophie's not much older than Olivia when she—"

"It was for Olivia." His eyes locked with hers. "Daniel had to be stopped."

She waited for him to say more, to make her understand.

"Will you still testify?"

"God is that all I am to you? A testimony?" She whirled away from him, the hollow inside her sucking away all air. Nothing. She meant nothing to him. Was just a means to an end. She swallowed the wedge of burning pain in her throat, keeping her back to him.

"I'll testify, but the terms have changed. One, the only time you will ever contact me is over case-related business. No more hotel visits or intrusions on my runs. Business only. Two, you will swear on Olivia's memory to get Riley out of Ireland beforehand. I mean it, Alec. He is safe, or I will not take the stand."

"Of course I won't leave him exposed. What kind of man do you think I am?"

She turned and fixed him with a stare. "I wouldn't know."

"You don't trust me? I'm not the one who disappeared, whose fingerprints were found on the gun."

She rose to her full height, her back taut in an effort to prevent tears. "I thought we could be something, Alec. But if you believe me capable of climbing into your bed after trying to kill you, I couldn't have been more wrong."

His fingers dragged through his hair, and his shoulders dropped. "You're right." He stepped closer. "I'm sorry, I—"

"Enough, we're done. I'd rather wait alone to be discharged. Let me know when Riley is safe." She turned away, clenching her hands together.

His gaze burnt into her back. Her body trembled, but she forced herself to remain where she was.

His footsteps moved to the exit. "I am sorry, Sarah. For ever involving you in this. I will keep you and your family safe, I swear on all Olivia meant to me." The door shut.

She pushed a fist against the searing pain threatening to tear her chest in half. Two days until court. Then she could leave this place behind forever.

TWENTY-FOUR

The police custody officer took Sarah's signed release form from the gap under the grey grated window. He exchanged it for a yellow envelope - the items that had been confiscated before they took her to the interrogation room. She slid her mother's wedding ring back on, pocketed the £200 from her dad, and headed for the station's exit. Two policemen escorted a shackled man towards her, his hair matted with blood. When he lifted his face, Sarah pulled in a breath.

"Liam, what did they do to you?" His right eye was almost swollen shut.

"I'm sorry, Miss Sarah. He made me say it was you." His good eye was stretched open wide, and his head shook back and forth. "But I didn't shoot that peeler. I promise. I didn't do it."

Sarah stepped into the policemen's path. They halted metres away, the short wiry one reaching for his belt.

"Officer, this man needs medical care."

The men, both constables in their mid-twenties, visibly relaxed.

"He was in this state when we found him."

Her gaze went straight to the short, wiry officer's clean knuckles. Then the taller man's. No damage, maybe they were telling the truth?

"And I've a doctor coming to check on him." The taller man pushed Liam to walk again. When he got within her reach, Liam rushed forward against the restraints.

"You've got to help me," he whispered, nostrils flaring. "I'll get killed in prison."

"Mam, I'll have to ask you to step aside."

She stared at the policeman. He tilted his head to the side in question. Her gaze flicked briefly to Liam's pleading face, her shoulders sank, and she shifted out of the way.

He twisted to get back to her, but the constables yanked him back on path. "Maybe some time alone in a holding cell—"

"No!"

"Liam, don't fight, please, you'll get hurt more."

The officers bent Liam's upper body back and down as he shouted and continued to try to wrench free

"Liam, stop!" Sarah stepped towards him. "I'll...I'll see what I can do."

He glanced her way. Once she nodded, his body slackened, and he allowed himself to be frogmarched through to the booking room.

Sarah stared at the closed doors. Why had she said that? She couldn't help herself, let alone Liam. She jammed her hands in her pockets, turned and walked out of the station into an overcast afternoon. Smoke from a coal fire laced the air, and traffic noise assaulted her ears. The world kept turning as if the events of the last three days had never occurred. She might be free now, but she was more caged than ever. Eyes were on her - Daniel's, Michael's, Alec's. She'd have to walk a very careful path until court, weigh up every move. She turned left out of the gate and set off at pace in the direction of her hotel. Four blocks later she found a corner store, bought a disposable mobile, sank to the shop's dusty steps and dialled.

The light trill of Sophie's laughter still rang in Sarah's ears. The physical grip on her chest had eased to an ache.

Warm air gushed across her back, escaping the automatic doors of the store. A group of teenage boys spilled out. With close shaven heads, baggy sportswear and narrowed eyes they could have been from either side. But their Ranger's blue shirts revealed their loyalties. The boys clustered on the footpath, looking her up and down, one nudging another. She scoped her surrounds. Faded red, white and blue paint coloured the gutters the whole way up the street of terraced red brick houses. British flags hung from poles. At the end of the block, an Ulster Defence Association mural had been painted depicting the Queen flanked by masked and armed men. The hairs on the back of Sarah's neck lifted. In her urgency to buy a phone, she'd strayed into Sandy Row, the heartland of the Protestant para-militaries.

Pushing quickly off the steps she threw out a broad-accented "G'day" in the boys' direction and crossed the road, resisting every screaming instinct to run. It might have been seventeen years since she was engaged to the brother of the head of the Real IRA, but people in Northern Ireland had long memories. When she stole a glance over her shoulder, a sigh wheezed from her mouth. The boys had forgotten her already, their attention directed to two teenage girls exiting a house further up the street.

Turning the corner, she spotted Belfast City Hospital in the distance, its modern Lego-like structure and yellow trims a beacon of neutrality against the grey of its surrounds. She picked up pace until her feet crossed the hospital boundary then she sat on a bench, pulled out her phone and dialled.

"Hello?" her son's deep voice filled the line.

"Riley, it's Mum. Do you have a minute?"

"Where were you all weekend?"

"Sorry I worried you."

"Max was worried," Riley's tone cooled. "I'm still annoyed."

"I'm sorry, honey. That's why I'm ringing. To say sorry for what I did to Siobhan." She twirled her finger around a loose piece of cotton on the seam of her top. Alec's top. She discarded the thread. The sooner she could get changed the better.

"Do you mean it this time?"

"One day I should explain what coming back to Northern Ireland is like for me. I told you I did aid work here but there was more." Silence filled the line. What was she doing? Excuses wouldn't smooth things over. She cleared her throat. "Are things okay between you and Siobhan?"

"She's gone home for two weeks. Her mother needed help."

Odd. Why would Daniel let Siobhan leave now, right when things were coming to a head?

Sarah massaged the back of her neck.

Not important now. For Wednesday's plan to work she needed Riley a hundred percent on side.

"Well perhaps we could get together when she returns, if she'll give me a second chance."

"A third chance."

"You're right. I promise I'll apologise and won't interfere again."

"And mean it?"

"Yes. She's important to you."

"She is." He cleared his throat. "I've got a day off on Saturday. Maybe I could come and visit you in Belfast? You could show me around."

"I'd like that."

She swallowed. He would be back in Australia by Saturday. Would her son forgive all the lies? A horn sounded in the background.

"I've gotta get back to training. I am glad you're okay, Mum. I do love you."

Her throat thickened. "Love you too sweetheart. Always."

She hung up and slouched back against the bench. Now it was up to Max and Padric. On Wednesday morning, they'd surprise Riley with a "camp-approved boys trip" to London but put him on a flight to Sydney instead. All she could do was wait.

Sarah stepped out of the shower cubicle into a steamy room and checked her phone. Still no message. She checked the time. 7:03 am. Two hours and twenty-seven minutes until her court appearance.

Sliding a towel from the rail she wrapped it tight around her shoulders. Were they on the ferry yet? Had Riley realised he'd been tricked?

Uncertainty slithered along the pit of her stomach. Padric had insisted if they told Riley the truth, he would refuse to leave her alone. She pulled the towel from her shoulders and dried off. Padric was right. Safety was more important than honesty at this point. She looked again at the phone.

Come on, Max.

Rolling on deodorant, she ran through the prosecutor's notes in her head. Stay calm. Don't slouch. Speak clearly. Her throat tightened. *Just get ready.*

She slipped on underwear and moved to the mirror, wiping off the mist with a tissue. Twirling her hair up into a bun, she pinned back every flyaway she could find. She smoothed on foundation, concentrating longest on the dark circles rimming her eyes. When she began applying mascara, her mind returned to her testimony. The wand trembled. How could she tell everyone what she'd done? She'd barely managed to relive it for Alec.

She poked the wand back in the mascara tube, pumping it a few times. He'd be there too, his unyielding stare following her every move.

She shook out her hands, then brought up the wand again and coated her lashes. In court she would concentrate on Gerry's parents. Their faces. They deserved to know what happened to their son. How brave Gerry had been.

A vibrating sound drew her attention. She seized her phone. *Ferry departed. All good. M.*

She sank onto the edge of the bath, closed her eyes, and allowed herself a moment to relish the release of tension. Her boy was free. Her father too. She rose to her feet and finished getting ready. Doing up the final button of her suit jacket, she moved to the full-length mirror. She took in the neat, structured, together woman in the reflection. Today was for Gerry, and for all those Daniel had silenced. On the stand she would be their voice.

Three raps sounded on her room door. Sarah checked the keyhole. Constable Taylor, her police escort to court, held up his identification. She collected her handbag and followed him to the tinted-window sedan waiting downstairs. He swung open the door, and her step stuttered. Alec, dressed in a deep-grey suit and teal tie, sat on the other side of the back seat.

Sarah tucked a non-existent hair behind her ear, forced her body to fold in two and climbed in. "Pulling out all the stops I see, Detective."

"Can't have our star witness getting lost on her way to court."

She shifted away, leaning her elbow on the door's armrest. *Star witness. It was all she'd ever been.* She took a deep breath and let it out. A white patch of condensation spread across the glass. Wiping it clear, her gaze went to Alec's reflection. His eyes were closed, the muscles of his neck ropy. Her jaw loosened. Today was for him and Olivia too. They'd been Daniel's victims as much as anyone else.

She turned to face him. "You've worked so hard for today, I hope it helps."

Guilt flashed across his features then his expression went

blank. "I assume you heard from Max? Padric confirmed every-thing went to plan."

She glanced back out the window. Television vans lined the road. They were close to court now. She ran her palms down her skirt.

Alec touched his hand to her thigh. "Thank you for going through with this." For a moment neither of them moved.

"I need to focus, Alec." She pulled gently away.

"Just tell the truth. That's all you have to do. Then you can say goodbye to Belfast for good."

She faced the window again until the car pulled into the courthouse parking lot. Her breathing shallowed.

This was it.

TWENTY-FIVE

"Do you swear by God almighty that the evidence you give to this court will be the truth, the whole truth and nothing but the truth?"

The bailiff's gruff voice circled in Sarah's head as she stared at his gnawed thumbnails curling over the bible.

"Ms Calhoun, you will need to answer for us to proceed."

Her attention lifted to the judge, sitting slightly higher and off to her right. His old-fashioned garb of scarlet gown and white horsehair wig was a huge contrast to the modern decor of the room – a Crown Court specially designed to accommodate terrorism-related trials.

"Yes, sir. Of course. Sorry." Sarah splayed her palm over the leather-bound book. "I will."

She allowed herself to look from the oak wood panelling of the witness stand past the microphone, and out into the room. Below, to her left, were the twelve jurors, seven women and five men, ranging from a blank-faced monkish looking man in his mid-twenties through to an elderly lady in a salmon-coloured cardigan whose unblinking stare seemed to be assessing every person in the room.

In front of her numerous officials sat on purple chairs at long oak benches. Each table was strewn with open laptops. Sarah's focus strayed to the gallery in the back third of the court, where a bulletproof glass wall separated observers from the main room. She paused there, on a slew of journalists in the front row, heads down, scratching at their notes.

Thank God for her suit coat. At least they couldn't report on the damp patch of sweat pooling under her arms.

Finally, she forced her gaze just forward of the gallery, to the dock where Daniel sat, boxed off from the rest of the court behind three metres of glass. He was in a black suit, relaxed and at ease, joking with the uniformed guard who had brought him in.

He turned, as if he felt her gaze, and his glare slid across her skin. Her breathing accelerated. He'd try to strike back at her from jail. Could she trust the procedures put in place by the Prosecutor and Police Commissioner to protect her?

She blinked slowly, severing the connection, and scanned to the left, just beyond the jurors, until she found Gerry's Dad, Giles McCann. He sat next to Alec, sequestered in a protected section for police and the victim's family. His deep-set silver eyes met hers, the same shape and colour as Gerry's. He tipped his head at her, in a gesture of thanks. With a brief smile, she nodded back then looked at her lap. She had to trust the system. She wouldn't let the McCann family down again.

After much chatting with his counterparts, the prosecutor, a thirty-something barrister with frameless glasses and a crooked nose, stood, straightened his black robes and turned her way.

"Ms Calhoun, as an Australian citizen, why were you in Northern Ireland during the summer of 1997?"

"When I completed my social work degree in 1995, I applied to work for a refugee aid program in Sierra Leone, but they rejected my application, saying they required experience in a western zone first. So I applied for and got a position here in Belfast with the Harmony Reconciliation Project."

"And what did they do?"

"They were a European Union cross-cultural aid program aimed at bringing together Catholic and Protestant teens, in particular those living in areas under the control of the paramilitaries."

"What exactly did your job there entail?"

"Objection." One of Daniel's defence barristers stood - a red-lipped woman with long blond hair flowing from beneath her powdered wig. Sarah had actively avoided looking at the defence table before but now she scanned the rest of the team. Michael wasn't amongst them. She searched every face in the court. Why wasn't Michael here?

"While Ms Calhoun's work was commendable, I'm sure," the defence barrister turned her condescending smile from Sarah to the jury, "I do not see how it is relevant to this case."

"Your Honour," the prosecutor approached the bench to argue but was silenced by a wave of the judge's hand.

"Objection overruled. Ms Calhoun," he nodded in her direction, "please continue."

She'd been warned that the defence would object regularly, to break her train of thought and make her appear confused and unreliable. Sarah folded her hands in her lap and focused directly on the jurors.

"I devised programs that highlighted the children's similarities, coached sports and helped them write plays. The objective was to open their minds to life beyond what they had been born into. For the older ones, I started an apprenticeship program, providing them with the opportunity to pursue a career rather than joining the ranks of the IRA or UVF and the like."

"And this is where you met Gerry McCann?"

"Yes, he was one of nine apprenticeship students, although his was more of a mentorship. He wanted to study law."

"Thank you, Ms Calhoun. That brings us to the night in question. Where were you on Friday July eighteenth, 1997?"

"I was at Strangford, helping to run a weekend camp. But I'd left a folder at home, so I borrowed a friend's car and drove back to fetch it."

"To thirteen Jerusalem Street, Botanic?"

"Yes, sir."

"At what time?"

"Objection, your Honour." The defence barrister stood again. When she glanced over her shoulder at Daniel, her robes parted to reveal an expensive, dusty-pink suit fitted firmly to a slender body. A look passed between the two that spoke of an intimacy beyond the courtroom. "This event occurred over seventeen years ago. Can we really be expected to believe Ms Calhoun can accurately remember the time?"

The judge's mouth thinned, and his forehead wrinkled. "Ms Murphy, I do hope you don't intend to waste this court's time with further grandstanding. Objection overruled. Ms Calhoun, please answer the question."

"It was around 9:30 pm. I know because I left straight after the evening workshop."

The prosecutor nodded. "And who was at your home when you arrived?"

"No one, the house was empty."

"What occurred next?"

"I ran upstairs to get the folder. I wanted to get back to camp as fast as I could to help with bedtime. While I was upstairs, I heard the front door bang open, then a howling scream. I was about to run downstairs when Daniel and Michael began yelling."

She dug her thumbnail into her palm, using the pinch of pain to stay in the present.

"And then?"

"Daniel sounded volatile. I thought it best not to let him know I was there. But then I heard moaning. I was terrified Daniel and Michael had come to blows, so I crept to the edge of the stairs and looked down." A trickle of sweat slid between her shoulder blades.

No turning back now.

She made herself look at Daniel. Pure hatred spewed her way. But she wasn't going to cower, not this time. A smirk spread across his face. Sarah's skin electrified with thousands of prickles. She glanced to Alec.

"You okay?" he mouthed.

She nodded and poured herself a glass of water from the jug to her left. The glass shook while she sipped. After placing the glass back on its coaster, her hands returned to her lap. She brushed down her skirt. Riley was safe. Daniel held no power over her anymore. She looked up to the prosecutor, and the man nodded, encouraging her to go on. In her periphery she registered a flurry of action in the gallery of the court. People standing, changing seats. A heavyset man moved along the front row. His head was tipped forward, but he had orange hair. A chill ran down Sarah's spine. She willed the man to show his face.

"Ms Calhoun, what happened next, after the brothers started yelling?"

The man looked up; Padric stared straight at her. The lurch in her stomach forced a surge of sick up her throat. He was supposed to be with Riley, getting him out of Ireland. Her eyes snapped to Alec, but Padric sat behind his line of vision. He still hadn't seen.

How could she have been so stupid? She hadn't even thought to question Riley's host dad's loyalties. Not when he had the superintendent's endorsement.

Was there no one she could trust?

Daniel looked over his shoulder, and Padric gave a nod.

Sarah's chest heaved. This couldn't be happening. Couldn't anyone else see what was going on? Her gaze shot to Daniel. He crossed his arms, and the corners of his mouth lifted. Blood roared through Sarah's ears, blocking all other sound. Heat stormed her body. She searched for Alec, but he was already running from the court.

"Ms Calhoun, what did you see when you looked down the stairs?"

Where were Riley and Max? What had Padric done to them?

Her gaze glued on the exits. There was no one to turn to. Nowhere to run. Spots danced before her eyes.

"Ms Calhoun, are you okay?"

What had she done? Her vision tunnelled. She had to find Riley. Had to get to her son. She rose from her chair. All sound retreated, the spots blurred into black, and she collapsed to the floor.

TWENTY-SIX

A woody scent burrowed into Sarah's subconscious. A hand caressed her hair. Then she remembered and reared up, bashing her skull against something solid.

"Shite," Alec rubbed his forehead, "you've a hard head."

Book-lined walls spun and settled. A framed law degree came into focus. It hung behind an oak desk that displayed a carved wooden bust wearing a wig. The judge's chambers. She gripped Alec's forearm. "Tell me you found Riley and Max. Tell me they are safe." Her voice thinned on the last word.

Alec paused, his eyes softened. "We're trying, but we've yet to make contact."

"Padric?"

"He slipped out of the courtroom when you collapsed. But the building was locked down almost immediately. He'd no time to get out. Officers are searching floor by floor."

"Where's my bag, my phone? Riley might have tried to call me." He indicated her bag next to the lounge. She found her phone. No message. Nothing. She rang Riley's number. Message bank. Then Max. Message again. She leant her elbows on her knees, pressed the phone against her forehead. "You said Padric had been vetted."

"No one had anything on him. He blindsided us all."

The large spirals on the Persian rug beneath her feet blurred. "What if we can't find them? What if Daniel has my father and my boy?"

Her shoulders caved in around the crushing pang at the centre of her ribs. There had to be something she could do. "What about the girls? Have you contacted them?" She leapt to her feet. "What if Daniel's gone after them too?" She paced the room and started dialling.

Alec stood and prised her phone from her hand. "Come and sit down."

She took in his stricken face. "What aren't you telling me?"

"Evan's not answering his phone, neither are his parents. But it's the middle of the night in Australia. I've rung the local police. They are driving out to the property as we speak."

She sank to the sofa. "I should have done everything Daniel said."

"Someone had to stop him."

A ringing phone cut in. Alec pulled a mobile out of his jacket pocket. "Stone. Aye." His gaze cut to Sarah. "You sure?" A tendon on his neck bulged, twitching with his pulse.

Sarah leant forward. "What? What's happening?"

He put up a finger and twisted away, giving one-word answers into the phone. Sarah's palms drew together at her mouth. She didn't move, didn't breathe. With each passing second Alec's back seemed to harden. But when he ended the call and turned, his face was blank.

"Have they found them?"

He removed his suit jacket from the chair and handed back her mobile, "I have to go and deal with something. Stay here until I get back."

"Stay here? Are you insane? What was that call about?"

"Police business." He opened the door. "I'll ring if there's any news."

Sarah stared at the door Alec had left through. He'd been gone for the longest five minutes of her life. She didn't know how much longer she could last.

She stood and paced again. What police business would draw him away, in the middle of everything going on? By the end of that call he'd shut down every hint of emotion, every tell on his face. She strode to the door and her hand paused on the handle. Where would she go? There was nothing she could do to help right now, other than sit here and wait. She dialled Riley's number again.

"*Riley here. Leave a message and I'll catch you later.*"

"Riley ring me as soon as you get this. Please. As soon as you can."

She checked the time. It might be the middle of the night in Australia, but she was done waiting to hear from the New South Wales police. She rang the girl's disposable.

"Hello?" Doug's voice croaked.

"Thank God. It's Sarah. Sorry to wake you, but I need to know if the girls are okay?"

"They're fast asleep."

"Could you please check on them to make sure?"

Sheets rustled. Sarah's hand rubbed at her sternum until Doug cleared his throat. "What's going on?"

"Nothing, I..." Enough lies. To keep her girls safe, he had to understand what they were up against. She released a breath. "This trip, Doug. It's not work. I've been testifying in a criminal case. But it's fallen apart."

"Well your girls are fine. I'm looking at them right now, sleeping peacefully. Do you want me to wake them?"

"No, no, just give them a hug and a kiss from me in the morning."

"You want to tell me what's going on love?"

"Honestly? I don't know. The man I'm testifying against is dangerous. Max and Riley - we can't contact them, but the police are searching. It's why Evan's under police protection in hospital."

"Are you okay?"

"I will be when I know the girls are hidden. Is there someplace you can go with them that would leave no trail, somewhere even I don't know? Please Doug, you and Wendy take them in the morning and tell no one, not even Evan. Buy a new phone. Send the number to this one. I won't use it unless I have to. I know it sounds crazy but please trust me."

"How will I know it's safe again?"

"I'll use a code word." It had to be something that couldn't be used accidentally. "How about Skydancer? That's Ally's favourite horse, right?"

"Someone's pulled up outside. Give me a sec." Sarah

nudged an upturned corner of the Persian rug back into place. Doug came back on the line. "It's a police car."

"The police here asked them to check on you."

"I don't understand. Is Riley okay? This doesn't seem real."

"Please Doug, you have to believe me. The girls' lives are in your hands."

"What's happening with Riley?"

"I'm going to find him. Trust no one, okay? If the code word isn't used, it's a trap. I'm so sorry."

"Let us know as soon as you have any news. And you get yourself back here safe. These girls need their mum."

Her nose stung. "Promise you'll take care of my babies?"

"With my life, Sarah, with my life. The sergeant is at the door. I better go." The line cut out. Sarah swallowed the knife in her throat. Doug was tough as nails. No one would get past him to her girls.

She moved to the window of the judge's chamber and scanned the courtyard below for any sign of Alec, or Padric, or anyone she knew. Why hadn't Alec returned yet? What was happening out there?

A blaring fire alarm pierced the silence. With her pulse spiking she crossed to the door and peeked out. Herds of people stampeded past, snippets of their agitated conversations spilling into the room. Then a leathery-faced man in police uniform blocked her view.

"Bomb scare, Ms Calhoun. We need to get you out."

"But I have to wait here for Detective Stone. He told me to stay no matter what."

"I hardly think he meant for you to sit through a potential explosion, Mam. Come with me. There's a car waiting."

She stilled, her mouth suddenly dry. "Please show me your credentials."

The officer flashed her his badge. All looked in order. "Ms Calhoun, we need to go."

Picking up her handbag, she reached in for her phone, to let Alec know she was leaving, but the officer gripped her elbow and hustled her across the crowd surging to the main exit. No one noticed where she was being taken. And badges could be faked. She slowed, tried to withdraw her arm, but the man held tight. Alec had told her to stay. She was getting further and further from where he'd look for her.

"Officer I think—"

The uniformed man pushed her out the staff entrance and she stumbled into a secure, armour-plated car park drizzling with rain. Wailing sirens approached the courthouse from all sides. A dark-coloured sedan pulled up. Sarah checked the surrounds. *Where was Alec? Why wasn't he here with her?*

"Here's your car, Mam. Constable Judson will escort you to your hotel room."

She bent down to look through the opened door of the unmarked car. A bright-eyed policewoman, looking barely old enough to drive, sat behind the steering wheel, her hand lifted in a wave. Thunder rumbled above.

"May I please see some ID?"

The officer flashed her warrant card. The male officer put his hand on Sarah's head and folded her into front passenger seat of the car.

When they drove from the courthouse Sarah checked the side mirror. No one seemed to be following. She rubbed at her arms to warm up.

The constable turned up the car's heating. "Damn bomb scare. Everyone is so over these eejits who can't seem to move on. They keep trying to turn back the clock. But I tell you, we've all had enough, so we have."

Damn bomb scare all right. Padric would have escaped in the crowds pouring out of the courthouse.

"I have to say I think the world of what you're doing, Ms Calhoun, standing up to the McNaulty's and all. Northern Ireland needs more like you."

Sarah smoothed her hand across the wet droplets in her hair. The swishing of the car's wipers grew in volume as the rain pelted harder at the windscreen.

"Thank you... sorry, I missed your name."

"Judson, but please, call me Ainslie."

A sheet of lightening lit up the dark sky. The car pulled up at a familiar intersection and then turned right. Sarah sat tall and her fingers moved to the door handle.

"Ainslie, my hotel is in the other direction."

"Aye, so it is, but I'm to take you to Stranmillis."

A crack of thunder jarred.

Alec's house. *Thank God.*

TWENTY-SEVEN

onversation ceased with the roaring rain. Ainslie bent
forward, squinting in an effort to see the road. Sarah
drew out her phone to try Riley again. The screen was blank.
She jabbed at the buttons. It must have gone flat. She rifled
through her handbag again and drew out the phone she'd
brought from Australia. The one she suspected Daniel might
have tracked. She powered it up. She'd text Riley and Alec, so
they'd know how to reach her. A voicemail box flashed on the
screen. From 9:55 am.

Call "101" you have one new voice message.

She checked the call log. Riley had tried to call her three
times. Panic surged. Why hadn't she checked this phone before?
Her fingers flew across the buttons. Riley's whispered message
crackled in and out.

"Mum...crazy...Max...scared...please..."

She scrambled to phone her son back. Voicemail.

Why? Why wasn't he answering?

241

Holding the phone tight to her ear, she played the message again, willing the belting rain to shut up so she could hear. Riley's voice tremored with fear. Sarah sucked in shallow breaths. Alec. Maybe he could trace Riley through his phone? She dialled him but his phone clicked straight to voicemail.

Damn it, Alec, I need you.

She hugged herself tight, her phone digging into her fingers. She had failed her son. When he needed her most she hadn't been there.

"Ms Calhoun, we're here." Sarah stared at Alec's house.

"Mam, are you okay? You're pale as death."

"Is Alec even here?"

"He's caught up at the station. Do you want me to call him?" Sarah nodded, her hands clenching tight in her lap. After a minute Ainslie hung up. "No answer."

An involuntary shudder jerked Sarah's body.

"I'll try again after we get you indoors." Ainslie dashed around and opened Sarah's door. "Sorry, but I've no umbrella." Sarah ducked her head and ran.

As she climbed the last stair, Alec opened the front door.

"You're soaked." He called around her. "It's okay, Judson, I've got this."

When his attention returned, something in his face, new grooves carved around his eyes and mouth, caused her to still. Why hadn't he answered his phone?

"Come in."

She remained rooted to the tan-coloured welcome mat. A rivulet of water trickled down her back. She shivered, her teeth chattered. She couldn't stop it, couldn't stop any of it.

Alec bent down and removed her waterlogged heels. With

an arm curled about her torso he led her to the lounge room. The fireplace crackled, but the heat didn't touch her. He pulled her body to his, holding tight until the trembling subsided. Leaning back, he looked into her eyes.

"I think we better sit." He took her hand, but she couldn't move.

"Tell me."

Alec held her shoulders. "It's Max. I'm so sorry. They found his body near Belfast Lough."

Her body went rigid, every muscle braced. She had to ask, but she couldn't bear to. What if the next answer was the one she couldn't survive?

"Riley?"

"There was no sign of him."

Her legs crumpled. Alec caught her, and they both sank to the ground. She struggled to breathe through the crippling pain beneath her breast.

"Max went down fighting. There were defensive bruises all over him."

A gaping hollow opened through her middle. Max. Her indestructible Dad.

"I shouldn't have drawn him into this. I'm like quicksand, Alec. You should stay away, or you'll be dragged under too."

"Don't you dare take the blame."

"Riley left me a message. Hours ago. He was terrified."

"We've got police combing the whole area. We'll find him."

She clung to his arm.

"Why hasn't Daniel contacted me? I'll do anything. I don't care what. I just want Riley back."

"Maybe Daniel doesn't have him. Max might have helped Riley escape."

"I'm not strong enough. If Riley's gone...I can't...I can't—"

"You look at me, Sarah. I've never met a stronger person in my life. Sophie and Ally are safe. I'll get Riley back to you, I swear."

Sarah locked her arms around her shins and lowered her head to her knees. When Alec's palm pressed into the small of her back, she pulled her legs in tighter, afraid if she looked up, if she let go of her hold, she might shatter completely.

TWENTY-EIGHT

S itting stiffly, gaze fixed on the black curtain closed across the viewing room's internal wall, Sarah's stomach churned. No noise filtered through from the mortuary but behind that material, just the other side of the glass, morgue staff were positioning a body for identification. For her verification. She pushed at the ache in her chest. Officials make mistakes all the time. It might not even be Max. Perhaps he and Riley were already in Germany. Together. Safe. Alive.

She rose to her feet and checked the clock above the door. The officer said she'd only be a minute. What was taking so long? She rubbed her hands up and down her arms.

Perhaps she shouldn't have asked Alec to wait in the car. What if he had news about Riley but couldn't reach her? She checked her phone. Full bars. No message.

The waiting room door swished open and the police liaison officer, a matronly woman with a soft smile, entered. "You ready love?"

Sarah hugged her cardigan tight about her body and moved next to the woman at the curtain.

"I have to warn you, his face has a bit of bruising."

Sarah's closed her eyes. *Please don't be him.*

The blinds opened with a whoosh, like the sound of a knife being sharpened. Sarah looked into the room, her left palm spreading across the frigid glass.

"Ms Calhoun, is this the body of your father Maximilian Angus Calhoun?"

A dam blocked her throat. She forced out a whispered "yes" and continued to stare at the body on the gurney. None of this felt real. "Can I go in there?"

"Of course." The officer opened a door, and Sarah coughed against the blast of bleach and sweet rot.

"It's easier if you breathe through your mouth." The officer's gentle voice was accompanied by a brief pat.

Sarah took shallow inhales through parted lips as she moved across the polished concrete floor. The officer walked to the exit. "I'm awfully sorry but I've another family to see to. Please take all the time you need. When you've finished, John here will escort you back to reception." She indicated a young, thin-faced man Sarah hadn't even noticed standing silently in the corner.

Sarah stepped to her Dad's side. A white sheet covered his body, leaving his head exposed. His face was mottled purple with bruising. Not one square inch had been left untouched.

Dad.

Touching her hand to his shoulder she lifted her chin and blinked against the blurring of the ceiling. Her breathing hiccupped and she fought to lock her pain inside. Max wouldn't want tears. Or time wasted on words. He'd want her to act.

Would demand she find Riley. She bent forward and pressed a kiss to his cheek, his skin cold against her lips.

"Thank you, Dad," her voice cracked. "I'll never forget what you gave to protect my boy."

She touched her forehead to his and squeezed her eyes shut.

I promise your sacrifice won't be in vain.

Forcing herself to stand tall, she smoothed out the sheet across her father's chest then stepped away to leave. The room was empty. Where had the orderly gone? He was supposed to show her out. Her lips pressed together. No more waiting, she needed to search for her son. She returned to the door through which she'd entered, crossed the threshold and froze. Adrenalin charged every muscle. Two bodies blocked her exit. Daniel's bodyguard Seamus, and, at his side, Siobhan.

Seamus stood at ease, his tattooed biceps bunching as a result of his folded arms.

Sarah glanced over her shoulder and back again. "The orderly will be back any minute."

"Ach, John won't be back for a while. He's our second cousin, so he is."

Siobhan slid her arm through Seamus's. "But sure, that's the thing with Belfast, you always know someone, wherever you go."

Blood pulsed at Sarah's temples. She tried to get hold of her breath.

"Give her a moment, sis," Seamus patted Siobhan's hand. "It's terrible hard to say goodbye to a loved one."

Sis. The family history Alec had given her for Siobhan hadn't mentioned a brother.

"Aye, but it'd be worse to see a boy on that there gurney, especially if he could have been saved."

"Have you no shame?" Sarah's gaze locked with Siobhan's. "Riley is only sixteen years old."

"You think that makes him special? We've lost two brothers to this war, one only twelve."

"The war's over."

"It'll never be over, you ignorant bitch, not until every Brit and Prod is gone for good." Siobhan's fevered eyes revealed the true ugliness of her soul.

Sarah's limbs vibrated with inaction. She turned to Seamus. "It's me you want. Not Riley, he's not a part of this."

Siobhan laughed. "You have it arse backwards. Riley is the key. You made it that way with your lies." She leant in, "Now who's not good enough for him, huh?"

Sarah lurched forward, ready to strangle every last breath from Siobhan's body. Seamus blocked her way, while Siobhan continued. "You may as well face it, you're beaten. Unless you give Daniel his alibi in court, Riley dies."

Sarah's gaze swung between Seamus and Siobhan. "How do I even know you have him?"

Siobhan thrust a photo into Sarah's face – Riley strapped to a chair, a copy of today's *Belfast Telegraph* placed in his lap. A red gash sliced across his cheek, but he was alive. Relief almost buckled her knees until she looked into his eyes. Her heart splintered. What had they done to him? What had he seen? Terror ripped through her. Even if she did testify, Daniel would kill Riley. He'd witnessed too much.

Seamus's phone pinged, and he checked it. "No sharing what we've told you with anyone, including that filthy peeler.

You do?" He looked up and moved into her space. "Both he and Riley die."

A trembling took hold of Sarah, but she refused to give any ground. Seamus smirked then turned away and shook a set of keys at his sister. "Time for us to slip out back." Light glinted off the Celtic symbol stamped on the brushed metal tag. It was identical to the keychain she'd found in Siobhan's bag. A replica of the heart-shaped harp carving behind Daniel's office desk. Why hadn't she put that together before?

Siobhan took Seamus's arm and left.

Sarah braced her arms against the doorjamb, the pain so acute in her chest she struggled to breathe. They were heading back to her son, and there was nothing she could do.

TWENTY-NINE

Sarah stumbled from the morgue visitor's exit and sucked in a huge gasp of fresh air. The cold stung but she took another, anything to get rid of the stink clinging to her lungs and throat.

"Sarah!" Alec crossed from the car park to her. She veiled her face as best she could. He jogged the last few steps. "I was on my way in. I've good news. We've found Riley, or he found us. Thirty minutes ago. He couldn't get through to either of our phones, so he called the Station. He's in Frankfurt boarding a plane to Tokyo where he'll change for a flight to Sydney. Sarah, did you hear me? Riley is safe."

Wind whipped around her head. Alec's voice seemed to come from afar. Riley wasn't safe, she'd seen proof.

"From now on we are taking no chances. You'll stay with me under police protection 'til you testify on Friday."

"No."

"You are the prime witness in a serious criminal case. You should have been under protection all along."

Her nails dug into her palms. She was the only one who knew Riley was in trouble. Under protection she'd be powerless to save him. "What about Padric? Why did he leave them and come to court?"

"Riley didn't mention Padric, and we've still not tracked him down. Maybe Daniel threatened Padric, thought he could trick you into doing what he wanted. I don't know."

"Did Riley say anything about Max?"

"Only that Max put him on the boat then decided to come back and help you."

How could Alec believe that? Her Dad would never have left Riley alone, not with his life at stake.

"The thinking now is Max's death was a robbery gone wrong. His wallet was missing when his body was found."

All neatly tied up. Daniel would get away with another murder. It was like he had a direct line to the devil. In a flat voice she whispered, "So the police search has been called off?"

"Of course." His gaze narrowed. "Are you okay?"

She swallowed the bile climbing her throat. "How do they know it was Riley? I want to talk to him."

"You can't. He's in the air. It was him, Sarah, the desk sergeant pulled up his file and asked identifying questions. Why aren't you relieved? Riley is finally out of Ireland."

His expression turned serious, searching and alert. If she wasn't careful, he would figure something was going on, and Daniel would carry out his threat. She had to shut this down.

"It is good news." She looked to her feet. Her vision blurred and her throat burned. "I just can't believe Max's gone."

His tone softened. "I'm sorry. At least he died knowing he got his grandson to safety."

A sob engulfed her. Max hadn't died knowing he'd saved Riley. He'd died fighting with everything he had to protect him. And failed. This was a nightmare. And nothing she did could wake her up. Max was dead. Riley was a prisoner, and no one was even looking for him. When her sobs finally faded, she stared across the car park.

Resolve hardened in her belly. She would do it. She would find her son and save him on her own. But she couldn't do it from protective custody. She dried her eyes with her sleeves and turned to Alec, whose hand had just left the middle of her back. "Could we go by Gerry's grave?"

"I don't think that's such a grand idea. You're exhausted. Let's get you back to my house where you'll be safe and can have a sleep."

She touched her fingers to his arm. "Please Alec, I think it will help. Remind me of why I came back to Belfast in the first place."

He reached for the car keys and nodded but she caught his second glance. She'd have to tread carefully.

Fresh flowers leant against Gerry's headstone. The chrysanthemums she'd left had been removed. Off to her side, sitting on the bench where they'd been together only last week, Alec sat rigid, scanning for potential threat. Sarah's throat thickened. He was too late.

Her fingers found her mother's ring. She twisted it round and round. Everything she had feared had come to pass. She'd protected no one. The secrets she thought would keep everyone safe had only made them all more vulnerable. What if she had told Michael? What if she had been honest with Evan? What if she hadn't come back? What if she had testified as Daniel ordered? *What if? What if? What if!*

If anyone should be dead, it was her. There's a 'what if'. What if she were no longer alive? There'd be no point to Daniel keeping Riley. Her arms fell limp at her sides. Daniel wouldn't let Riley go. Even then there'd be a price. She rocked back on her heels and stared up at the storm clouds bearing down on the city. Riley was counting on her; there was no one else. She'd need her computer from the hotel, to search for properties owned by the McNaultys.

Alec checked his phone. Now was her one chance to give him the slip. If she took off, she could run to the hotel. It wasn't that far. But he would be faster in the car. She pushed her shoulders back. She'd get the keys off him, drive the car back herself. That would give her a thirty-minute head start. It would have to be enough.

She pulled her scarf tighter about her neck, hunched her shoulders against the howling wind and set off back to the car park, Alec trailing behind her.

They reached the deserted car park, and she turned to him. "I need a minute to ring Evan, to tell him about Max."

"You can call him from my house."

"No, I need to get it over and done with, or I'll lose all courage. Do you mind if I ring from the car? The wind's picking up, it'll be harder to hear out here."

He fixed her with a stare, searching her face.

"I just need a minute and then we can go to your house. I'm desperate for a shower. I can still smell the morgue."

His stance loosened. He handed over his keys and pointed behind. "I'll wait over there."

Sarah fished out her phone and made to walk off.

"Damn, my phone is flat." She showed him the dead screen. "Can I borrow yours?"

She wet her lips as Alec dug in his pocket and passed her his mobile. That would delay him further, not being able to call for reinforcements.

He pulled his collar up. "Don't be long." He turned and walked to the bench.

She slid into the driver's seat and slipped the key in the ignition.

"Sarah!" Alec was charging for the car.

She twisted the key and shoved the car into gear. Alec's hand bashed on the boot, but she stepped on the accelerator and roared from the kerb, heart ricocheting against her ribcage. She'd broken any tenuous link they had left. He would never trust her again.

Sarah rushed around the hotel room, throwing things into an overnight bag. She glanced at the clock. Time to go.

A loud bang on the door stilled her. No way. He couldn't have gotten here that fast. She zipped up her overnight bag and placed it by the door. The beating became more insistent. She checked the peephole, and her forehead sank against the door.

"I know you're in there, Sarah. Open up."

Pulling in a deep breath she opened the door a crack.

"Sorry, Alec, it's not a good time."

He burst through, knocking her back, and slammed the door behind him. "I don't give a damn what time it is! What the hell's going on?"

He was breathing hard, his face shiny with sweat. His green eyes blazed with fury. She had to get rid of him before he discovered the truth. She crossed to the table and picked up her handbag.

"I have somewhere I need to be." She tried to push past him, to get to the door, but he used all 6"4' of his might to block her way. "You're supposed to be under police protection, my protection. It's only for two days, do you hate me that much?"

"I don't hate you. I'll go nuts hiding away. Besides, I need to organise Dad's funeral, his transport back to Australia. I'm going to ask for the case to be delayed."

"I thought you wanted to end this?"

Riley needed her to find him now. She had no time for this. "After my collapse yesterday, the doctor gave me a week to get back on my feet. I've decided to take it. Now please, let me past."

He paced the exit, his anger flush across his face. "But we had it all sorted. You are so close to being free."

Colour burst in front of her eyes. "Free? Are you insane? You and Michael and Daniel, you'll never let me go. We'll never be safe no matter what I do!" She charged forward but Alec spotted the overnight bag by the door.

"Where are you going?"

"I need a break!"

"Bollocks!" His gaze narrowed on hers, the piercing cold slamming straight through her. "He's got to you, hasn't he? Like he always does. What was it with you, Sarah? Money? To keep your mouth shut?" He prowled towards her. "Or was it Michael, the great love of your life? Did he fuck you into submission?"

She slapped his face, the sound of the crack reverberating through the room. "Get out."

"Do you think he'll protect you?" Alec's hands tore through his hair, "You'll just be another one of his whores, sacrificing her kids, just like Chloe."

Sarah's body shook, vibrating with indignation. Her hands clenched into fists, and she met his glare. "Don't you ever come near me again." She ignored the burning in her throat, snatched up her bag and stepped towards the door.

Alec blocked her path. "Sit your arse on that there bed. Try to leave again, and I will arrest you. Do you understand? It's my job to make sure you make it to court on Friday. Even if you don't care about doing what's right, I do. You will testify." He dragged the lounge across, barricading the door. "Better make yourself comfortable. We are not leaving this room."

THIRTY

S arah jerked awake, the scream still bouncing around her skull. She kicked away the sweat-soaked bedclothes and sat up. The last image in her dream, the one where a bullet blew out the back of Riley's head, wouldn't fade. She reached for the glass sitting on the nightstand, gulped a mouthful of water then struggled to swallow it down. She checked the bedside clock. 2:00 am. Thirty-two hours until Alec delivered her back to court. She couldn't have stuffed things up more if she'd tried.

Snagging the quilt around her shoulders she moved to the window and peeked around the drapes. Clouds veiled the moon, leaving the street below in black. Anyone could be out there watching. Did Daniel know Alec was staying the night in her room? Would he punish her for it?

Wind whistled through the tiny gaps in the window's frame. She pulled the quilt tighter, the threat of tears stinging her nose. Riley had been gone almost a day. How could Alec detain her when her son's life was in very real danger? Her gaze flashed to

257

him. He lay asleep on the lounge, one knee bent up, an arm
flung over his eyes. It would break him when he discovered his
actions had actively aided Daniel's plans.

She pinned her arms across her stomach. This was her fault.
All of it. Alec believed he was doing the right thing. Just like
Evan. Just like Max. Wouldn't she ever learn? She turned back
to the window, seeing nothing but the dark. Her attempts at
controlling the situation had failed. It was time to stop. She
needed to tell Alec about Riley. Give him the chance to make
his own choices, whatever the risks.

Outside, a street sweeper rumbled past, its brushes stirring
up ponded water in the gutter but achieving little else. Just like
her lies. Her manipulations.

How different would things be if she'd given Michael a
choice, all those years ago? The street below her blurred then
dimmed...

*Sarah retched into the toilet bowl, the muscles of her stomach
convulsing against air. When it ended, she pulled herself up to
the sink and stared out the bathroom window to the morning
sky, its bleak grey cut into quarter-moons by the curls of barbed
wire placed around the neighbour's roof. The same spiky halo
rimmed most Belfast homes, installed to prevent rioters gaining
a vantage point. But it never stopped them. They threw their
petrol bombs from wherever they wanted, sometimes even
storing the petrol cans, bottles and rags in pre-prepared crates
on those very same roofs. A dull ache pressed down on her
chest. Could she really settle down with a family amongst this
chaos?*

Two raps sounded on the door. "*Mo chroi*, are you okay in there?"

"I will be. I think I might have caught a bug." Her empty gut churned with the lie. Every morning for two weeks straight she had knelt at the toilet. And the blood tests yesterday had confirmed it. "I'm going to take the day off. You should leave for work. I'll be okay."

"Why don't I stay home, look after you?"

The concern in his voice worked away at her resolve. "I'll be fine."

"You sure? I could play doctor for the day."

She couldn't help but laugh. "I think not."

"You're no fun. Seriously though, I'll only go if you promise to ring me if you're in need."

Her hand pressed at her chest. "I will."

"Do you want me to bring home dinner?"

"No, it's okay." He continued to hover on the other side of the door. "Michael, you better go, or you'll be late."

"Are you sure there's nothing I can do?"

"I'll be fine."

"Love you, *mo chroi*."

"Love you too."

She bent over the sink and splashed her face with water. It wasn't like they hadn't talked about having kids, but they'd planned to be married first. She slid a towel from the rail and pressed it to her skin. This was just awful timing. Michael had been so engrossed in Daniel's problems these past few weeks, so distant and removed.

But Daniel was heading back to Crossmaglen tonight. Michael would be hers again; they would sort things out. She *loaded a toothbrush with paste and brushed away the sour taste from her tongue. Michael wanted a family. He would be happy. He would. She'd tell him once Daniel left. She rinsed and met her own sunken eyes in the mirror. No matter what happened, she was going to be a mother. Whatever she did now had to be in the best interest of her child.*

She scooped the dirty washing into a basket, opened the bathroom door and bumped straight into Daniel.

"A tad off-colour, are we?"

Sarah stilled. How much had he heard?

"I'm fine, just a bug." She pushed by him, using the basket as a buffer, and darted to the laundry downstairs. While she loaded the machine, her pulse tripped. The last thing she needed was Daniel figuring things out, especially before she told Michael. She needed to play nice.

"Daniel," she called out, "do you need to throw a few things in the wash before you head south?"

A small smile fought its way through. Almost there. In eight hours they would have their home back. Just her and Michael. She threw a scoop of powder on top of the load.

"Ach no," came Daniel's voice from behind, "It seems you'll have my company for a while yet, I've another job here in Belfast."

She pivoted on the spot. He stood a ruler length away, his spicy cologne causing her emptied stomach to pitch.

"But sure, I'm welcome here, am I not?"

Michael said she didn't understand Daniel. He was wrong. She understood all too well. Her focus skidded from his stare.

"Yes, of course. Let me know if you'll be here for dinner." She turned back to the machine and jabbed at the controls.

Daniel's hand clamped on her wrist and twisted her around. "What's Michael's is mine, Sarah. He'll never turn me out." He leant closer and his breath burnt across her face. "I am all he has."

She pulled free, ramming herself back into the corner of the machine. Ignoring the pain, she straightened.

"You're wrong. Michael has me."

"Yes, for now,' Daniel's mouth thinned, "but I will still be here when you are just some whore from his past." He stomped away.

Heat flared up her neck while retorts burnt on her tongue. The front door slammed. Why couldn't Michael see? Why wouldn't he listen? Tears welled. She had to rid them of Daniel, or he would destroy them all. She wouldn't let that happen...

Sarah's gaze came back into focus as the garbage truck's brake lights disappeared around the corner. No way Daniel had figured it out that day or he would have hunted her down as soon as she ran. He never would have allowed a McNaulty to escape his control.

She caught the flesh of her cheek and rolled it between her teeth. Where would Michael's loyalty lie - to a son he never knew existed or to a brother to whom he'd devoted his life? What if Riley got hurt, and then Michael found he'd played a role? Didn't he have a right to choose, knowing all the facts? The idea sat like a foreign body under her skin, scratchy and uncomfortable. Yet the longer she let it be, the more she settled. And began to hope. Perhaps it was the safe way to get Riley out. Somewhere inside him, the old Michael existed. His strong beliefs about family. Surely, he would choose to save his only son.

She let the drapes fall back into place and a warm sensation branched out across her back. Turning she found Alec watching her with acute concentration. She sat on the end of the bed, swallowed the reflex to protect herself and faced him. "There's something I need to tell you."

THIRTY-ONE

"So, Michael has no idea he's Riley's father? Does he know Daniel's kidnapped him?"

"I've no idea how involved Michael is. There's a small chance he already knows. Someone sent that envelope with Riley's birth certificate to my hotel room." Sarah tucked her hands beneath her thighs and bounced her heels against the carpet.

Alec snagged the chair from the desk and sat in front of her, bending forward, elbows to knees. "Have you thought this through? Michael could run straight to Daniel."

"We tried putting our trust in the 'right' people and look where that got us. At least I know family is important to Michael. Riley is his only child." She picked at a piece of jagged thumbnail, fighting the uncertainty swelling in her chest. "He needs to know that the choices he makes could harm his son."

Alec's hand lifted briefly, then withdrew to rub behind his neck. He leant back against his chair.

"Michael never shies from stretching the law when defending his brother, but Gerry's death is the first crime he's directly linked to. Trusting him is a huge risk."

"What other options do we have?" She threaded her fingers together in her lap and looked at him. "Are you going to tell the Commissioner I'm compromised as a witness?"

"I may as well pull the trigger on Riley myself if I do that."

She flinched, the dream image still too vivid in her mind. Alec leant in and covered her hands with his.

"I'm telling no one."

"But your job?"

"The Super himself vouched for Padric. We've no idea who to trust. Let's hope you're right about Michael."

After all she'd done - the lies, the manipulations, the cowardice - Alec was still prepared to stand at her side. She entwined her fingers with his. "Thank you. You deserve so much more than that, but thank you."

For longer than was comfortable he held her stare, then with a quick squeeze, he released her hands and stood. "We need a plan."

Meeting at the Cave Hill car park had been Alec's idea. Anyone watching Sarah this morning would have assumed she was going on her daily run. Instead she'd slipped through a peace wall gate into the protestant Shankill, through the back of St Andrews church, and was now hidden behind a hedge of brambles, their musky scent tickling her throat as she waited. Alec was picking up Michael from his law office, supposedly taking him in for questioning.

Sarah peeked out to check down the road. A loud crack punctured the air. She dropped to a crouch and her gaze whirled, searching out the shooter. An old Volkswagen pulled away from the parking lot, its tailpipe backfiring again down the hill. She let out a huge breath, rolled her shoulders and stood again behind the hedge.

Movement down the road caught her eye. The flash of Alec's silver Audi revealed two solid men in the front seats. Adrenalin lashed her pulse. She reset her baseball cap. *Game time.*

The car reversed into a parking spot, ready to roar off at a moment's notice. She opened the back door and slid in.

Michael's fists rammed against the console. "I knew it, so I did. The big detective wouldn't lower himself to transporting the likes of me." Michael turned, eyes narrowing in on Sarah. "Then again maybe you lower yourself enough on him that he'll do anything."

"Shut your mouth."

"It's okay, Alec. Michael's every right to be angry."

"Fuck you, Sarah." Michael crossed his arms and turned back to Alec. "This is illegal detainment."

"I never arrested you."

"No, you said Sarah had been re-arrested, needed my counsel."

The high-pitched cawing of a buzzard filled the thick silence. Sarah cleared her throat. "Alec, I think it might be better if you wait outside."

"No."

"Alec, please."

He paused, fixing Michael with a savage glare, then he

yanked the keys from the ignition and settled against a tree a few metres away. Sarah exhaled. Michael stared out the windshield, the summery waft of his aftershave the only hint of warmth in the car.

"I'm sorry we tricked you Michael, but Daniel couldn't know we were meeting."

"I'll be informing him myself as soon as your peeler sees fit to let me go."

"Could you at least hear me out?"

"What the fuck have you got to say to me that hasn't already been said?" He squared his back to her. "We're done. You never loved me. I'm over it. Moved on. When you left—"

"I was pregnant."

Michael's head shot round. "What?"

She met his shocked gaze. "Pregnant. Carrying your child, Michael. His name is Riley." She reached in her pocket and offered him a photo. He snatched it. His head bent down, exposing the corded muscles at the back of his neck. Sarah twisted her mother's ring. He had to recognise the truth.

Michael waved the photo, his mouth pinched in a thin line. "This proves nothing."

"Please Michael. The eyes. They're the same as yours. You must be able to see."

He shook his head. "You would have told me at the time."

"The week before I left, I tried time and again to tell you. Remember the night we went for dinner? I was going to tell you when we got home, but there was the riot, and then Daniel took you away."

"A boy had been killed. Everyone was getting arrested. What did you want me to do?"

"Daniel knew. He kept you away from me."

"If this is going to be a Daniel bashing, I'm done. He was fighting for what he believed in."

"What about what you believed in? The power of the law, what was best for us?"

"Daniel was my responsibility. He needed me."

Heat burnt Sarah's ears. Her tone dropped an octave. "I was there, Michael."

"What?"

"The night Daniel murdered Gerry McCann, I was there."

Michael frowned.

"You were in Strangford."

"No, I was upstairs. I saw what Daniel did, and you stood by, Michael. You did nothing." She indicated Riley's school photo, still clenched in Michael's hand. "He's why I ran. I'd lost you forever, but I needed to protect our child from that life. I get in some twisted way you believed you were protecting family, but Riley is your family too. Your blood. Now you know, you can't turn away."

She held her breath as her words hung in the air. A car horn beeped further down the hill, and she glanced briefly in that direction. When she looked back, Michael still stared at the photo.

"What is it you think I can do?"

She leant towards him, her fingers digging into the back of his seat. "Daniel is holding Riley prisoner. He's forcing me to be his alibi, to swear that on the night of Gerry's murder, I was with him in his bed. If I don't, he'll kill Riley." Her voice cracked. "But he'll kill him anyway, to punish me, and hurt you. I need you to rescue our son."

"Daniel's not a monster."

"Didn't you listen to a word I said? He's the fucking Devil! He kidnapped my sixteen-year-old son. Our son. Did he warn you of his plan?"

Michael's gaze broke away from hers and his head turned away. Daniel hadn't told him anything.

"I think Daniel knows you are Riley's father, he's probably known for years. Now he's holding your son hostage." She touched his shoulder. "Please Michael, we never had a chance, but Riley is innocent. He's just a boy."

"Stop." Michael shrugged away, went quiet. Sarah sat back, gripped her hands together in her lap and forced herself to wait for him to speak.

Michael's cold tone sliced through any hope. "Daniel warned me how manipulative you were, that you'd do anything to get your way. But this is low, Sarah, to pretend that boy is my son. Just do as Daniel says, and your son will be fine. Daniel will keep his word." Michael got out, the slam of his door like a slap across her face. She leapt out the car.

"What the hell happened to you?"

Michael's step paused; his back stiffened, then Sarah's lungs emptied with an anguished scream as her only hope walked away.

THIRTY-TWO

S arah slapped her palms against the roof of the car. *Damn Michael. Damn him to hell.* There was nothing left of the man she had loved. Daniel had thoroughly destroyed him. She replayed the conversation in her head. Did she miss something, anything, to give her hope? Michael's eyes had flared when she showed him the photo of Riley.

A stick snapped to her right, her chest swelled. She spun around, but it was Alec, not Michael, who walked towards her.

"You okay?"

"I've no idea what he's going to do. He could be headed straight to Daniel to tell him everything. If he does, Riley's as good as dead. Then Daniel will come for you."

"I don't think so. Daniel needs us for court tomorrow. We have twenty-four hours to find Riley ourselves." His tone gentled and he leant a hip against the car. "I need you to think back to your days with the McNultys. Anywhere they visited, any other property they had."

She pressed the heels of her hands into her eyes. But nothing came. She was trying to save the life of her son and she couldn't remember one single thing to help.

"Wouldn't the police have more up-to-date information?"

"All database searches are logged and tracked. I don't want to tip off anyone that has Daniel's files flagged."

Her palms ran back over her hair. A gust of blustery wind whipped up scattered leaves into a swirl across the car park. The scent of late season heather lingered in its wake. Memories stirred of picnics near a farm in County Armagh, alongside Slieve Gullion's rolling purple and pink fields.

"There was the family farm where they grew up, but I think it might have been sold." She pushed from the car's cold metal, a surge of heat flushing her neck. "I can't remember anything useful!"

She turned away and tramped up the dirt path towards the peak of Cave Hill. When tears stung her eyes she broke into a run. Max, Gerry, Olivia, Liam. How many more lives would Daniel destroy? She lurched to a stop.

"Alec!" He charged the final metres to reach her. She reached for his forearm. "I know who can help."

Alec, still trying to regain his breath, gestured for her to continue. "Liam. He'd know where Daniel's holding Riley."

"Liam's a criminal. He can't be trusted."

"He said he didn't shoot you Alec, and I believe him. I think Daniel set him up to take the fall."

"Even if he did—"

"What other options do we have? We can't go to the police, Michael refused to help, and Daniel's had Riley for over a day now. Who knows what is being done to him?"

"I know Sarah, I know, but we have to go about it in the right way or we might make things worse."

"It's worth a try isn't it? We're running out of time. I can't do nothing." She inhaled deeply, then slowed her words. "What if we could help Liam somehow, in exchange for information?"

"It's a risk."

"No more than approaching Michael. Please, Alec, I need your help."

"Liam's on remand in Maghaberry Prison. But I couldn't go in with you."

"I don't think you should. When I passed him at the police station, he begged me for help. I think I can reach him."

Alec checked his watch. "Two hours 'til visiting ends. I've a friend who's a guard. He can bypass the booking system and get you in. But there are eyes and ears everywhere inside. You'll have to be careful, or you'll get Liam killed."

She grabbed his arm. "I can do this." She pulled him towards the path and ran back to the car.

The prison's sniffer dog took one last pass around her and moved on to investigate the next person. Sarah stepped through the door of the visiting area and came up short. The room was open plan, exposing her to the scrutiny of every waiting prisoner. Any one of them could report her visit to Daniel. She quickly scanned the numbered wall plaques and dipped her chin, allowing her hair to veil her face while she made her way to area seven. A gaunt-looking Liam Breen waited in a booth that looked like it had been borrowed from a fast-food chain. She sat on the yellowed bench seat opposite him.

"Well, what about ye Miss Sarah?"

Liam's voice boomed with a cocky confidence, but the performance barely masked his fragility. Her chest expanded. She was in with a chance.

"How are you Liam?"

"Dead on." He leant back, arms stretched along the top of the backrest.

"I've left money for you at the desk. Would you like a cola and crisps?"

"That'd be grand."

She walked to the dispensing machine like she had a rod through her back. When she bent to collect her purchases, a cool sensation crept across her skin. Twisting to check, she found the stare of a heavyset man with a spider web tattoo covering his entire neck. He looked her up and down. When his mouth lifted in a smirk, her fist loosened on the crisp packet. The man was just a slimy creep, not one of Daniel's henchmen.

She returned to Liam, handed over the treats and slid back into her seat. He pushed her offerings to the side, unopened. She waited for him to make eye contact.

"I'm here because of what you said at the station, Liam. I have a friend who can help." She paused, until Liam gave a slow nod. "But we need something first."

Liam's eyes rolled. "Always a catch."

"Just information. Someone important to me is staying with an acquaintance of yours. I'd like to visit them."

He blanched. "I'm no tout."

"Think Liam. My friend can give you options, a new start."

"I doubt that."

"Think, have I ever broken my word to you?"

Liam snatched up the bottle of cola, the fizz when he twisted the lid open filling the hanging silence. His tense grip dented the plastic bottle from all sides. After guzzling a mouthful, he stared into the swirling contents. He wanted time to think this through, time she didn't have.

She slid her downturned hand forward, pressing at the centre of the table. "This is about family, do you understand?"

Liam gnawed at his fingernails. The clickety-clack of tottering heels drew Sarah's attention. A skinny woman in a short denim skirt and tight tank had rushed through the visitor's entrance. She made her way directly to the man with the spider web tattoo.

Sarah looked back at Liam. His pupils had dilated, yet there was something other than fear in his gaze when it flicked about the room. He waited until a crescendo built in the surrounding noise.

"They've a big party planned. A blast of an event, much bigger than The Twelfth we shared. Your friend is sleeping beside the supplies."

The Twelfth? Did he mean the Twelfth of July? The Protestant Orange Parades? In 1997, the year Liam attended her camp, the Twelfth had erupted into riots all over Northern Ireland. Talk spread of a huge bomb attack planned for Belfast's city centre, but it never happened. Her pulse quickened.

"The rumours?"

He nodded. "Double the size. Party's tomorrow."

"What!"

Heads twisted in their direction. Liam smothered her shriek with a forced laugh. When everyone turned away, he whispered through gritted teeth, "Catch yourself on, or you'll do us both in."

Sarah stared at her lap. If Daniel set off a bomb in Belfast tomorrow the city would be full of innocent people.

"You need to tell me where they are."

Liam's eyes widened. A guard appeared at their booth, his pocked-marked face etched in hard lines of suspicion and contempt. Sarah checked his name badge. Charles Lowry.

"You alright here?"

"All's fine, officer." She smiled widely, hoping the guard couldn't hear her thumping heart.

From the corner of the room a different guard bellowed, "Get off him you skanky munter!"

Prison officers descended from all directions to the epicentre of the commotion, two booths behind Liam. The skinny woman had straddled her prisoner, and they were making out. The guard who'd been questioning Sarah charged over and wrenched the woman off. They dragged her away and, as she screamed all manner of obscenities, Liam leant in, his voice barely audible.

"They're at Lennoch Farm, just outside Cross. But be prepared. All his friends are invited."

Sarah reached her fingers across and touched them briefly to his. "Thank you, Liam. I always knew you had a good heart."

Colour rushed into his cheeks, and for a brief moment he looked like the ten-year-old she remembered. His expression shifted. "You promise you'll get me out."

"My friend's working on it as we speak."

She checked the metal caged clock above the exit. Midday.

She needed to get back to Alec. "We better make this look like it ended badly. To keep you safe."

Liam nodded.

"How could you?" She slapped his face so hard her hand stung. Liam pulled back, her finger marks bright red below his still bruised eye.

An older guard charged in their direction. "What's going on?"

"Get me away from him. I can't believe I wasted my time."

"It's alright, Mam. Come this way. And you," he pointed at Liam, "Charlie will take your sorry arse back to your cell."

The prison transport minibus pulled into the visitor car park. Sarah waited until last to disembark and pretended to retie her shoelace while she watched the other passengers climb into their cars. The bus chugged away, joining the convoy of vehicles peeling out onto the main road. Finally, she was alone. She darted to the back of the old Quaker Visitor Centre and dashed left through the surrounding farmlands.

After ten minutes sprinting at full pelt, she reached their meeting point. Alec paced outside the abandoned factory. He swivelled round at the crunch of her shoes.

She bent over and sucked in oxygen.

"It's bad," her lungs heaved, "worse than bad." Sweat slid from her temple, dripped from her nose and pooled in a small dark patch on the asphalt as she tried to regain control of her breath. "Daniel is sending a bomb to Belfast tomorrow. Double '97."

"But that'll take out a whole city block."

She braced her hands on her hips and stood tall. "We've got to tell your police chief. They have to get Riley out now."

A young woman, barely out of her teens, bustled down the lane with a pram and toddler in tow. Alec grasped Sarah's waist and guided her to his car, his sharp look insisting on silence. When they'd slid in and closed the doors, he turned to her.

"We can't tell the chief. Anything to do with Daniel gets handled once it's passed up the chain. If we call, Daniel will receive a tip off, and we'll all be dead."

"But Riley's right next to the bomb!"

He bracketed her face with his hands. His steady gaze and even breaths helping to bridle the panic rushing through her veins.

"We have to be smart. Did Liam tell you Daniel's exact location?"

"Lennoch farm. Did you get anywhere with the prosecutor?"

He nodded. "He already had doubts about Liam's confession."

"Alec, we have to get Riley out."

His hands dropped to her shoulders and gave a squeeze. "We will." He sat back and concentrated on a point beyond the windshield. She stared out too. Granite grey clouds closed in across the blue sky.

"We'll extract Riley, then call in the media." He turned over the engine. "They can notify the police. That way the situation can't be handled. We'll also tip off the Garda Station across the border."

"You'll lose your job."

"There are more important things."

Sarah closed her eyes. Again, she'd given Alec a choice, and he hadn't abandoned her. In the turmoil of her swarming emotions, she zeroed in on that, drew on its strength.

His palm touched her thigh. "It's not going to be easy to get around Daniel's security. Are you up for this?"

"When do we leave?"

"We'll go by my house for supplies then wait until dark."

Her body vibrated with the need to get started. She wanted this done. Finished for good. She looked over to Alec as he pulled the car onto the road. The muscles in his neck flexed. He was worried, but she believed in him. He would do whatever it took to rescue her son and prevent the attack.

THIRTY-THREE

Sarah followed Alec into his book-lined study. The room's window looked out over an untended cottage garden of purple, white and pink. Pushed up to the window's edge was a large pine desk, its surface clear of all clutter except a computer screen and keyboard. He pulled the window shut, blocking the wintry wind and its lavender scent.

"Paper and pens are in the draw. Do you need anything else?"

Darkness circled his eyes, stubble graced his chin. This was taking them both to the brink. It would be even worse for Riley. She shook her head sharply. Imagining her son's situation wasn't going to help.

Alec turned away, taking her head shake as the answer to his question. His footsteps retreated from the room. She sat in the high-backed office chair, switched on the computer and concentrated on finding the farm. She trawled the Internet for any references to Lennoch farm, its exact location, and for satellite imagery they could use to devise an approach.

An hour later she stood and rolled the cricks from her neck. Displayed on the screen was Google Map's earth view of the huge property right near the North-South border. She'd zoomed in on the one long, weaving lane for getting in and out. It was lined with hedgerows. Entering through there would be suicide. They'd have to set up in the heavily wooded area about a kilometre away, hide the car, and make their way on foot behind the natural ridge. From one hundred and fifty metres away, they'd have to run through an open field to the property's only cluster of buildings - a two-storey farmhouse with a large courtyard leading to what looked like stables and a barn. The most logical place to store explosives would be in the furthest structure from the main house. So, they'd check the barn first.

She bent forward to stretch out her hamstrings. When she unfolded, she was struck by mingling scents of leather, wood and coffee. Turning, she found Alec studying her. She caught a look of utter vulnerability on his face before he slid his mask in place. He handed her a steaming cup of espresso.

"I picked up the hire car. You find the farm?"

She discarded the drink and re-sat at the computer. Alec moved behind her.

"That's it, there." She pointed to the screen, then zoomed out on the map. "And the barn, where the explosives are most likely stored. We can set up back here," her finger moved to the woods, "and work our way through here to the property."

Alec bent forward to get a better look. "We'll be totally exposed crossing here." He pointed to the last hundred and fifty metres and leant in closer. His chest brushed her back. They both stilled and his breath fanned her hair. Her lungs ached, but she didn't want to make it any more difficult for him to rein himself in. After what seemed an eternity cold air replaced the heat, and Alec's gravelly voice came from the doorway. "It'll get dark around 9:00 pm. We both need to eat, then rest 'til then."

"There's no way I can sleep."

"You're running on empty. We'll have stew, a dram of whisky, and then you will go to bed. I need you rested and alert for tonight." His request, spoken as a command, opened her to the tiredness of her body, her gritty eyes and the emptiness in her belly.

"I'll try."

"Good. Save the maps in a file and send them to our phones. I'll be in the kitchen."

After waking from a restless sleep Sarah rolled to her back and checked the clock. 7:00 pm. Not long now. She had one more task to do, just in case she didn't make it back.

Jumping out of bed, she threw on the black pants and hoodie Alec had bought her and made her way downstairs. She checked in on a sleeping Alec before sitting at the desk in the study. She pulled out four sheets of paper.

The words to her children flowed easily; her greatest memories with each one, favourite times shared, their individual strengths – Riley's generosity, Ally's quick wit, Sophie's sense of humour.

She moved to the last sheet of paper. Her pen hovered, motionless, above the page, until she put aside all doubts and questions, her fears and pride, and shared everything she'd been holding in tight.

When she finished, she folded each letter into an envelope, gathered them in a neat pile and sat back. A hammering water pipe drew her attention. Alec must be awake. She still had to check on the girls before leaving. Picking up her disposable phone, she dialled Doug.

"Sarah?"

"Hi Doug."

"How are Max and Riley?"

Her eyes winced closed. He didn't know about Max, but she couldn't go there, not now. She licked her lips and answered. "We're putting Riley on a plane home tomorrow."

"Good. That's good. Any idea when we can head back home?"

"I'll know more tomorrow, I promise."

"Evan comes out of hospital today. He and Felicity want to see the girls."

"I know, but it's not safe yet. Just give me another day, please." She pressed at a black knot in the surface of the desk.

"Do you want me to put the girls on?"

"Thank you, Doug. I don't know what I would have done without your and Wendy's help."

"No need for thanks, love. You're family." Doug's voice left the phone. "Ally!" Shuffling sounds filled the silence.

"Hi Mum." Sarah cradled the phone against her ear, wishing she could crawl down the line. "Hey, how come this phone works? Pop says mine won't work here."

"Listen to your Pop, honey, he knows what's best."

"I just want to talk to my friends. Pop's being all 'this is a no devices holiday' which sucks."

"Ally, don't give him a hard time."

"But when can we go home? I want to go back to school."

Sarah smiled briefly. "Never thought I'd hear you say that."

"I miss my friends. And you. I even miss Riley. Is he there?"

Sarah's hand fluttered to the base of her neck. "He's not here right now. I just wanted to say hi and tell you I love you. Lots and lots."

"Love you too, Mum. Wait. Sophie's being a pain. She wants to tell you a joke."

A hand muffled the receiver.

"What do you call a smelly Father Christmas?"

"I don't know, what?"

"Farter Claus. Get it?" Sophie's laughter tinkled down the phone. Sarah's throat thickened. "Mummy?"

Sarah forced out a laugh. "I miss your jokes."

"I miss you, but don't worry, we're having fun with Pops and Gran. And guess what? I can ride really well now. Before we left the farm, Pop said I was ready for proper jumps."

"Jumps, wow. Do you have a favourite horse?" Sarah closed her eyes, blocking out everything but her girl.

"Shadow. He's brown with a black mark the shape of a cloud on his side. He's beautiful." Silence filled the line. "Mum, when are you coming home? You've been away ages."

"I know honey. I'm trying really hard to finish up the job. You know how much I love you, don't you?"

"Yes, but I love you the mostest."

"Not possible, 'cause I love you more."

Sarah needed to get off the phone before her voice cracked

and Sophie heard. But she couldn't bring herself to break the tie. A hand squeezed her shoulder. She looked up. Alec stood next to her, concern softening his face.

"Sophie, honey, I better go."

"Okay, see you soon, Mummy!"

"See you soon." Sarah hung up and hugged the phone to her chest. Her girls were safe. And they would stay that way. If something happened to her tonight, they would have Evan and their grandparents. It was Riley who needed her now. He was all alone.

Alec withdrew, leaving behind an imprint of heat on her shoulder. The skin on her back tingled as he studied her from behind. Squaring her shoulders, she turned the chair to face him. He perched awkwardly on the edge of the lounge.

"How're your girls?"

"Missing me and home, but safe. Even I wouldn't be able to find where they are. Evan's parents have been amazing. I owe them."

"Ally and Sophie are their grandchildren."

"I guess."

Alec smoothed a non-existent crease from his black pants and cleared his throat. "Change of plans. I'm going alone tonight."

"What?"

"You should stay here. I'll get Riley out then send photos of the bomb components to you. That way you can forward them to the media straight away."

"No."

"It'll be safer."

"Safer for who?"

"I have the training."

"No."

"Hear me out. If something goes wrong, I have nothing to lose, no one relying on me."

She jumped to her feet. "I said no! The girls have Evan, but Riley is alone. If you don't take me, I'll make my own way there."

He stood, his body rigid and stiff. "This isn't open for discussion. You are staying here."

"Daniel needs to be stopped, and I need to be a part of that, for a whole heap of reasons including Max and Gerry. But most of all I need to do what's right. I haven't come this far to hide now."

His gaze bore into her. When she stared back, he broke away to the bookshelf. "If Daniel catches us, he'll show no mercy." His fingers touched a photo of Olivia. "You're staying here."

"I have to be there for Riley. Please Alec, who knows what state he'll be in."

"Exactly. How do I know you won't fall apart if Riley is hurt?"

"Don't. I'm strong, you know that."

"You're a mother, not a soldier."

She stepped in, getting right up in his face. "You show me a soldier who would fight harder than me to save my son."

The words hung in the air. The rise and fall of her chest the only movement between them.

He grasped her shoulders. "You do as I say. Everything I say. If you so much as pause before following a directive, I'll secure you in the car." When she nodded, he released his grip.

"Grab your stuff. We need to hit the road." And he marched out the door.

Sarah turned to the desk, and with unsteady hands spread the letters in a row. Then she picked up her backpack and ran for the car.

THIRTY-FOUR

S wathed in the night-time blackness of the rented four-wheel drive, Sarah snuck a look at Alec. His stare hadn't deviated from the road since leaving. They were almost at Crossmaglen, and he had driven silent the whole way.

Sarah took another shallow breath attempting to avoid the sickly floral scent oozing from the rental's upholstery. She had tried opening the window, but the outside temperature had dropped. Her stomach turned again. The stench wasn't the real problem. She was wavering. For all her bravado about taking Daniel down, about needing to be there, she wondered what on earth she was doing. Was her insistence on taking part going to put Riley's rescue at risk?

A vehicle approached fast from behind, lighting up their interior then screamed by. For a moment its headlights caught on a not-so-old green, white and orange IRA sign affixed to a telegraph pole. An old board below declared they had reached Bandit Country.

Her fingers reached to the axis of her jaw and rolled in circles. On her arrival to this town in 1996, she'd passed similar signs, and worse, like the "Sniper at Work" triangle hung where a British soldier had been shot dead. Their car passed through the village square, and up the road on her right she spotted the tall towers of the old British Army base, now a police station, still dwarfing the youth centre where she had worked.

Her circling fingers pressed harder and changed direction, but she couldn't dislodge the memories reaching for her. Trying to run activities while the pounding rotors of army helicopters shook the building around them. Children in her care falling silent as armed foot patrols in full fatigues and kit passed through the middle of their group. Ignoring the kneeling soldier who trained his gun on her when she crossed to the corner store. Being dragged to a meeting with prominent locals on her first day in town, after she responded "Hi" to a patrolling soldier's greeting - *You're either with us, or against us. There is no in between.* They'd used those exact words. At the time, the whole them and us had seemed like a game.

Until the first riot, the first death.

They drove out the other side of the township, and she forced her lungs to inflate. She couldn't afford to get buried in the past.

Alec turned off the main road and entered a narrow tree lined lane, big enough for only one vehicle. He slowed their speed. From now on, they'd be on back roads until they found the wooded area to hide the car.

What was going through his head? Was he wishing he'd left her behind? After all, she didn't have the skill set for an extraction. Who was she kidding? She'd never even used that word before except about teeth. Her hands clasped together in her lap. But she did know her son. If everything went to hell, she was the best person to guide Riley through. She chewed at her cheek. Better go over the plan again in her head.

With her heart inching up her throat, Sarah watched Alec make his way across a cowpat-littered field towards Daniel's barn. Leaving the car in the woods, they had followed a narrow path parallel to the road for eight hundred metres until they reached a small stream. After crossing the trickle of water, they'd climbed the embankment into the hedges rimming the open field – a thorny row of briars where she now lay on her front, wishing she hadn't obeyed Alec's command to wait while he scouted for Riley.

Alec reached the edge of the barn and slipped around the corner, disappearing from sight. Nature's night chorus filled Sarah's ears – a hooting owl, a scratching fox, the trickling of the stream. Each second ticked over as if it were moving through molasses. Had Alec found Riley yet? Were they both okay?

She stiffened. A ray of blue moonlight caught on movement in the stable's shadows. A human form, too stocky to be Alec, crept its way to the corner of the barn where Alec had disappeared. Her fingers gripped the grass, her heart thumping faster and faster with each step the man took. *Come on Alec. Where are you?*

From behind came the crack of a stick. Every muscle in her body tensed for flight. Something touched her leg. She whirled to her back and only just stifled her scream when Alec removed his black balaclava. Air whooshed from her lungs. He put his finger to his lips and motioned for her to follow him. She followed his soundless retreat across the stream, back down the path and into the dense foliage of the trees.

With each step her anxiety grew, swelling like a balloon in her torso. When they reached the car, she could stand it no longer. "Was Riley there? Did you find him? Was he okay?"

"He's in an abandoned stall at the back-right corner of the barn. His leg is shackled to a wooden post, but he looked unharmed."

Her hands tented over her mouth. "Did you talk to him?"

"I couldn't. I only spied him through a crack in the slat wall." He opened the car door, pulled out a water bottle and drank a gulp down. "There were constant patrols. They're going to be a problem, even later tonight. We'll need a distraction to lure them away."

"Maybe we should call in the media and police now?"

"We can't. Riley could get caught in the crossfire. We have to get him out first. Besides we have no proof of the bomb, not yet. We need to get in and take photos."

She leant back on the car's bonnet and toed a rock in the dirt. Riley needed her head in the game. She had to use her fear, direct its energy, make it work for her. She drew in a lungful of cold air and looked back up at Alec.

"What kind of distraction?"

"There's an abandoned car on the other side of the main house. A well-aimed Molotov cocktail could set it alight. The car's exploding petrol tank would definitely attract attention."

She raised her eyebrows. "A Molotov cocktail?"

He shrugged, a grin lighting his face. "A misspent youth."

"Right." She pushed off the car and tucked her hands in the

warmth of her armpits. "What do you need me to do? Siphon out petrol?"

"No, I brought a full jerry can in case. And glass bottles. And cloth." Sarah laughed. He raised two fingers to his temple. "Dib Dib Dib and all that."

Sarah's smile faded. They were really going to do this. She stomped her feet to restart circulation. When she rubbed her gloved hands together Alec closed the distance between them and cupped them to his mouth. He filled her gloves with a warm rush of breath. Her gaze locked to his, lips parting to speak. But before she could fully form the thoughts, he broke away and shoved his hands into his pockets.

"There's a thermos of coffee in the car to warm you up. And some cards for a game of Patience. I'm doing another perimeter check." He marched off.

Two hours later she stood by Alec's side, staring up the embankment that would take them back to Daniel's land. A rustling of leaves to their left produced a grey-haired bunny. Its twitching nose poked out from between two bushes then it darted away. If it had chanted, "I'm late, I'm late", she wouldn't have been surprised.

The night had such a surreal air - the ninja black clothes, the stakeout, the plan to breach Daniel's hideout. It certainly didn't fit with the safe controlled life she'd fought so hard to maintain, and yet she was exactly where she needed to be. She stole a glance at Alec. His shoulders were taut, his face pinched with strain.

He reached over and pulled a woollen beanie down over her

head. His calloused fingers grazed her neck and tucked in the wispy hairs that had escaped. She looked into his face, this man who had stepped up like no one ever had before. She owed him everything. "Thank you."

His gaze met hers, his Adam's apple shifted. Curling his hand at the back of her neck, he pulled her body to his. Her arms encircled his waist and held tight. They stood wrapped together, until their breathing settled.

"We need to go."

Alec clung on tighter, pressed a kiss hard against her temple. "Please be careful. I can't lose you too."

She eased back. "The plan's going to work. We're all going to be okay."

The corners of his mouth lifted, but the smile didn't reach his eyes. He resettled her beanie, then cradled her face. "You know what to do? When you hear the first smash of glass?" She nodded, but he continued. "Sprint to the barn. There is a hole on the left side you can crawl through."

"I know. I have the bolt cutters. I have to get in and out as fast as possible."

"Don't forget to take the photos, but don't spend too long. You'll have two minutes tops before they start sweeping for trouble. When you get out, Riley might be a bit slow. Don't wait for me. Just get across the damn field, and you'll be in the clear."

"Alec, I can do this. You take care of you."

He leant his forehead to hers, his breath brushing her lips.

"Let's go." He broke away and ran up the incline. Sarah scrambled up behind him but when she reached the top he'd already disappeared. She pulled her backpack straps tighter on her torso and waited for her cue.

THIRTY-FIVE

S arah flattened against the wooden slats of the large barn, the boom of the explosion ringing in her ears, her chest heaving from the sprint across the field. Poor Riley. What must he be thinking happened? A flash of him at six years old, buried in Evan's chest, palms shielding his ears as the cannons of the William Tell Overture shook the ground beneath them.

Block it out honey, just like back then.

She inched along the barn's rear, sticking to the shadows, and craned her neck around the corner. Clear. She spied the gap that would lead her to Riley.

Hold on sweetheart, I'm almost there.

She edged around the corner and slipped through the hole. A musty smell lingered but when she moved further in, the sulphuric reek of diesel fuel overpowered the hay's scent. Dust swirled with her soundless steps, lit by shafts of moonlight peeking through the ramshackle roof. Eerie shadows formed on the hay-covered ground. Rusty farm tools hung from the bearing posts, the hooks like outstretched limbs ready to grasp her as she passed.

A scuffling sound froze her feet to the spot. She whirled about, sweeping the barn with her torch, its beam of light finding nothing, but a mountain of industrial-sized white bags set against the barn's back wall. Ammonium Nitrate fertiliser. A tonne of it. She grabbed her phone, almost dropping it in her haste, took photos of the white bags, then narrowed the camera's focus on the plasticine-like block of brown Semtex.

She forwarded the images to Alec's phone, left hidden in the glove box of their car. They had to stop Daniel. Belfast would be heaving tomorrow. Workers. Families. Babies. Her chest jammed. A flash of Riley as a newborn, asleep on her chest, the honeyed scent of his scalp.

Leaving the bags, she crept past a row of horse stalls, glancing in each before passing. Finally, she reached the horse stall at the far corner of the barn, rounded the wall and faltered. She looked behind and back again into the stall. *Where was he?* Alec had seen him here three hours ago. She did a scout of the rest of the barn. Time sped up.

She could push it a minute longer; dart to the stables and if Riley wasn't there she'd return to the car. She edged to the front door of the barn, her neck strained as she scanned for sound then she stepped into the courtyard. A sudden flood of light captured her in its glare.

"Going somewhere?"

Sarah stilled, limbs momentarily paralysed, then she dropped the bolt cutters and torch and ran back into the building. She dived through the gap in the slats and fled to the right, through a yard of discarded farm equipment. With Daniel's men following, she couldn't return to the car. Alec and Riley might be there. She bolted in the opposite direction. If she could stay ahead of her pursuer's thudding steps, she would outrun them over distance.

Pumping her arms and legs, she increased her speed. The accelerating footsteps of a sprinter closed in. Her vision tunnelled. Every ounce of her energy and strength narrowed in on escape. She cranked up the pace of her strides.

Flying down the rocky driveway, she turned left and cut across a vegetable patch. Hissing exhales moved closer from behind. She had to make a break for it now, or she'd be caught.

A wooden fence came into view and she ran at full pelt, vaulted it and landed, still running, on the other side.

She darted into a scruff of trees, ignoring the branches whipping at her face. The root-infested ground tested her balance, but she pushed harder. Her calf muscles screamed in pain.

Suddenly a hand wrapped around her ankle, jerking her back mid-stride. Her torso catapulted like a loaded slingshot against the ground, and she smashed her head with a hard crunch against a rock.

Everything went blank.

THIRTY-SIX

She came to lying prone on a scratchy bed of hay. Pain stabbed at her skull as she worked to regain her vision. When she reached her fingers up to her forehead, they came away wet. Her swollen nose pulsed and the grazes along her cheek stung. The bruising imprints of her attacker's fingers smarted around her ankle.

She lifted her head and glanced down. A padlocked metal chain secured her to a wooden post.

The barn spun.

She lay back down, curled on her side facing the post. Silence hissed in her ears. The fog in her brain evaporated when she read a scratching. *Riley*. Her boy had dug his name into the pole. She checked the padlock chaining her leg. No signs of blood. And it hadn't been scratched or broken. Either the lock was new, or its key had been used to release Riley.

And that meant Daniel still had him.

The pressure in her head crippled her back to lying flat. Her son had been here, right here. She stared up through the roof's cracks into the star-littered sky.

Please be okay, Riley. *Please be alive.*

The pain roared, and the roof began to whirl.

When brightness hit the back of her lids, she opened her eyes and cringed. Light poured through every crack in the barn. Morning. She must have passed out.

She blinked until her pupils adjusted, spread her palms on the ground and pushed up to her knees.

Her nose wrinkled. The diesel fumes were stronger than she remembered. She tested her head, twisting it carefully. It still pounded, but at least she could move. She pulled her restrained leg up, foot flat to the floor, pressed both hands against her knee and willed herself to stand. After a sway or two, she found balance. She stretched the chain as far as it would go and peered over the side of the stall. Breath wheezed out her lungs.

The pile of fertiliser bags was gone. That's why the reek of diesel was so strong. They must have mixed the diesel with the ammonium nitrate pellets. They'd assembled the bomb.

The morning peak hour. All those people.

She closed her eyes. Maybe Alec had stopped it. That would explain where he was, why he hadn't rescued her yet. He could've been the one to unshackle Riley. Any moment now the media vans could arrive.

She yanked at the chain again and again. It clanked and clunked but didn't give way. Tears pricked her eyes.

She would not give up.

Kneeling on the ground she dug through the hay, sifting for

a stick or a rock or anything she could use to break the lock apart.

Muffled footsteps padded towards the stall, closer and closer. Fast quiet steps, as if someone didn't want to be heard. Sarah braced herself.

Michael rounded the corner and she scrambled away, like a cornered cat. "Get away from me. You leave me alone."

The muscles of Michael's neck flexed. He checked over his shoulder. "You need to trust me Sarah, we haven't got long." He pulled a key from his pocket and bent down to her leg. His brown eyes checked hers then heavy footsteps thumped toward the stall.

Michael reared away and stood up tall. Seamus appeared. "Daniel wants her in the courtyard now."

With Seamus at his back, Michael looked at Sarah. Every crevice of his face deepened. Sorrow coloured his eyes. Had he come to help her? Is that why he asked her to trust him?

His face shuttered. He turned to Seamus and shook the key. "And I'm after collecting her, just like Daniel asked."

Michael ignored her while he slipped the key in the padlock, but as he slid the chain from her ankle he whispered, "Riley is gone."

Sarah blinked. Gone? Did Michael mean escaped, or gone as in dead?

Seamus clamped a meaty hand around her wrist and yanked her towards the door. Her gaze shot to Michael, but he'd turned his back. She struggled and dragged against Seamus's grip. She had to get to Michael to ask him what he meant.

She kicked and bucked but Seamus wrenched her sideways and slammed her up on his hip. Her struggle had no effect. She forced her body to go limp, to conserve the energy she had left.

They reached the gate of the compound and Seamus dumped her feet back on the ground then shoved her forward. She fell, landing at a pair of expensive leather boots.

She looked up into Daniel's icy blue glare.

He wrinkled his nose and stepped back. "Ach, Sarah, you've seen better days."

She scoured the courtyard for any sign of rescue, any option for escape. The ruthless indifference of nine sets of eyes burnt through her. Four men she'd never seen before stood at the back of a white van perpendicular to where she lay – feet shoulder width apart, arms folded across their chest, all wearing a uniform of sportswear and trainers.

At Daniel's right side stood Siobhan, haughty glare aimed at Sarah, her presence so small amongst the men, her overdone make up and high heels so out of place.

And yet how hugely she'd made her mark.

Sarah bit down on the surging need to tackle the girl to the ground. There'd be no point. Padric stood at her side. How could the two of them have spent so much time with her son, with all Riley was, and be so unaffected by what they'd done to him?

Seamus and Michael moved in from behind.

Sarah sucked up every bit of courage she could find and clambered to standing. "Charming as always, Daniel. Now would you please release me? We have court today, and I need to get cleaned up."

"You hear that boys?" Siobhan laughed, her desperation to impress, to put herself at the centre of things, almost palpable.

Daniel stepped closer to Sarah, the scent of his spicy cologne an invasion. "There'll be no court today. The plan has changed."

She held his gaze. *The bomb.*

"Couldn't keep your nose out of my business, could you? But it's just as well as I need your assistance."

"There is nothing that could make me help you."

"No?" Daniel paced around her. "Not even if I offer you a trade? Your life for your son's?"

She waited until he stood in front of her again, needing eye contact to read his reaction to her next statement. Her voice vibrating a solid strength she didn't feel, she answered, "You don't have Riley. He is on a plane to Australia as we speak, and Alec is on his way here with the media and Garda in tow. It's over Daniel. Once they get here you're finished. They'll lock you up and throw away the key."

A delighted squeal from Siobhan sent a chill sweeping through Sarah. Daniel's lips stretched in a closed smile. He turned his back on her and walked behind the van.

The air around her went thick.

Daniel reappeared dragging a bloodied Alec by the scruff of his shirt. A cry escaped Sarah's mouth. When Daniel let go, Alec's body crumpled like a rag doll. Motionless and broken.

"I don't think Stone will be troubling us now, do you?"

THIRTY-SEVEN

Sarah dived to Alec, a hiss escaping her mouth when a rock tore a gash in her knee. She ignored the throbbing sting and clambered to his side. Above, powerful winds drove in clouds of battleship grey, darkening the courtyard. Six men moved in her direction, but for Sarah the world had fallen away.

Be alive, Alec. Please be alive.

She bent her cheek to his lips. When a breath brushed against her skin, her eyes welled.

With her hands hovering around his face she took in the damage. Purple bruising swelled around his eyes and nose. Red rivulets smeared across his skin, crusting in pools at his nostrils and mouth. She traced her fingers around the back of his skull. Behind his left ear, she found matted hair, sticky to the touch, and a bulbous lump underneath.

"Alec," she grazed her knuckles down his cheek.

When he didn't respond she bent down to whisper in his ear. "Alec, it's Sarah. Please, I need you to wake."

Warm air skimmed her cheek, but he didn't stir. He was alive but who knew for how long. "It's okay." She pressed her lips lightly to his. "You stay alive, I'll figure something out."

Dark shadows fell over her. Her belly lurched at the stink of cat piss and fuel.

She searched past the circle of men. Past Padric, his expression cold and flinty now he'd abandoned the mask of affability; past a preening Siobhan, overconfident in her own importance amongst the adult men; past Michael who, for a brief moment back in the barn had given her a flicker of hope, but now wouldn't meet her gaze. She gripped Alec's hand and glared at Daniel.

His smirk injected a stab of cold into her blood. "Throw Stone in the van."

"No!" Sarah leapt to her feet, assuming a fighting pose above Alec's body, ready to tear to shreds anyone who tried to touch him. Four of Daniel's men stepped in, each grabbing for one of Alec's limbs. She punched and slapped at them, fighting with everything she had to keep them away. Suddenly large arms locked around her middle and wrenched her from the tussle. Air oomphed from her mouth when she collided with a wall of chest. Michael's citrusy scent filled her sinuses.

"Get off me!" She kicked out. "Get your filthy hands off me!"

Michael gripped tighter. "Stop." He growled in her ear. "You're going to get yourself killed."

She twisted against him. Striking and jabbing anywhere she could. He lifted her feet off the ground.

"You're doing Stone no good. Daniel will kill him now if you don't stop."

Her gaze shot to Daniel's beet red face. His fists were clenched at his side.

Alec landed with a thud in the van's cargo hold. Sarah recoiled at the sickening crunch of bone against metal then went slack.

There was no fighting her way out of this. She inhaled deeply to slow the adrenalin flooding her veins.

Her eyes searched the courtyard and settled on the house. She'd bet her life that's where they had moved Riley.

If he was still alive.

Her breath hitched. What was Daniel's plan for her son? He was the man's nephew, of his blood. Would that be enough to protect Riley once she was dead?

She shrugged from Michael's loosened hold. She needed to do something. Push Daniel. Expose his true character.

If the men saw Daniel break...she scanned the courtyard. Forget Seamus, Padric and Siobhan. But Michael and the other men. They were the key. If she could convince even one to question Daniel's motives or plans, they might help. If not her, then at least Riley. She licked her lips. It was a long shot but what else did she have?

She stepped forward. "Why do you all trust Daniel?"

Seamus drew in a loud hack of saliva.

She crossed her arms, tucking her shaking palms into her armpits. "Don't you realise you're all pawns in his game?"

A gob of spittle thwacked to the ground at her feet.

She forced herself not to flinch. From the corner of her eye she could see Daniel. But his attention wasn't on her. He studied his men, all lined up, looking past her with the impassive stare of soldiers waiting for their next command. A self-satisfied smile tugged at the corner of Daniel's mouth. Then he frowned. His focus had moved to Michael, whose gaze was fixed on Sarah.

Her heart sped up. A chink. Michael's history with her was Daniel's weakness. Time to force a reaction. She lengthened each vertebra.

"Think about it. Liam's been a loyal soldier for years and where is he now? Stuck in jail, framed for a crime he didn't commit." She swivelled to Michael. "And what about you? Haven't you wondered why Daniel brought me here? I was in Australia, no threat on the other side of the world, but he forced me to come back to Belfast. Why? To testify in his court case? I don't think so."

Siobhan slid next to Michael, her fingers curled around his bicep. Panther-like. Possessive. Had Michael slept with the girl who had betrayed his only child?

Michael yanked his arm back, pitching Siobhan away.

Sarah raised her voice, every word shaking with restrained fury. "Daniel knew you had a son, but he kept it from you. Now he is holding him hostage. Riley is yours, Michael. He's Daniel's nephew, but even that won't keep him safe."

Michael's features stayed blank. What the hell was wrong with him, with all of them?

She turned, sweeping her arm in a circle. "Don't you remember Omagh? Even the most loyal republicans couldn't stomach that. And yet Daniel wants you to do it again. Killing innocents will make you lepers. You'll lose. But Daniel won't, not with all his money and connections. He doesn't care about a united Ireland. He doesn't care about family or about you. He's a psychopath, a conman—"

The back of a hand cracked across her face, knocking her to the ground.

Pain slashed through her cheek where Daniel's ring had ripped through the flesh. But what did it matter? He would kill her anyway. Kill Alec, then her, then Riley. Her ribcage heaved.

No, not Riley.

She would make Michael see exactly how unhinged his brother was. She blocked the voice in her head screaming at her to stop and pushed up to her knees.

"See? If I'm not speaking the truth, why is he so angry?"

Daniel glowered, the waves of threat billowing her way.

"He doesn't trust you to make your own decisions. He's not a real leader, or even a real man."

Daniel reached to the back of his trousers.

"Without violence, he is pathetic and weak. He is nothing but a coward, a traitor—" She braced for the fist swinging her way but found herself staring down the black metal barrel of a gun.

THIRTY-EIGHT

"Shut the fuck up!" The pistol shook in Daniel's white-knuckled grip. "Shut up right now or I'll blow your fucking head off."

Every muscle of her body trembled, but she held Daniel's glare. Movement flashed in her peripheral vision. "Daniel, bro, calm down. They were just words."

"I'm no coward or traitor." A swollen vein pulsed in Daniel's neck. Michael stepped in front of Sarah, putting himself between the gun and her head.

"Dan, leave her be. She's talking gobshite."

Daniel's glare sliced to his brother. "Is that so? Bro." His gun hand lowered. "She's after throwing herself on top of another man, a peeler for fuck's sake. He's been screwing her brains out for weeks, but you're still trying to protect her. The bitch destroyed you once already. What the fuck does she have, a shining cunt of gold?"

"Leave it, Daniel. Leave her alone."

"Or what, Michael? What are you going to do? Fuck, you are such a disappointment. For years I've been waiting for you to man up."

Michael went completely still. Then his body swelled in height and width. "I've done everything you asked, Daniel. Everything you demanded. I promised to stand by you if you let Sarah be. And then you kidnap her son? My son? Were you never going to tell me? I've spent the last seventeen years at your beck and call, cleaning up every filthy mess you've gotten into. You're the disappointment. Ma and Pa would hate who you've become."

Daniel's torso arced forward, like he had an invisible leash restraining his waist. "You made sure they didn't trust me."

"Your idiocy got Da lifted."

"And there it is."

"If you hadn't joined the 'RA, the peelers never would have hauled Da in for interrogation. Ma wouldn't have been driving them back from the army barracks. They wouldn't have been there for the accident."

"Da was proud of what I was doing."

"Are you insane? He hated it. He stayed up every night wondering how he could get you to stop. Ma cried herself to sleep every time you slipped out to do a raid."

"No more!" Daniel swung the gun up and pointed it at Michael's chest. Sarah's body flooded with heat. "Pick that bitch up, Michael, and throw her in the van."

"What are you doing? You'll not shoot me."

"I said, pick her up."

"No."

Daniel cocked the slide, unclipped the safety. He wouldn't. Michael was his brother. The only family he had left. "Now!"

Michael crossed his arms. "No."

Daniel's gun hand shook, his fury vibrating through the yard. Each second stretched into the next. His focus jumped from Michael to Sarah.

Her lungs locked.

When his gaze settled on Michael, Daniel pulled in a deep breath. The tension melted from his shoulders.

Her whole world shrunk to the barrel of his gun.

"Ach then, Michael, we'll do it your way."

Light flared, a crack snapped through the air.

Michael jerked back and fell, landing across her legs. The scent of sulphur and fresh blood filled her nose. A high-pitched ringing echoed in her ears. She couldn't move. Her gaze locked on the gun, waiting for it to swing her way, while the sticky wetness of Michael's blood slid down her face.

THIRTY-NINE

Siobhan's scream splintered the shocked silence. She lunged to Michael's side and pulled him from Sarah. "Leave him be!"

"Stop moving him. We have to stem the bleeding, or he'll bleed to death."

"This is your fault. I'll tear your head off if you touch him again." Siobhan's spittle sprayed in a mist across Sarah's face. "Why couldn't you just leave him alone?"

Sarah inched backwards. A tug of war wouldn't help Michael. The crying, ranting girl pulled him to her breast. He groaned. Sarah's hands flew to her mouth to smother her protest.

"You bastard!" Siobhan yelled at Daniel.

"Shut your sister's whining, Seamus, or I will." Daniel wiped the gun back and forth across his thigh, his breaths labouring loud, his nostrils flaring.

Seamus hooked his arms under his sister's armpits and hauled her to the farmhouse. Only when the girl's wailing screams dulled with the closing of the front door did Sarah dare risk scrambling over to Michael again. The sweet scent of his spilt blood hit her like a bat to the belly. His breath gurgled, the sounds of a drowning man. With flat palms she applied pressure to the wound, but warm blood gushed out over her fingers. Too much. Too fast.

She had no idea what to do next. "Please Daniel, ring for an ambulance. You have to help me save him."

Daniel marched back and forth, his gun swinging wildly through the air.

"For God's sake, he is your brother." Her raised voice tore at her vocal cords. "Please!"

She held still while Daniel stared through her.

He stalked away, yelling orders as he disappeared behind the van. Sarah clenched her jaw, damming her erupting scream. She studied Michael. His skin had turned a translucent shade of grey. Her lungs bucked.

Oh God, he was dying.

"I'm so sorry. I didn't know. All these years, you sacrificed everything, and I didn't know." She had to push aside her own regrets, find a way to ease his pain. Edging her legs under his head, she cradled him in her lap.

Michael sucked in another ragged breath.

Gently, she brushed his hair back from his forehead, repeating the motion again and again, soothing him with her palm.

"Remember the night when we convinced Quinn to return to school instead of joining the Belfast Brigade?"

Michael's gaze locked with hers. She forced her lips into a smile. "Remember? We climbed to the peak of Cave Hill."

A shudder racked him.

She cupped his cheek. "It was that night we made our son. In all that hope. Riley got the best of both of us." Her voice caught. "He still is."

"Riley," he whispered.

Her eyes welled, and she nodded. "Your son."

A groan leaked from Michael's mouth.

"Shhh, it's okay."

"He won't stop." Michael's voice, barely audible now, rasped with pain. His eyes clouded over, closed, and then fluttered open again. He strained to find focus, fighting to tell her something.

She bent lower. "What is it?"

"Riley." Michael's taut body softened. His last exhale whispered across her cheek and she felt her son's father, the man she had loved for a lifetime, pass over into death.

Icy droplets of rain splattered on Sarah's skin, drawing her back to the courtyard. Daniel left the van and marched her way. Her body trembled. "What did you do? Michael loved you, he gave you everything."

"Michael gave me nothing."

"He did everything you demanded."

"He never gave up you."

Clarity hit her like a wash of icy water. Daniel would keep on coming, and there was nothing she could do. She stared at her blood-soaked hands. Daniel would kill her, but even then, he wouldn't leave Riley be.

She slid from under Michael's lifeless weight and scrubbed her hands down her jeans. Her gaze turned away from the smears of red, and she swallowed hard. Is that what Michael had meant? *He won't stop.* Did he mean Daniel? The last horror-filled hour replayed in her head. In the barn Michael had said Riley was gone. Just now he kept repeating Riley's name. He'd been trying to tell her something. But what?

Her body vibrated with indecision.

If Riley had escaped, she could surprise Daniel, tackle him for his gun. At least she'd die taking him down. But what if Michael only meant gone from the barn? What if, right now, Riley lay shackled in the house, still vulnerable? If she attacked, Daniel could kill her son. Her only option was to bluff. Force Daniel to reveal Riley to her.

She dragged herself to standing once more and stared into the sharp angles of Daniel's hate-savaged face.

"I've a job for you," he said.

"I want to see my son first. If you allow me to see Riley, I will do whatever you ask of me."

"You'll do as I say, without condition, if you want your son to live." Daniel moved right up into her space. "Riley is mine now. He's no need of you anymore."

Her insides seared with heat and her muscles retracted. Every fibre of her being wanted to charge Daniel, claw his eyes out, beat him into non-existence, but she couldn't. He was goading her. She dug her fingernails into her palms. "What do you want me to do?"

FORTY

At Daniel's demand, she walked towards the van. Drizzle settled its damp weight into her clothes. The muscles of her body protested each step, but she overruled them with pure will. If there was a chance she could save Riley, she had to take it.

The slam of the van's side door jarred through her bones. The vehicle looked innocent enough. Used. Old. White, except for corroded dents and the green lettering across the sides and back – The Garden Whisperer. No one would have a problem with the reek of fertiliser, not when it emanated from a beaten-up gardening van.

When she neared its rear, she craned her neck to study the cargo hold, but Daniel's men drew together, forming a solid wall of muscle. She laid her palm to the vehicle's side panel. *Stay alive, Alec.*

A chill passed between her shoulder blades. Daniel had closed in, his presence hovering scarcely off her back.

"Do you remember when we met?" His voice slithered across her ear. She scoured her memories, her drumming heartbeat muddying her ability to recall. Then it came. She turned. His arms caged her against the van.

She locked her knees, lifted her chin. "You attended my leader training camp. Said you wanted to help kids."

"Before Michael."

"I met him when he came to pick you up."

"I saw you first."

"What? No. We barely spoke at that camp."

"Michael had everything. He wasn't getting you too."

Realisation dawned. This had nothing to do with her, it was all about some sick competition Daniel had with his brother. Her mouth twisted in disgust. Daniel's gaze locked on her lips.

Before she had time to react, he smashed his mouth on hers. She tried to push him away, but he ground in further, his teeth bruising her lips. Boiling fury surged up from her feet. He rammed his tongue in her mouth, and she bit down, drawing blood. Daniel grasped her head and cracked it back into the steel wall of the van. Pain radiated through her skull.

"You weren't worth it. Michael should have listened to me."

She lurched at him, fists flying.

Daniel's right hand punched through her flailing arms and seized her neck. She froze. The vee between his thumb and forefinger jammed into her windpipe. Any harder, and she wouldn't be able to breathe.

The back door of the van slammed shut.

"It's ready," Seamus called out.

Daniel released his grip and stepped away. Sarah bent forward, gasping and coughing for air.

"Get in." Daniel threw open the driver's door and gestured to the seat.

A pungent slap of fuel and fertiliser rammed down her bruised throat. Her feet wouldn't move.

"You're driving this here bomb through the front doors of Victoria Square Shopping Centre. The ones directly opposite Laganside Courts."

"No." She staggered back, her head agitating side to side.

"Get her son out here. Now!"

Padric turned and marched into the house.

"As soon as Riley steps out that door he is dead." Daniel withdrew the pistol he had used to kill Michael. "No begging, no second chances." He released the safety. "I will shoot him on sight."

Every one of her organs wedged under her chin. Bonds of family, of blood, meant nothing to Daniel. A burning sensation filled her eyes. She had no choice. She could not watch her son die.

"Tell him to stop. I'll get in. I'll get in!" She climbed up onto the seat. A locking sound clicked, terror paralysed every muscle.

"You just depressed a weight-activated sensor connected to the bomb. If you lift so much as one arse cheek, it'll blow." Daniel leaned in. "Check your watch."

Buzzing droned in her ears, but she did as she was told. 8:15 am.

"The device will detonate in seventy-five minutes. If you've not smashed into the centre by then, I'll put a bullet through your son's head."

She gripped the steering wheel with shaking hands.

"And then I'll go after your girls."

Her right hand slid to the ignition.

"That's it." He nodded as she twisted the key. Fat drops of rain thwacked on the windscreen.

"You see a battle is all about how far someone will go. That's why I always win." He braced his arms across the top of the doorframe. "And so, we come to the rest of my plan."

The rest?

"This attack is a practice run. I've the supplies for twelve more bombs. In one month's time, all across the cities of England and the North, simultaneous explosions will bring the Brits to their knees. Then we will win this war for good." He angled closer. "And you, Sarah, will be remembered for starting it all."

FORTY-ONE

Sarah steered the van down the potholed and puddled driveway, every bump and bounce rattling her rigid body. At the junction with the pebbled lane she braked to a stop and risked twisting her upper torso to check on Alec. All she could see were the toes of his bound feet.

"Alec? Can you hear me?"

She strained to detect anything – a cry, a groan – but the pelting rain drowned out all sound. The wipers slashed across the windscreen, back and forth, closing her in. She emptied her lungs and fought for control. She couldn't let Max's and Michael's sacrifice be for nothing.

Inching the van out onto road she scanned for anyone who could help. But the rain had driven everyone indoors. She drove and drove, not passing another car. She swallowed against the coppery taste on her tongue. It wasn't supposed to end this way.

Green paddocks flashed past until she reached an intersection. Sarah glanced at the time. 8:25 am. A trail of sweat slid down her backbone. Left to Dublin, right to Belfast. She wiped clammy hands down her legs and turned right. The rain lightened over the next few kilometres, allowing her a clearer view of the surrounding fields and woodland. Up ahead, she recognised a two-lane road. The last one before the motorway. She tried to picture herself driving at full speed into the glass doors of the shopping centre, but the image refused to form.

Off to her right, on the shoulder of the road, a patch of dirt backed onto a thicket of silver birch. She eased her foot onto the brake and turned in, wincing when the van jostled over a large rock. Bringing the vehicle to a complete stop, she left the engine idling.

Now what?

She stared, unseeing, at the trees. She should drive to a police station. But what if they couldn't diffuse the bomb? They'd die and the people in the surrounding houses would too.

Heat swirled in her gut.

She had to do something. Warn someone about the rest of Daniel's plan. But how? She was trapped, and if she weren't in Belfast on time, he'd definitely kill Riley. Her vision blurred. The burning inside her flared to white-hot flame. She hit her fists against the wheel, and a scream ripped through the flesh of her throat.

A loud bang from behind silenced her. Her gaze snapped to the rear vision mirror.

"Alec?"

He kicked his bound feet against the rear door again. The van rocked.

"Alec, stop!"

"There's a bomb, Sarah. Get out of the van."

"I can't. My seat is booby trapped."

"My vision's blurry. I can't read the timer. Do you know how long's left?"

"Fifty-one minutes."

Silence. Her pulse skipped. That last sentence, he'd slightly slurred his words. She couldn't let him pass out again.

"Alec? Did you hear me?"

"The bomb's secured to the van. I'm checking for tripwires." He bashed against the metal floor and walls as he twisted his bound body about. She stilled, ears alert for the clink or snap of another trigger. He met her stare in the mirror. "I can't see any. I'm going to break the doors open, okay?"

"Okay."

There was a grunt followed by the pounding of his feet against the back doors. Her shoulders bunched higher and higher with each bang.

The sounds of twittering birds and distant traffic flooded the van. She drew in a huge breath. Alec would escape the blast. He could still get to Riley and prevent the other bombs.

The sounds of violent retching sent a chill through her. She wound down the window.

"Alec. Alec!"

Thudding jumps came up the side of the van, then he slouched into her door - his swollen face flushed with effort and lined with pain. "Are you okay?" he asked.

"I couldn't stop him, Alec. He killed Michael, and I never found Riley." Her voice caught. "Daniel said he'd shoot him if I refused to drive the bomb to Belfast. But I can't murder innocent people." Her hands covered her face. "I can't."

"Daniel doesn't have Riley."

"What?" Sarah's head jerked up.

"Michael got him out minutes after I sighted him in the barn. Quinn helped."

"Quinn?"

"Michael has sheltered him from the IRA ever since you left. Quinn already has Riley across the Irish Sea."

"Can he be trusted?"

"Michael had no doubts. They've been working together all along to protect both you and Riley.

"How do you know?"

"He snuck in to see me, just after I was captured, and told me himself. The day you turned up in Quinn's bar asking for Liam, Quinn rang Michael."

"That's why Michael came to my room straight after. But why didn't he just tell me?"

"I don't know, but by keeping you in the dark, he did keep you safe. Daniel didn't suspect something was going on. Not until the end."

Sarah pressed her palms together and held them at her lips. "So, Michael saved our son?"

Alec nodded. "And stayed behind to rescue you."

Her head tipped back against the seat rest. Michael had saved Riley. Because of him their son would live. Her eyes brimmed with tears. Daniel was wrong. She might die, but she had won.

Alec's upper arms bulged with effort, fighting the restraints holding his hands behind his back.

"Sarah, I need a sharp rock to cut these zip ties. But I'll be straight back, okay?" He shuffled to the trees – beaten, bloodied and bruised but still fighting.

She closed her eyes. Daniel believed he would win because he was prepared to go as far as it took. But just like he'd underestimated his brother, he had underestimated her. She'd sworn to do anything to keep her children safe. Trade everything to protect them from harm. It was time to honour that oath.

FORTY-TWO

Alec staggered from the tree line. He wrenched open her
door and stopped, palms braced on the door jamb.

"Your seat's booby trapped? Are you sure?"

"I heard the sensor click when Daniel forced me in the
van."

"I'm going to check, okay?"

Without waiting for her answer, he crouched down on his
knees and looked under her seat. He leant closer. The twin lines
between his brows deepened. "Goddamn it!" His hands ripped
through his hair and he stood.

"It's okay, Alec."

"It's not fucking okay." He charged around the back of the
van. It pitched and rattled when he climbed in. Her hands
clenched in her lap

"What are you doing?"

"Diffusing the bomb."

She couldn't see what he was doing in the mirror, only his

curved back as he bent into the bomb. His muttering and cursing increased. She held her breath trying not to think of what would happen if he touched the wrong thing.

"Have you done this before?"

"In training."

"But have you ever actually done it?"

"Not live."

She stared at the oval shaped badge on the steering wheel. The fingers of her left hand reached for her mother's ring and twirled it round and round. She knew what she had to do. It was the only choice. She blew out a deep breath.

Alec had gone quiet. His gaze locked to hers in the mirror. "I have to call in the bomb squad."

"How? Daniel took our phones. We're in the middle of nowhere."

"I'll flag down a car or find a house."

"There's only twenty minutes left. Even if you find a phone, the squad won't make it. I have to drive the van deeper into the woods."

"But then the bomb will go off. I won't stand by and watch you die. We have to get you out."

He came back around to the door and knelt on the ground beside her. But even if he managed to disconnect the sensor, what then? Daniel would never give up. While he had breath in his body, he'd keep on coming for her. And for her kids. Even jail wouldn't get in his way. And then there were the other bombs.

Alec looked up at her. Sweat beaded above his lip. "How much longer?"

She checked her watch, eighteen minutes. "Alec, enough."

He crouched forward, getting as close as he could to whatever lay under her seat.

"Alec. Stop."

"Fuck it." He reared to his feet. "I'll find some rocks. We can replace your weight with theirs."

"What if you get the balance wrong?"

"I have to try."

"It's over."

"No. I can't lose you too."

She had to take control of this. Make him see there was no other way. "Come here."

He leant in, his pupils huge, pleading.

She held his face in her hands. "I am so grateful for everything you've done." Her thumbs caressed his cheekbones. "I need you to live, to tell my children how much I love them. I left letters in your office. Please make sure they get them."

"Don't give up on me, Sarah. I can do this, I'm getting you out."

"There's only seventeen minutes left."

He stepped away, rubbing his mouth with an open palm.

"Listen to me. Daniel has twelve more bombs. He's going to detonate them all over Britain. If I drive this bomb back to the farm, I can take him and his supplies out. He'll be gone for good, won't hurt anyone else."

"There has to be another way."

"Unless I stop him, he'll keep on coming. Riley and the girls will never be safe."

His chest caved in on itself, and his shoulders rose and fell. When he looked back up a vein had swelled in his forehead. "I can't just let you die."

"Alec, I'm just one life."

He crouched down to check again under the seat.

She stroked her palm across the crown of his head. "If I had done the right thing and reported Gerry's murder when it happened, we wouldn't be here now. Michael and Max and Olivia wouldn't be dead."

"But it wasn't your fault."

"I won't lose anyone else."

He looked up into her eyes. "Please don't make me do this."

She masked the ache tearing at her with a faint smile. "There is no other way." She removed her mother's wedding ring and curled his fingers around it.

"Give this to my girls." Her throat burnt. She was leaving them alone. Riley too. Would they ever forgive her? "Promise you'll watch over my children?"

His hand balled into a fist.

"Alec, please."

He lowered his chin but gave a jerky nod, and then pocketed the ring.

She combed back his hair. When he reached for her wrist, she wrapped her hand at the back of his neck and pulled him up to meet her lips. His fingers pressed into the flesh of her cheeks as he held on with both hands and deepened the kiss. She slid her palm from his bunched shoulders, down his chest, flattening it over his thumping heart and gently pulled away. "I have to leave."

The muscles of his throat convulsed. He angled back and pushed the door closed. But his fingers gripped the window frame tight.

"If I could swap places—"

The corners of her mouth lifted, and she shook her head. "I wouldn't let you."

She put the van into gear. Alec stepped back, arms clutching his head.

Sarah tore her focus from him, pressed her foot to the accelerator and swung the van towards the farm.

FORTY-THREE

On her final turn, the smooth bitumen narrowed to a pebbled lane. The sun pushed through the empty clouds, its golden rays warming the morning gloom. She drove on, the cab of the van vibrating and humming around her. The roadway thinned again, its hedges like landing lights guiding her in. Darts of energy pulsed from her feet, up her calves, through her core and zinged out her fingertips. What she wouldn't give to go on just one more run. To experience the freedom it brought one last time.

Barrelling back down the lane to the farm she kept a keen eye on the clock. With each closing metre her heartbeat slowed.

Two minutes to go.

She brought the van to a halt at the bottom of the driveway and unhooked her seatbelt. A strange stillness settled over her. Daniel McNaulty would do no more harm.

Thirty seconds to go.

She gripped the steering wheel and floored it up the hill.

Her left hand pressed down on the horn.

Twenty seconds to go.

Daniel and his men charged into the courtyard, guns drawn. They froze with baffled impotence.

Ten seconds to go.

She closed her eyes and pictured her children safe and re-united.

Five seconds to go.

She met Daniel's disbelieving stare and mouthed, "It's over."

Two seconds to go.

She unlatched her door and dived.

Kilometres away, the ground shook under Alec's feet. A moment's pause, then another blast. The mushroom cloud of fire, black smoke and debris drove him to his knees.

A continent away, Riley disembarked from his flight into the terminal at Frankfurt Airport. He tried calling his mother's phone, but it went straight to message bank. Bewildered, he dialled again.

A world away, outside a caravan parked somewhere in central New South Wales, Evan, Felicity, Doug and Wendy huddled around the phone. Riley was on the line, safe and on his way back to Australia. Relief and celebration swept the group. Until Riley asked if they had heard from his mum.

FORTY-FOUR

After a day of questions at the station, Alec was dropped home. He stumbled through the door of his study and lurched for a bottle of whiskey. Throwing the cap aside he guzzled straight from its neck. The amber liquid blazed down his throat, but still he shivered with cold. He drained another slug, allowed his eyes to close. The stink of gasoline and smoke wafted from his clothes.

He charged forward and flung the window wide open, sucking in deep hacks of the cold night air. A shudder shook him, and he slumped onto the chair. Four envelopes lay in a line on his desk.

Shifting upright, he pushed the whisky bottle aside and reached for the envelope labelled with his name. He removed a single sheet of paper.

Dear Alec,
   If you are reading this, it means you made it out, and

for that I am so thankful. In such a short space of time you gave me so much. You taught me to believe again, in other people and in myself.

Please take these letters to my children. Tell them how much I loved them, and if you can, keep watch over them. Especially Riley. No one but you will understand what he has endured.

My last request is an oath that I want you to swear to right now. When you are ready, promise you'll go out into the world and embrace the fullness of life, all its joys, blessings and challenges. Don't let my legacy be your withdrawal from everything that matters. Live Alec, love again, be happy in life, for me.

With Love,

Sarah

Alec held the paper between his hands, staring out into the dark. After a long while he refolded it into the envelope, laid it back in place and retreated to the shower upstairs. When he had washed the grime of the day away, he threw his black smeared clothes in the bin, seized the letters and headed back to the intensive care waiting room.

That damn woman could deliver the letters herself.

FORTY-FIVE

Sarah hobbled about the private hospital room, throwing the last of her toiletries into her case. Her leg ached from the plaster boot weighing down her foot, but she wouldn't waste any more time. She'd fought hard for release from the hospital. After three long weeks she needed to get back to her kids.

"What do you think you're doing?" Alec entered the room, gripped her elbow and sat her on the bed.

"Packing."

"I said I'd help you with that."

"I know, but I just want to get out of here before they change their minds."

"You're that eager to be away?"

"My kids need me. Evan said Riley is recovering okay, but I need to see for myself."

"It's only been three weeks. Two weeks ago, you were still in intensive care."

"The doctors have given me written permission to fly."

"But your lungs—"

"Are healed enough. The specialist said in a year there'll be no sign of damage. And before you ask, the pin in my ankle is healing. The orthopaedic surgeon has referred me to a specialist in Sydney for follow up."

"And your ears? What about the pressure on the plane?"

"The ringing could stay for months. The doctors wouldn't let me fly if it was too risky."

He stepped in, tucked a strand of hair behind her ear. "I don't think they could say no to you."

"Alec, I have to go home."

"Of course, of course." He stood back tall, hands shoved in his pockets. "I just wish you'd let me come with you."

"I've paid a nurse, I'll be fine." Sarah patted the bed and, once he sat, turned her torso to him.

"Before I leave, I wanted to thank you for everything you've done for me."

He lifted his chin but maintained eye contact. "That sounds like a goodbye."

"I live in Australia. My family, my life, everything is there."

"I could take time off and—"

Sarah shook her head, clasped her hands together in her lap. "I've made so many mistakes. I have to focus my energy and attention on my children. Get Riley fully healed, help him deal with what he saw happen to Max. I don't want my son's life destroyed because of what I let happen to him."

"It wasn't your fault."

"I need to explain everything, including Michael. I can't let anything distract me from that." The words hung in the air.

"And I'm a distraction."

"You're an incredible man who deserves a committed partner. That's not me, it's not in my future."

"When I've sorted out the mess of this case, I'll come visit. Maybe then—"

"No, Alec. I am so grateful for everything you did, for what we shared, but I think it's best if we make a clean break. You need to move on."

His chest rose and fell with the effort of containing whatever he was thinking. He sighed. "You're wrong about this Sarah, about us, but I'll respect your wishes." He stood. "When you come to your senses, find me. I'll be waiting."

Her lips pinched together, and she turned to zip up her bag. He needed to forget her, not wait. She'd never be the woman for him. For anyone.

Standing, she braced herself for further argument, but Alec skimmed his hands down her arms and leant in. Her eyes fluttered closed, and his lips brushed her left cheek. She held her breath as his warmth disappeared. When she opened her eyes, he was almost at the door.

He stared back to her, his face tight, his scar pinched up with the effort of control. "Take care of yourself, Sarah."

FORTY-SIX

Sᴠᴅɴᴇʏ, Aᴜsᴛʀᴀʟɪᴀ. Tᴡᴏ ʏᴇᴀʀs ʟᴀᴛᴇʀ.

Sarah pushed off from the ocean pool's wall and revelled in the muted silence of the glide. Her tinnitus had cleared months ago, but the absence of the ringing was still pure bliss. She surfaced to finish her last of forty laps. At the end, she gripped the wall and heaved in air. Gentle waves lapped over the edge of the swim lane as the soundscape of children and seagulls squawking returned to her ears. She rotated her left ankle in the water. It ached where they'd secured the bone with a pin, but her range of motion was improving.

Using the metal handrails to exit the pool she walked to the grass area where she'd left her things. Riley stood there holding out her towel, a hesitant smile on his face. He was tanned, and the gaunt look that had pinched his features for so long was finally beginning to fade.

"Well this is a lovely surprise." Sarah reached up and kissed his cheek. "How did training go?"

"It's good to be back on the field, finding my feet again."

"No pun intended?"

Riley rolled his eyes good-humouredly. "Coach is pretty sure I'll be ready to try out for the state squad in Feb, as long as I can manage the load with university."

"Any more thoughts on that?" Sarah dried her hair with the towel.

"Actually, it's what I came down here to talk to you about. The future and stuff." Riley rubbed the back of his neck. "I've been talking through my options in therapy, and I came to a decision this week."

"Okay." A gust of wind blew, and Sarah shivered.

"Why don't you get changed first?" Riley held out her bag. "I'll meet you over there." He pointed to an empty wooden bench down the path, facing the water.

Sarah walked to the amenities block and redressed in her work clothes. Her stomach tightened with nerves. She could tell by the way he was talking he had something serious to discuss. But at least he'd come to her. For the past two years, she had made it clear she was there for him. To question, to blame. And therapy had definitely helped them both. Although she wished the concern she spotted every time he looked her way would disappear. He didn't need to protect her, that was her job.

Throwing her swimmers and towel in her bag she hurried from the change room towards her son. Whatever he had to discuss, she had to show him that she was strong.

He squinted. "Your limp is barely noticeable now."

"It's always better after I swim."

"How's the rehab going?"

"Good."

"That's good."

A flock of seagulls cawed and fought over chips being thrown to them by the man on the next bench. Riley gnawed at the corner of his thumbnail.

"Honey," Sarah patted his leg, "it's okay. Whatever you want to talk about, just take a breath and get it out."

"I don't want to upset you."

"I won't break. I'm much tougher than I look."

"I know but after everything that—"

"We both had things to deal with after what happened, but I promise I'm fine." She bumped his shoulder. "And I'm still your overbearing, bossy mum, so spit it out."

"I want to get a gravestone made for my birth father."

Sarah's heart skittered. "They didn't find Michael's body, honey."

"I know, but we could get a memorial plaque made for him. I researched. They could add it to his parent's gravesite."

Sarah focused on a wave crashing, the white foam rushing to the shore then retreating from the sand.

"It's a lovely idea. I'm sure Quinn would help get it organised. He could send over photos when it's done."

"That's the thing, Mum, I want to be there when the plaque is unveiled. I need to be there in person. He was my father, and I didn't get to thank him for what he did."

"He did it to protect you. He wouldn't expect you to go back over there."

"Except that's exactly what I need to do. To put everything to rest, before I move onto university and law and

335

stuff. My counsellor said she thought it was the right move."

She forced breath in and out, just like the therapist had her practise. After a few rounds, the grip on her ribs gave way. She was able to drop her shoulders into place. Her own counsellor had suggested returning to Belfast, placing a line under everything in order to move on.

"What does your Dad think about all of this?"

"He agrees with the psychologist that it would help, but he had two conditions. We have to confirm that it is absolutely safe for me to be there. Dad was going to contact Detective Stone for me."

Sarah rubbed at a mark on her pants, ignoring the twinge in her chest. "And the other?"

"That you are one hundred percent on board and comfortable."

"You're eighteen. I couldn't stop you even if I wanted to."

"I know, but I want you to be okay. In fact, what I really want, what I'm really hoping, is that you'll come with me. That we can do this together."

Sarah leant forward, elbows to knees, hands tented over her mouth. Far above the horizon, the first star had appeared in the still-light sky. She checked her watch. "If you can pick up the girls from dance, I'll go and talk to Dad."

"And?"

"And as long as the trip is deemed safe, I would be honoured to accompany you. I'm so proud of the way you've dealt with things, honey, with everything." Riley wrapped his arm around her shoulders and pulled her into a side hug.

"I'm so happy you're coming."

"You better get a wriggle on, or you'll have to deal with Ally's wrath for being late."

"Love you, Mum."

"Love you, too."

Sarah's lungs expanded to their full depth and released. It was just like Riley to confront things head on. It was time she did the same.

She fished her mobile out of the bag and dialled. After two rings, he answered. "Evan, can I come over?"

Felicity answered the door wearing a floaty dress of yellow and a wide smile. "Hello!" She leant in and gave Sarah a hug. "We still on for girl's movie night tomorrow?"

"Can't wait." If someone had told Sarah two years ago that her ex-husband's wife would become one of her closest friends, she'd have scoffed. But Felicity had been a gift to their family. She had gone above and beyond in supporting them all through recovery, and their friendship had grown into one of shared secrets and many a laugh.

"Fantastic. I'll pick you up at 6:30 pm, then we can swing past and grab Yasmine." Felicity stepped back allowing Sarah to enter the house. Standing next to her Sarah felt like some kind of Amazonian, especially now, when Felicity had foregone her normal heels.

"Evan, Sarah's here!" Felicity closed the door and led Sarah through the beautifully renovated Edwardian home. In the kitchen, fabric samples were strewn all over the table. "How's the new collection going?"

"We're really happy with it. Did you see the top I gave Ally last week? That's already sold out."

Sarah's gaze drifted to the balcony that overlooked Bondi Beach.

"So, this talk you're having with Evan, is it a wine, champagne or coffee kind of discussion?" She weighed a crystal glass in one hand and a ceramic mug in the other.

"Definitely wine."

Felicity poured two glasses, handed both to Sarah and gathered up the scattered material in her arms. Sarah tilted a glass in her direction.

"You can stay if you like. This will end up involving you, I'm sure."

"Thanks, but I think I'll leave the two of you to it. For now, at least." Felicity left the room.

"Sarah." Evan's warm voice came from behind her. She turned and smiled. It was good to see him looking so relaxed in jeans and a slogan T-shirt. He gave her a quick peck on the cheek.

"Salty," he smacked his lips together. "You must have come straight from swimming." He took the offered glass of wine. "How's the ankle going?"

"Better. They've reduced my weight sessions to four times a week, and as long as I swim and walk each day, I'm almost ready to give up hydro."

"That must be a relief."

He gestured to the seats placed next to each other on the balcony. The few clouds above the ocean glowed with hues of orange and pink. Sarah sipped at her glass. "So I suppose you know why I'm here."

Evan nodded.

"What do you think about Riley's idea, honestly?"

"I spoke to his therapist, with Riley's permission of course. She thinks it's what he needs."

"I can't move past the danger. From Daniel's family and others. Would he be safe?"

"That was my first concern too, but I spoke to Alec and—"

"I didn't know you two were in contact."

"Off and on. When you were in the hospital, he kept us up-to-date on your progress. And we've swapped a few emails since, whenever Riley had questions he needed answered."

"I wish he'd trusted me enough to ask."

"He didn't want to upset you, Sarah. He blamed himself for what happened. The physical pain you were in. And Max."

"I told him it wasn't his fault."

"I know, but he believed if he hadn't gone to Dublin—"

"He was a child. It was my actions—"

"We've all taken too big a share of blame. The most important thing now is to move forward."

"You're right. I just hate that he's carrying around any burden."

They both sipped at their red wine, looking out at the purple shades now tinting the gossamer clouds.

He placed his glass on the table. "Alec asked about you, you know. When I spoke with him." Her breathing paused. She lifted her drink back to her lips. "You deserve to be happy, too, Sarah. You are so focused on all of us, making sure we are all okay, but—"

"Relationships and I just don't work."

"But—"

"Please Evan, I don't want to talk about it."

He sighed and his shoulders dropped. "Okay."

"What did Alec say about the safety of Riley returning?"

"Apparently Daniel's wife and children moved to Spain to escape the media and backlash after his death."

"There's still the Superintendent and Fairview and Morton and all the other corrupt police we don't even know about."

"That's what Alec has spent the last two years investigating. He exposed a gang of corrupt officers working for organised crime, which led to convictions and a purge of both the PSNI and the Garda. The ex-officers you mentioned are all in jail. As is Siobhan's Dad."

"What about Padric's family, some of them—"

"His wife and kids moved to Dingle to live with her mother. There is no one else."

"So Alec thinks it would be safe?"

"He swore on his life that neither of you would come to harm. Will you go with Riley?"

"I couldn't bear to let him go on his own. I just hope I can stay strong for him."

"You are one of the strongest people I know, Sarah."

"And the girls? Ally's barely forgiven me for last time I left."

"They are more resilient than you give them credit for. As long as we are honest with them about why you're going, and they know without a doubt you will be safe, they'll be fine."

"And you? Does it bother you that Riley wants to honour Michael?"

"I always knew he wasn't mine, biologically speaking."

"You're still his dad."

Evan smiled. "Riley said the same." He removed his glasses,

cleaned the lenses with his shirt, and returned them to his face. He shifted back in his seat. "I would like to know one thing."

"Yes?"

"Why didn't you confide in me when you came back in '97? Instead of saying you were pregnant from a one-night stand. I still would have adopted Riley, you know."

She reached for his forearm and squeezed. "I was scared and ashamed. I'm so sorry. You deserved better."

"I was angry with you at first. But Felicity helped me understand. You thought you were protecting us all by keeping us in the dark." He took up his red wine and looked at her. "I just hope you realise now that you don't have to do everything on your own. I can come to Belfast too, if you need me there for support."

"It's Riley and me that need to go. The girls will need you here."

"You're doing the right thing."

She smiled and shook her head. "What did I do to deserve you in my life?"

"You gave me three gorgeous kids. Speaking of which," he stood, "Riley should have the girls back here any minute. Why don't you all stay for dinner? We could get pizza?"

"I'd love that." She caught his wrist as he walked past. "Thank you, Evan."

FORTY-SEVEN

"Your destination is 200 metres ahead."

Sarah muted the posh English voice of the navigation system and drove up the last of the incline leading to St Mary parish. She glanced over to check on Riley, but his head was turned away, facing the stone wall lining the side of the road. She had to keep telling herself he needed this, or she'd turn the car around, to save him from the pain.

A whitewashed church came into view and Sarah straightened. They'd agreed to meet Quinn here, at the top of the stairs, so he could lead them to Michael's parents' plot. She pulled into a parking spot and switched off the engine.

Neither she nor Riley moved. Instead they stared out at the town in the distance and into the light-grey sky hovering above.

Her mouth dried. Alec would be at the plot site. She would greet him as she would any old acquaintance. Shake his hand, ask how he was. She wound her scarf about her neck.

"You okay, Mum?"

"I'm the one who is supposed to be asking you that."

"I know this must be hard."

"Honey, I wouldn't be anywhere else." Riley unclipped his seatbelt. She reached over and touched her palm to his leg. "I'm so in awe of you, facing your fears after everything you experienced. You have a much better handle on life than I did at your age." Sarah threaded her fingers through his and squeezed. "Michael would be so proud of the man you've become. Max would too."

Riley swallowed. After a moment of silence, he sighed, and gave her a brief smile. "Shall we do this?"

"Let's go."

The door flew open hard in the strong wind. She tucked her flying hair into her scarf then hooked her arm through Riley's offered elbow. They rounded the corner, and Quinn's face broke into a warm smile. "Ach, I was about to send the cavalry."

Sarah left Riley's side and gave Quinn a bear hug. Over his shoulder her gaze came to rest on Alec. He stood off to the side, straight-backed in a deep-blue suit and striped tie. He was exactly as she remembered, except for the slightly longer hair. His stare met hers.

She blinked away and retreated from Quinn's hug. Riley walked over to Alec and offered his hand.

"Detective Stone? It's so good to meet you, sir, after all our talks on the phone."

"You too, but enough of the 'sir', okay? Call me Alec."

His lopsided smile sent a flutter to Sarah's belly. She

brushed her palms down her coat and turned to Quinn. "Is Liam not coming?"

"No, his boss couldn't find another mechanic to replace his shift. But he'll be at dinner tonight."

Quinn stepped from Sarah and pulled Riley into his arms. She couldn't make out what Riley said but Quinn's large hands slapped her son's back in warmth and pulled him in tighter. The two had stayed in regular contact, ever since Quinn got Riley out of the country on that awful day. Lines of strain dulled Quinn's smile. Sarah swallowed. This day was important to him as well. Michael had been his mentor and a huge loss from his life.

"Sarah."

Her heart raced. Alec had moved in next to her. She pasted on a smile. "Thank you for coming today. It means so much to Riley."

His gaze searched her face, then he nodded and moved away.

"The caretaker has everything prepared. Shall we?" Quinn directed them to the stairs.

Sarah took Riley's arm again, and they followed the others down. Riley rolled his shoulders. She turned to look at her son. He had dressed so carefully this morning - the dark suit, the navy tie. "You're very quiet. You okay?"

"I'm kinda nervous, which is weird."

"I don't think it's weird. It's a lot to process."

"I guess."

The old fields of weathered stone and towering ornate crosses gave way to more organised, systematic rows and sections where the markers rose no further than a metre high.

Sarah pulled her son's arm in closer as Quinn came to a stop. The double plot was headed with a gravestone engraved to Nancy and Sean McNaulty. The interior area was overlaid with small pebbles, and in the middle sat a covered plaque. Sarah's hand lifted with Riley's deep breath. Alec closed in on her son's other side.

Quinn indicated the muslin covering, acknowledging Sarah's slight head shake when he shifted his attention to Riley. "You gonna do the honours?"

Her son knelt one knee on the ground and drew away the white material to reveal a shiny black square of marble. His finger traced the engraving.

Michael McNaulty
You gave us life, you gave us hope
Gone, but not forgotten

An ache hit the back of Sarah's throat. Riley's chin dropped to his chest, and she placed her hand on his back. When he opened his mouth to speak, nothing came out. His shoulders shuddered. Sarah's gaze searched out Alec's, pleading.

He cleared his throat. "I was wrong about you, McNaulty. You were a good man. Thank you for trying to protect me in that basement. I wish I could've done the same for you."

Riley's head stayed lowered.

Sarah exchanged a look with Quinn, who undid his coat and moved in to fill the spot Alec had vacated.

"Michael, it was an honour to know you. Thank you for everything you did when I was a kid, helping me become the man I am today. I promise to continue your work with the youth centre. Rest in peace, brother."

Sarah inhaled, the scent of freshly-cut grass filling her nostrils. She spoke through the thickness in her throat. "Michael, I can never thank you enough for what you did, the sacrifice you made. I'm sorry I didn't believe in you more. That I never gave you an opportunity to get to know your son. I regret that so much. Rest in peace *mo chroi*."

Sarah crouched and wrapped her arms around Riley's shoulders.

After a minute he eased from her hold and wiped his tears away. His voice came out clear and strong. "I wish I'd known who you were when you snuck me out of that house. I was scared and hurt, and terrified for my mum, and you and Quinn saved me. I will be forever grateful.

Thank you also for keeping my Mum safe—I would have broken without her." Riley's Adam's apple bobbed. It took all of Sarah's strength not to reach for her son.

"I'm lucky to have had two fathers– one who raised me and one who stepped up when I needed him the most." Riley cleared his throat. "While I didn't get much time with you, you played a huge role in who I am today, and the man I want to be. I'm going to study international law, just like you. And I swear I will do everything in my power to live a life you would be proud of. Thank you for giving me the chance." He placed his hand on the plaque then stood.

Sarah gathered her son into her arms, and they held onto each other tight. When his breathing settled Sarah reached into her pocket and placed a ring in Riley's hand. A cool hard silver band with two hands embracing a heart.

"This was the engagement ring Michael gave me. It was given to his mother by his Dad, and to his grandmother by his grandfather before that." She closed his fingers around it. "He would want you to have it."

Riley kissed Sarah's cheek. "I want to stay a while longer, spend some time alone with him. Is that okay?"

"Whatever you need, honey."

He sank back to his knees at the grave. Sarah stepped away, turning to Quinn who stood off to the side. When she searched further afield, her stomach twisted.

"He's gone." Quinn waved towards the exit. "Left when you were handing over the ring."

Sarah cleared her throat. "Was he okay?"

Quinn shrugged. "Why don't you find him and ask him yourself?"

"I don't think he'd be interested in talking to me."

"You might be surprised."

Sarah adjusted her scarf. Stepped foot to foot.

"What about you?" Quinn asked.

"The kids are settled, especially now I'm spending less time with rehab."

He gave her a sideways look and shook his head. "That's not what I mean, but sure you knew that."

"I wanted to thank you again for everything you did for me and my family. Getting Riley out safely, watching over me in intensive care."

"You're welcome, but it wasn't me who barely left your side when you were in that coma."

"I couldn't stay, Quinn, you know that. My children had been through hell. I had to go home and help everyone heal."

"And today? It looks to me as if Riley is doing well. And you yourself said the girls were settled. So, what's your excuse for not living your own life now?"

"There's no point. I live on the other side of the world."

He re-buttoned his coat, adjusted the collar. "He's moving, you know. No clue where but his house is for sale, and he's taken a year's leave from work."

Quinn's words played over in her head on the long trip back to Belfast. If she didn't act now, she'd lose the chance forever. Sarah pulled up outside the hotel and turned to her son. "Riley? Will you be okay if I visit someone for a while?"

He shrugged. "I was going to have a sleep anyway. The jetlag's catching up."

"You have my number if you need me." She passed him the hotel key. "I'll be back before we have to leave for dinner. Love you."

"Love you too. And Mum?"

"Yes?"

"Good luck."

Sarah's face warmed. She gave him a quick wave and drove off.

Sarah turned the rented Renault into the driveway, passing the "For Sale" sign and the beautifully restored garden. Gravel crunched under the car's braking tyres. She switched the engine off and licked her lips, wishing she'd gone into the hotel to change. Then she laughed. He'd had seen her in a much worse state than this.

She checked her face in the mirror, wiped away the mascara

that had run, then exited the car and climbed the stairs. When she lifted her hand to knock the door swung inwards. Alec's gaze swept over her, settling on her eyes.

Sarah cleared her throat. "You left without saying goodbye."

He remained silent, and her feet shifted on the spot. "Quinn said you were moving, that you're taking a year off?"

Alec's focus didn't move from her face.

She gestured to the garden. "The house looks amazing."

He leant against the door frame. "What do you want, Sarah?"

Looking to the ground, she took a breath. Everyone kept telling her it was time to live again. To take a risk. What was the worst that could happen?

She met his gaze. "I want to go for a drink with you."

He stared a moment, expression unchanged, then the corners of his mouth lifted. "It's your shout."

AUTHOR'S NOTE

When I landed in Northern Ireland in 1997, I arrived as a naive aid worker with dreams of changing the world. Very quickly it became clear how little understanding I had of The Troubles (as the Northern Irish conflict was known). Oh, I'd done all the reading, researching the history, delving into the culture of memoirs and music; after all, U2 had been my favourite band in the eighties. I thought I understood all the nuances, until I experienced living there.

At first it felt so oppressive, being under surveillance and suspicion by all sides. But after working at the Crossmaglen Youth Centre, and engaging with the young people, their families and my co-workers, I came to realise that people the world over have more in common than not. We all need security for ourselves and our family; we long to feel safe and want to believe the actions of those in charge are just. We require injustice, and any resulting suffering and pain, to be acknowledged in order to heal. I'm not referring to those in power. I'm talking about the average person on the street, living day to day - surviving, loving and creating families.

Every person I met in Crossmaglen shared a story of a close family member being victimised, sometimes horrifically, by those assigned to protect them. When I moved to Belfast, I mentored disadvantaged youth, many children of the paramilitaries – such as the IRA (Irish Republican Army) and UVF (Ulster Volunteer Force). The people I met from both sides of that divide mirrored each other in their needs, wants and hurts. A short time later I worked alongside the son of an RUC policeman, who shared the same needs. Then I met the child of a British army officer, then a migrant Indian take-away owner - you get the drift.

With these similarities in mind I believe it's important to point out I could have assigned the antagonists in this novel to either side of the paramilitary divide - the Protestant UVF or the Republican IRA – and the essence of the story would have remained the same. I chose to use the IRA, or actually it's offshoot, the Real IRA, as this organisation is more commonly known around the world, therefore making it easier for readers to connect with the story.

Throughout the novel I have used a number of Northern Irish slang words and spellings and have written in Australian/British English as that is the setting of the story. I have also played a little with street and business names so as not to slander anyone.

The Good Mother is a work of fiction, and while I drew on my experiences in Northern Ireland, not one character is based on a real person. Any similarities are purely coincidental.

For those interested in learning more about The Troubles, please visit my website www.raecairns.com for links to resources I found useful. You can also join my 'Crime With Heart' club to receive photos from my research trips to Northern Ireland as well as a few from my time living there in 1997.

PLEASE LEAVE A REVIEW

Thank you for reading *The Good Mother*. If you enjoyed the story I would really appreciate you taking the time to help other readers discover this book by posting a review at Goodreads, Amazon or wherever you purchased this copy.

Word of mouth is such an important tool for authors and even a one or two sentence review can make a huge difference.

Thank you.

ALSO BY RAE

THE EMPTY CHAIR
A stand-alone thriller coming March 2022

Ten years ago Geneva Leighton was ready to conquer the world – until she received a phone call that irrevocably changed her life. Her terrified sister, Amber, was trapped in the boot of a car, arms and legs bound, begging Geneva for help. Police traced the open line but the call dropped out and Amber was never heard from again. Instead of graduating from journalism studies, Geneva found work as a tele-marketer so she could help her brother-in-law, Hugh, raise three traumatised children.

Hugh Leighton fell apart when his wife went missing. It should have been him in the dark supermarket car park, with a shopping bag of nappies. Instead, he was out partying. When the police found him passed out in a hotel room naked and alone the following day, he could barely remember what he'd done the night before. These days he is a recovered gambling addict, drowning in hidden debt to a loan shark, fighting to keep the outward veneer of his successful life intact.

Constable Jesse Johns' life altered course that night too. His inability to rescue the young mother begging for her life and his failure to keep a naive vow to her children to find her, have haunted him ever since. Now working for Police Youth Command, he dedicates every second of his life to the job and the children he works with, in an attempt to make some kind of amends.

When Amber's remains are discovered on the Windsor property of a deceased recluse, Geneva, Hugh and Jesse work to unravel the truth behind her disappearance, unaware that each clue they uncover draws them one step closer to the crosshairs of a ruthless and determined enemy who will pitch them against one another in order to destroy them all.

JOIN RAE'S 'CRIME WITH HEART' CLUB

Join my 'Crime With Heart' club at www.raecairns.com to receive specially curated images of the settings from The Good Mother, behind the scenes photos of my time as an aid worker in Northern Ireland and from my more recent research trips.

Members are always first to hear about my new books and giveaways.

It is completely free to sign up and you will never be spammed by me. It is also easy to opt out at any time.

I look forward to meeting you in the club!

ACKNOWLEDGEMENTS

So many people have contributed to the final version of this novel with their generous encouragement, guidance and support. Thank you for the role each and every one of you have played in helping me achieve my dream of getting this novel to publication.

To my friends and colleagues in Northern Ireland, thank you for sharing your stories with me. Your resilience, compassion, laughter, tales of the absurd, generosity and willingness to place trust in me forever changed who I am and for that I'll be eternally grateful.

To Mark Lamprell, the first professional storyteller to hear the story I wanted to write, thank you for your generosity and encouragement. Your enthusiasm galvanised me to complete my manuscript, to develop my writing skills, and then to pursue publication.

To Kathryn Heyman, I couldn't have asked for a better mentor. You taught me so much about the craft of writing and for that I will be forever appreciative.

To Margaret Connolly, thank you for taking me on as a client. Your faith in my writing helped me build confidence in my work.

To Haylee Nash, thank you for taking me into your agency.

It may not have gone the way we hoped but your passionate support gave me the courage to plow on, and your wise counsel on character and story was invaluable.

To my cover art designer, David Perryman, your creativity and ability to interpret my messy ideas gave me the basis for a cover I am thrilled with.

To my cover designer, Sarah Paige of Opium House Creatives, you are a gem. You took my brief and created the exact cover I was hoping for.

To my editor and proof reader, Laura Boon of It's All Write Editing, thank you for your extraordinary attention to detail and for teaching me so much about the editing process.

To the designer of my gorgeous new website, Michelle Barraclough of Fresh Web Design, thank you, I adore everything about it.

To the readers of my first, very rough draft - Peter Vercoe, Sue Vercoe, Kim Egelton, Lynda Parry, Jan Cairns, Ian Cairns and Peter Cairns - thank you for your kind and sensitive feedback. You managed to give me honest, accurate feedback without crushing my dreams.

To the many writers and professionals who have guided, encouraged and supported me throughout this process, thank you. In particular I'd like to thank Chrissie Mios, Madeleine Eskedahl, Kirsten McKenzie, Lindy Cameron, Jacky Grámosi Collins, Craig Sisterson, Kel Butler, Steve Lewis, Lisa Ireland, Rachael Johns, Kelly Rimmer, Sulari Gentill, Sara Foster and Natasha Lester. Each of you have helped me at a time when I needed it. A special shout out to Candice Fox - thank you for Facebook Write Club, it has kept me on track for book two. And to Michael and Vivienne Robotham, you may not know it but you came along at time when I really needed the words you had for me.

To Sisters in Crime, Writers NSW, the Romance Writers of Australia, the Writers' Studio, the Australian Writers' Centre, the Sydney Writers' Festival, BAD Sydney Crime and Rotorua Noir, thank you for hosting courses and panels that have significantly contributed to my skills and growth as a writer.

To my amazingly talented and supportive writers' group, The Ink Wells - Pamela Cook, Terri Green, Laura Boon, Joanna Nell, Penelope Janu, Michelle Barraclough and Angella Whitton - I am so lucky to have such an incredible group of women in my life who are not only valuable colleagues but adored friends. The joy of life, humour, experience, insights and exceptional talents you bring to my world have kept me motivated and sane. To Pam, thank you for always being on the end of the phone to brainstorm plot, character and publishing. Your perceptive feedback and endless support have made me a better writer and mean the world to me. Terri, your astute observations, especially on the dialogue of teens, have been invaluable, as has your eternal optimism and quirky humour. Laura, thank you for your generous guidance on all things publicity and marketing, for your unwavering support, and for being my 'dealer' of romance novels. Michelle, I'm so grateful for your intuition, insight and artistic eye. Pen your shrewd feedback and hilarious banter bring me joy each day. Jo, I am so grateful for your wit, generous encouragement and wisdom.

Thank you to Monique McDonell for inviting me along to my first writers' group. You transformed my writing experience from one of isolation to one of community. Your generous guidance through social media, marketing and the world of publishing has been invaluable.

Thank you to my mum, Lynda Parry, for always enthusiastically supporting my creative pursuits, and for putting up with me in Bali while I feverishly worked on the edits I had due. Your insights into human behaviour and how the mind works have been absolutely invaluable, I'm so lucky to have you to bounce ideas around with.

To my sister, Kim, thank you for always supporting and encouraging your arty sister. Your scientific mind must often think I'm barmy but you're always there for me, regardless.

To my in-laws, Jan and Ian Cairns, thank you for your support and encouragement.

To my friends Melissa Doyle, Sue Vercoe, Jen Potter, Leanne Johnstone, Ainslie Fuchs, Tiffany Judson and Cath Pemberton - you have been the best cheer squad a girl could ever hope for. Your feedback, belief in me and encouragement to follow my dreams (and the copious laughter and wine) have kept me buoyed through the ups and downs of getting this story to print.

To Alfie, my gorgeous dog, who has kept me company from the very first page. Thank you for the cuddles and nudges to go for walks. You got me through some of the more challenging times.

To Ben and Amy, the best 'creations' of my life. Watching you grow into incredible, compassionate and beautiful humans has been a joy and privilege. Your continued support for my writing has been a huge motivation for me to complete this novel. Amy, when you read my book and loved it, it had a huge impact on me. Your diligence, empathy and wacky sense of fun inspire me and fill our lives with joy. Ben thank you for helping me find the jokes for my first draft. Your sense of humour, compassion and inquisitiveness bring so much wonder and joy to our family.

And to Peter, my husband, my best friend and my biggest support, thank you for challenging me to get on with it when I suggested I might want to write a book. You have always been in my corner, cheering me on, and listening to me endlessly ramble on about my imaginary friends. I am so grateful we met upon my return from Northern Ireland - your sense of humour, integrity, and love of family showed me I could be safe again.

Finally to you, the readers of this novel, thank you for taking a chance on my book. I hope you enjoyed it and would love to hear your thoughts. You can find me at

www.raecairns.com
www.facebook.com/raecairnsauthor
Instagram @raecairnswrites

First published by Bandrui Publishing in 2020
ISBN **9780648999508**

THE GOOD MOTHER
© 2020 by Rae Cairns
The moral right of the author has been asserted.

This book is a work of fiction. Names, characters, places and incidents are either the product of the author's imagination or are used fictitiously and any resemblance to actual persons living or dead, business establishments, events, or locales is entirely coincidental.

This edition published by
Bandrui Publishing
www.raecairns.com

A catalogue record for this book is available from the National Library of Australia www.librariesaustralia.nla.gov.au

Made in the USA
Monee, IL
07 December 2020

51149959R00215